GILES KURNS: ROGUE OPERATOR

GILES KURNS: ROGUE OPERATOR

CONFESSIONS OF A SPACE ANTHROPOLOGIST™ BOOK 1

ELL LEIGH CLARKE

MICHAEL ANDERLE

DISRUPTIVE IMAGINATION

To everyone who ever dreamed of making a dent in the universe.

— Ellie

To Family, Friends and
Those Who Love
To Read.
May We All Enjoy Grace
To Live The Life We Are
Called.

— Michael

THE ROGUE OPERATOR TEAM

Thanks to our JIT and Beta Readers

Micky Cocker
James Caplan
Paul Westman
Kelly ODonnell
Daniel Weigert
Joshua Ahles
Kimberly Boyer
Tim Bischoff
Peter Manis
Larry Omans
Thomas Ogden
AbH Belxjander Draconis Serechai
Keith Verret

If we missed anyone, please let us know!

Edited by

Joe Brewer

LMBPN Publishing
PMB 196, 2540 South Maryland Pkwy
Las Vegas, NV 89109

First US edition, November 2017
Version 1.03, December 2018
Print ISBN: 978-1-64971-813-6

PROLOGUE

Question: how do you tame a rogue space archaeologist?

Answer: You don't.

When Professor Giles Kurns discovered a crucial piece of intel while being held prisoner by the exiled former Zhyn High Marshall, he returned to the ArchAngel command ship with a compelling argument for him to be allowed to reopen an old research project.

But this time, it was more than intellectual curiosity.

This time, the continued existence of the Federation, and perhaps all species in the Loop and Pan Galaxies were at stake.

Having convinced General Lance Reynolds of the imminent significance of his findings, Giles and his partner in crime, Arlene Bailey, set out to the Orn System for a spot of tomb raiding.

Together with the Empress's old covert ops warship, fully equipped with Gate technology and a rather spunky AI, they embark on a swashbuckling adventure of danger and intrigue to uncover the truth about the Ascension Myth.

CHAPTER 1

Gaitune-67, Safe House

The safe house was a buzz of activity.

Joel could barely contain his enthusiasm for the return of their old friends. "I can't believe it!" he exclaimed, clasping hands with Giles in a manly handshake.

He called over to Molly, the boss of their operation, but couldn't take his eyes off Giles. "You go to the university to do a recruitment talk, and you come back with the Gilester...and Arlene!" he exclaimed, seeing Arlene following Molly out of the basement door from the hangar deck and into the safe house. The pair disappeared off on a hush-hush mission months ago, without so much as a goodbye, leaving the crew of the Sanguine Squadron intrigued as to what they were up to.

And missing their friends.

They'd been through some intense and interesting times, fighting side by side for survival, and to keep war from breaking out between the Federation and the Zhyn Empire.

And now, they seemed to be back. But for how long remained to be seen.

Joel shook his head in amazement as Paige, the budding business person, integral team member and self-elected hostess, breezed past quickly and began fussing around the common area to give their guests somewhere to sit.

Crash and Pieter were quickly persuaded to pause their holo games. They weren't that concerned, on account of Oz (the AI) thrashing them mercilessly. Paige started picking up their beer bottles, her heels clipping busily as Giles and Arlene hugged the ever-growing spontaneous welcome party as news of their arrival back on the asteroid, Gaitune-67, spread through the base.

Paige strode out to the kitchen, carrying empty bottles and trash. "If you want to keep playing," she called back to Crash and Pieter, "just take it down to the workshop."

Pieter stood up stiffly. The first time in about four hours. "Are you kidding? And miss this?" he called back as she disappeared. Giles caught his eye and headed over, giving him a man-hug.

"How you doing, kid?" he asked, patting Pieter on the back firmly in a hug a little too tight for Pieter's liking.

"Ugh. I'm ok," he said awkwardly as Giles released him. "So where've you been? You just disappeared from the ArchAngel."

Giles looked caught off-guard. "Well yes. We er... had pressing business to attend to." Pieter nearly rolled his eyes at the standard company line.

Paige had resurfaced from the kitchen carrying beers and a new trash bag to grab the rest of the trash that had been left strewn around by the boys having a game night.

"Let him get in and sit down before you start grilling him," she fussed at Pieter, shuffling him out of the way so she could continue with mission-hospitality.

Giles pushed his glasses up his nose as Paige thrust an obligatory beer into his hand. "Thanks!" he said, trying to smile amongst the kerfuffle.

Pieter didn't budge. He stood awkwardly still looking at Giles. He ruffled his hair trying to think of what else to say.

"Let him sit down," Paige's voice instructed him again as she scooped up an empty pizza box along with some more empty bottles and disappeared into the kitchen for the second time.

Pieter moved out of the way to let Giles into the lounge area. But Giles was also distracted, scanning the faces that had shown up and were lining up to embrace Arlene.

Arlene was clearly more popular, he noticed.

Jack and Maya had just been released from hello hugs and were heading his way. But Giles was looking for someone else.

Before he knew it Maya had snuck up on him and was squeezing him tight. Giles tried not to spill his beer. "Hi!" she greeted him. "Long time, stranger. How have the adventures been?"

Giles grunted and bobbed his head agreeably. "Yes, all going-" His response was interrupted by Jack stepping in to hug him. She was a little more polite in her distance and quickly released him. "Yes, it was good," he continued. "Some success. But we hit a dead end, which is why we're back... for now..." he answered to the expectant faces looking back at him.

Maya's eyes lit up as she glanced briefly back at Arlene,

now talking with Molly and Brock, who had just emerged from the basement with screen-face. He'd obviously been taking the time to continue on with whatever pet project he had permission for. It was a stark contrast from his normal, bubbly self.

Maya peeled her attention back to Giles. "So you'll be staying?" she inquired enthusiastically. Her eyes darted back to her as yet oblivious, but would-be mentor, Arlene.

Giles put one hand in his pocket and tried to feign politeness. "Yes. For a little while, at least. Tell me, is Sean about?"

Maya took a second to process the question, her distraction now evident even to Giles. "Er… yeah he should be," she said.

Jack interjected. "I think he was down in the gym. The base gym," she relayed helpfully.

Maya snapped out of her distraction and back into her usual 'helping' mode. "Lemme go find him for you. You relax," she told him, indicating to Jack and Giles to sit. "I'll be right back," she added as she scurried off between her teammates chattering away with Arlene.

Within about twenty minutes Crash and Joel had brought Giles's and Arlene's overnight bags up to the safe house, leaving the *Scamp Princess* powered down on the hangar deck.

The team sat around in the common area, which Paige had managed to return to some semblance of order only to have a new set of empty beer bottles materializing on the mocha table.

"So come on," Pieter insisted. "Tell us about what happened," he pressed now that everyone was settled down and had a drink in hand.

Arlene looked at Giles. "I think you're the better story teller," she winked, pleased with herself with how she deftly moved the responsibility of recounting the last couple of months over to him.

Giles narrowed his eyes, completely aware of her tactic. He leaned forward, taking a deep breath and placing his beer bottle on the table. "Well," he started, "I have no doubt that Arlene will interrupt at appropriate points, but I'll at least start the story." His eyes had a glimmer of humor in it as he glanced around the assembled team. His gaze landed on Molly, who looked equally intrigued as the others to know what they had missed while he had been out of communication. He felt a flutter in his chest knowing that she was paying attention.

"So, as you know," he continued,"after we all got back from the Zhyn mission Arlene and I continued doing some digging into the mysteries of the talisman that Sean and I had retrieved from Teshov."

Brock interjected. "Ah, yes, we never did get to hear about what happened there."

Pieter chuckled, his beer bottle almost to his lips. "Yeah, Royale is nearly as tight lipped as Crash," he interjected.

Crash glanced at him, narrowing his eyes and then pointing two fingers at his eyes and then at a slightly tipsy Pieter.

Just then Sean arrived, his hair still wet from the

shower and wearing a track suit with a towel around his neck. He wandered into the lounge area, poking his ear with one end of the towel.

Giles looked up at him. "Speak of the devil!" he grinned, springing to his feet and stepping over Pieter and Crash's legs to greet Sean. This was clearly the person he'd been waiting for.

"I knew my ears were burning for a reason!" Sean chuckled, clamping his hand in Giles's and then pulling him closer for one of his famous bear hugs. The two men slapped each other on the back in a show of mutual appreciation.

"How the devil are you?" Giles grinned back.

Sean bobbed his head excitedly and repeatedly. "You know, can't complain," he told him. "No one would listen even if I did," he said dryly. "Besides, this lot keeps me busy," he said, nodding affectionately in Molly and Joel's direction.

Paige handed Sean a beer and moved over to give him some space to share the couch she and Brock were occupying.

Molly squinted at the pair. "Since when did you two become so chummy?" she asked.

Joel added his commentary. "Yeah, and how come we're just noticing it now?"

Sean did a little wink as he sat down and took a swig of beer.

Giles answered the question. "It was probably since he saved my life on our Teshov mission," he mused. "I've heard stories about the great Sean Royale, but until that moment I just assumed he was a jerk."

Sean stopped with his beer bottle at his lips and lowered it, his mouth open in mock amazement. Then he pretended to look hurt, his eyes drooping at the sides. He clutched his hand to his chest. "You kill me with your words, Kurns!"

Giles chuckled. "Come on, you've got to admit it, even the AIs don't like you!"

Sean chuckled. "You know that's just coz they're jealous about how much everyone else likes me, right?"

Giles grinned, picking up his beer bottle, pointing at him. "Yeah, whatever helps you sleep at night," he told him, jokingly.

Sean finally took another sip of his beer and then set it down, lounging back on the sofa. "Yeah, whatever, mate. Weren't you about to explain your mysterious disappearance without saying goodbye?"

Giles composed himself. "Yes. Yes I was…"

Brock pointed at him. "Hey, and then you have to tell us about Teshov. Sean Royale has a habit of keeping secrets, so we still don't know what happened there while we were all busting our asses on the Shaa mission."

Giles nodded. "Ok. I'll come back to that shortly, because actually, it's kind of relevant to our mission after the ArchAngel."

He settled down and continued his story. "So, as I was saying, the reason we left the ArchAngel so quickly was because the General gave us the 'OK' for a mission that was prompted by something I discovered while I was being held captive by that Shaa asshole." He shuddered at the thought of the escapade where he had narrowly escaped with his life.

Sean chuckled playfully. "Ah yes, the one we had to rescue your reprobate ass from…"

Giles nodded. "The one and the same."

Molly had been quiet, taking it all in and exhausted by the evening's events. Only now did her curiosity prompt her to interject. "So what did you discover?" she asked. This was the first she was hearing about the lead and it was likely that if it had anything to do with the talisman stuff Giles had shared with her, it might also hold some answers to her realm jumping abilities she was still learning to control.

Giles waved his hands. "More of what I shared with you in that first meeting when Uncle Lance brought you to the lecture theater," he told her. "But perhaps I should start at the very beginning, to catch everyone else up?"

Molly nodded her agreement, and everyone settled in for the story.

"So there's something that I didn't explain to you," Giles continued, looking over at Molly with a serious expression on his face.

Molly indicated that he should continue.

"You see," he explained, "I was… economical with the full story because it wasn't relevant at the time." His eyes dropped to his beer bottle and he fiddled with the label as he spoke now. "It's not like it was a big secret. Uncle Lance knew the crux of it… but not the details I shared with you when we were first talking about it."

Molly regarded him with a narrowed eye, trying to read between the lines of what he was saying. "You're referring to the talisman I take it?"

"Yes, exactly," he confirmed, still studying the bottle in his hands.

Sean cut in. "The one we went to retrieve?"

"Exactly," Giles nodded, only now looking up to meet Sean's eyes, and not Molly's. "Except at the time I had led you to believe that the story started where I was asked to look after it by the Estarians. But that wasn't the whole story."

Molly frowned, glancing briefly at Joel for his reaction. "So what is the whole story?" she pressed.

Joel's expression was blank as he awaited the details.

"Well it all began many many years ago," Giles explained. "Long before even Arlene and I crossed paths. I was included on a mission to Earth; the place on the other side of the Gate where our ancestors came from."

Paige's eyes lit up. "You're talking about the origin of the humans?"

Giles nodded, smiling at her perception of his race. "Yes. Humans," he confirmed.

Paige was half human and half Estarian, but because of her blue skin most folks just assumed she was a bizarre looking Estarian rather than anything else. Apart from anything it meant it was nearly impossible for humans and Estarians to mate because of their DNA structure. Nevertheless, Paige was a miracle. And an anomaly.

Giles now held everyone in rapt attention - as he so often did when he lectures.

"The mission was to swing back to Earth to build up its defenses against another Kurtherian assault. And to rescue a certain vampire. This vampire will remain nameless, but he had been stranded there since the war against the Kurtherians broke out."

"Why nameless?" Brock asked, leaning forward and shuffling his butt back into the sofa a bit more to get comfortable.

"Because this particular vampire wouldn't like the idea of being rescued by anyone. And, besides," Giles added, "he'd probably tell the story quite differently... like he wasn't being rescued."

Brock grinned. "Ah, but we know it is a *he* then!"

Giles pointed with his beer bottle in hand. "Or," he added, "maybe I'm just throwing you off track?" He winked before trying to return to his story.

"Hang on," Brock interrupted again. "I thought earth was destroyed?"

Giles nodded. "It was," he replied simply. "Pretty much, at least."

Pieter frowned, confused. "Well hang on, was this before or after it was destroyed then?"

"After," Giles confirmed. "The vampire survived being blown up by a nuke - apparently. I never did get the full story from him. He's not the most talky-talky of people."

Brock and Pieter looked at each other, processing this new intel and trying to slot it into what they'd each learned in the limited time allocated to human history back on Estaria. Brock immediately jumped to the question they were both thinking. "Well hang on then... how old are you?"

Giles grinned and glanced over in Sean's direction. "That's classified. Right Sean?"

Sean grunted from behind his beer bottle. "Right."

Brock shook his head, knowing full-well the game that Sean had been playing with them, not telling him how old he really was.

Pieter was still enthralled by the discourse. "So then what happened on Earth?"

"Well... let's just say that during a swash-buckling adventure," Giles revealed glibly. "I ended up helping the team who was responsible for finding and assembling a Sacred Clan's ship left over from when the Empress kicked their asses the first time before she left Earth."

There was a hush amongst the team. All movement stopped. What Giles was talking about was legendary — so legendary that not one of them really knew the details of what had happened.

Giles waved his hand ironically, now looking uncomfortable at all the attention he was suddenly receiving, despite this being his main driver normally. "Only... well, you don't need the details. But let's just say there was an artifact on board that everyone else thought was just junk."

Molly regarded him carefully. "But *you* didn't?" she emphasized, pressing him for as much information as she could glean.

"Exactly," Giles agreed, smiling at the recognition that Molly had bestowed upon him. "Though I was still a young buck by Federation standards, I had already done my share of book-worming and adventuring, and I knew that it must have some significance. Although what the sacred clan was doing with it we'll probably never know," he mused as his thoughts drifted momentarily.

He pulled his attention back to the task in hand. "Anyway, it turned out it was some kind of talisman, likely originating on the planet itself from the crude scans we could do with the onboard material analysis at the time. And this was the talisman Sean and I retrieved on Teshov."

Molly nodded. "So the Estarian Elders didn't entrust you with it?" she asked rather skeptical of him once again.

Giles's eyes looked concerned. "No no," he protested. "It's not like that. Yes, they entrusted it to me, but several decades after I'd given it to them for safe keeping. You see, it turns out that this talisman had certain... *magical* properties."

Brock raised his eyebrows, looking skeptical and a little anxious at the same time. Paige and Maya were wide-eyed, hanging on Giles's every word.

Molly looked blankly. "What do you mean... 'magical properties'?"

Giles nodded at Arlene. "That's not my area. Arlene? Want to take this one?" he suggested.

Arlene nodded, stretching her legs out in front of her for a moment, and then putting her palms together between her knees as she leaned forward and pulled her legs back in and stretching her back. "I guess the easiest way to describe it is that all things have a power to them. A property, like entropy. Or temperature," she explained. "Some objects, or places, or people, have more of this power than others. Like Neechie..." she added, the sphinx having just at that moment come into the middle of the group and was sitting directly in front of her between the mocha table and her feet.

Paige and Maya seemed to be getting more and more excited at what they were hearing.

Arlene continued. "Some places have a ground energy,

too, meaning that it is easier to manifest certain things in that place than others. Estaria has a slightly higher power than most planets, and that's why they have such a high incidence of their ancestors having been able to ascend and realm-walk."

Brock's eyes were also wide now, and he was looking around anxiously as if afraid of ghosts appearing behind him.

Arlene brought the conversation back to the talisman. "And sometimes objects have so much power that someone who is attuned can pull energy from it, and use it to move things around in this realm."

Molly frowned. "Move things around? Like telekinesis?"

Arlene tilted her head from side to side. "Yes and no. I was talking more about making things happen, or transmuting matter or energy into one form of another."

Molly frowned. "Give me the science," she asked without any real energy on the request.

"Well," Arlene explained, "It's kind of like this. Your brain emits certain frequencies, depending on the thoughts you think. But for those who have total control and awareness of the frequencies they have, they can use this to resonate with, and affect, matter in the physical world." She smiled. "I just prefer to call it magic because not everyone can do it!" She winked playfully.

Molly bobbed her head, contemplating what Arlene had just told her. It fit perfectly with what she had been teaching her all those months ago out in the deserted landscape of the asteroid.

Arlene chuckled to herself. "Anyway," she added, "It

comes in handy now and again. Especially on missions with this one," she added, nodding her head in Giles's direction.

Giles took that as a cue to continue with the story. "Quite," he agreed dutifully. "So this talisman had power, and I had learned enough to be able to feel it. Not straight away, but after a while of having it in my possession. So when I met the Estarian elders sometime later I explained this to them, and they suggested they look after it. I for one was happy to not have it with me when I was doing my gallivanting. Way too easy to get into all kinds of trouble I didn't know how to get myself out of."

Arlene nodded in agreement. "Yeah, it is a little like walking around with a target on your back," she confirmed.

Giles chuckled. "Yeah, all was safe until I got involved with a woman who was ruthless and cruel and would stop at noth-"

"Alright. Alright!" Arlene interrupted him. "You don't need to lay it on so thick!"

"Hang on," Molly interjected looking at Arlene with her eyes wide and horrified. "YOU were the woman?" she asked.

Arlene rolled her eyes at herself. "We were young and reckless. He makes it sound like I was an evil sorcerer or something."

Giles leaned over in a low voice and whispered in the direction of Joel and Pieter. "Oh, she totally was."

Arlene gave him a stern look.

Giles straightened up again. "Yeah, okay, we'll skip that

bit about how you tried to kill me to get your hands on it," he said.

The rest of the team could barely believe what they were hearing.

Joel chirped up, looking at Arlene. "Is that true?".

Arlene nodded. "Yep."

Giles waved his hand dismissively. "All water under the bridge now. Anyway, the rest," he said now looking at Molly, "of what I told you about the elders, and how they were killed and having to find another hiding place for the talisman, is all accurate."

Molly nodded, pushing her bottom lip out contemplating the information.

Giles pulled his lips to one side. "Are we good?"

Molly shrugged. "Sure," she said simply. "You're right. It wasn't relevant to anything we needed to know at the time and it doesn't change anything."

Giles's face relaxed and his shoulders dropped about two inches. "Good," he said, smiling now. "So," he continued, turning back to his story, "when we started putting all this data together I started wondering if there were other talismans, like the one I'd found on the ship. And the six sections on it looked awfully like constellations as seen from areas like Earth, Estaria and the original planet of the Zhyn Empire - Zhyn."

He made eye contact with each member of his enraptured audience as he spoke. "That, together with the uncanny DNA similarities between the Estarians and the Zhyn made me wonder if there weren't some other association between them. So, while I was in prison that other captive we rescued shared with me a nursery rhyme about the Moons of Orn. It got me wondering if that was where the Zhyn talisman might be hiding, and when Arlene checked the constellations on the talisman - taking into account the 100,000-year lag time - it looked like that could very well have been the constellations looking from the Moons of Orn, back into space as seen from Earth, in the Pan Galaxy, pointing back in the direction of this spot." He paused for breath, his excitement at his string of discoveries getting the better of him.

Brock screwed his face up. "You mean these two sets of regressed constellations both point to the same area of space, as viewed from these points?"

Giles nodded. "Seems more than just a coincidence."

Oz piped up over the base intercom. "I can run the probability of that being a coincidence if you like."

Giles chuckled. "No need, thanks Oz. Though very kind of you to offer. We understand it is astronomically low... and then if you factor in the rest of my theory, I think we can safely say we're onto something."

Oz laughed too, clearly enjoying the whole team being together and being a part of things. "As you wish," he conceded, the audio channel going quiet again.

"So, after you guys kindly saved my life from that infernal hole," Giles continued, "Arlene and I were pretty sure that our next stop should be the Moons of Orn. And when the General gave us the go ahead it was deemed to be of utmost importance to the Federation and we just had to scarper."

Molly nodded. "Seems reasonable," she agreed.

Joel looked at her, amazed. "How can you not be even a little bit hurt that he didn't say goodbye?"

Molly shrugged. "He had a job to do," she said blankly.

Joel eyed her carefully as the conversation moved on. He could sense that there was a chance her cool exterior and analytical assessment was still just her protection mechanism for keeping people at a distance. He just hoped that she hadn't reverted. He didn't know what might have gone on between her and Giles, but he sensed there was a commonality that the pair shared... both being outsiders, and both being too smart for their own good.

Brock was enthralled. "So what happened next?"

CHAPTER 2

Gaitune-67, Safe House

"So there we were, having got special permission for a ship with Gate technology. I can probably count on one hand the number of times the General has given me access to such tech… and never before without a special forces Federation escort."

Arlene bobbed her head as Giles explained the situation. "Just goes to show how much he thinks this talisman might be a threat to the Federation," she added in.

"Either that," Sean added, "or an opportunity for us."

Giles pulled his lips to one side. It wasn't something he hadn't considered before, but he liked to think more of Lance. "In any case," he continued, "there we were, Arlene and I, on our way to the Zhyn Empire."

Aboard the *Scamp Princess*, Koin Star System

"Adjusting course for Kurilia," Scamp announced.

Arlene looked up at Giles from her console. "Kurilia?" she queried.

Giles's attention was elsewhere. "Huh?" he grunted absently.

"We're going to Kurilia?" Arlene clarified.

"Yeah," Giles responded, pressing buttons on his console and cross-checking the reference coordinates he had been working on. "We're going to ask someone for permission."

"Permission? For what?" Arlene's blue complexion glinted in the dim light of the cockpit, accentuating her expression of confusion.

Giles still didn't look round. "For visiting the Moons of Orn on our quest," he told her.

Arlene frowned, turning in her antigrav chair to face Giles, who had his back to her sitting at his console at the front of the ship's cockpit.

"Bit old-fashioned," she commented.

"Yeah," he agreed. "But it's all about honor and respect with these guys," he explained, still engrossed in what he was doing.

"Hmm," she grumped. "More like it's all about covering your ass," she muttered under her breath.

"That too," he confessed. "ADAM, set up a meeting for us on the down low... we're meeting with the Justicar himself."

Arlene was intrigued. She got up out of her chair and ambled over to where Giles was working, perching on the console next to him to see his face as he spoke. "Why him specifically?" she asked.

Giles looked up at her, his hand mid-way to another button in the holo-display he was working on. "Well, the

Emperor himself doesn't handle these kind of trivial matters. It normally falls to some random official in his court, but given Molly's diplomatic relations had gone so well in the past with him and the Justicar, ADAM reached out to them directly. Turns out the Emperor and Justicar had rather warmed to her... and by extension, humans in general."

Arlene squinted one eye suspiciously. "And what about Estarians?"

Giles chortled quietly, his attention mostly back on his work.

"What?" Arlene pressed.

He smiled up at her briefly before turning back to the holo-console. "I don't think they have any bad feelings towards you," he said slowly.

"But?"

"But..." he continued, "I think they just have you down as a rather ugly version of themselves."

Arlene looked horrified as she swiped at his nearest arm. Giles managed to lean back and dodge, still chuckling. "Don't worry Arlene, I still think you're cute!"

"Humpft," she retorted, turning her attention back to her console and nursing her ego. "Ugly version... we'll see about that!"

She stomped back to her console to continue her analysis of the constellations she had been working through.

It took a little time before they were finally within striking distance of Kurilia. Scamp piped up over the cockpit intercom. "Giles, Arlene, will you be wanting to land, or would you like to take the skylift down to the surface?"

Giles had just come back into the cockpit. "I'm not sure," he said contemplating the two options. "Which is easiest?"

Scamp chuckled over the audio. "For who?" he asked cheekily.

Giles suddenly remembered why he had always had interesting relationship with AIs. "Let's say for us," he suggested.

Scamp's chuckling subsided. "I'd say the skylift is the better option. You'd still need to meet with your official liaisons, but landing will take more time and lots more walking by my calculations."

Giles smiled. "Ok. Skylift it is then," he responded.

Scamp seemed to compute something else. "There is an additional variable to consider," he added.

"What's that then?" Giles asked.

"Well," Scamp explained, "I understand from data shared by Emma that Molly and her crew would jump down onto the skylift platform as the ship passed by it in an off-kilter kind of geo-orbit."

Arlene frowned. "Hang on, who is Emma?"

"The EI that runs Molly's ship, the Empress," Scamp explained.

"Ah," Arlene murmured, allowing Scamp to continue.

Giles was considering the new information. "What do you mean, they would *jump* down" he asked.

"You know," Scamp explained playfully, "tuck and roll style, down to the platform."

"You're kidding?" Giles asked, now contemplating if it were indeed possible for an EI to be running irony as some kind of uncontrolled sub-routine. "What speed was the ship passing at?" he tried to clarify.

Scamp's tone was giving nothing away on the irony front. "Maybe a couple of meters per second," he responded matter-of-factly.

Giles glanced over at Arlene. Arlene was shaking her head. "No frikkin way!" she exclaimed, clearly taking Scamp's suggestion as a serious one.

"I'm afraid," Giles informed Scamp with a degree of relief in his voice now, "we're going to have to go with the parking-up option. Sorry," he added, his tone clearly not remorseful about his decision.

Scamp chuffed back over the intercom. "As you wish, Mr. Kurns. I'll make preparations for entry into orbit and coordinate with their orbital control unit to dock."

"Thank you Scamp," Giles responded politely, while exchanging disbelieving looks with Arlene.

Scamp's intercom clicked off.

"Did you believe that?" Giles exclaimed, still wondering if he had imagined what Scamp was suggesting.

Arlene was still shaking her head. "You mean that they just jumped? I can't. I mean, what if they missed the platform? That would just be it for them, right?"

Giles thought for a moment. "It's either a long way down, or a hell of a way to go from atmospheric exposure."

Arlene shook her head, her expression suddenly much more serious than it had been. "Well, you'd know about that," she muttered quietly.

Giles grinned. "Yeah, and I know how painful it is, with or without nanocytes to heal you."

Arlene shuddered. "Ok. Conversation over. I don't want to even think about it. Do you think we need suits to head down?"

Giles shook his head. "Probably not. But after this conversation, I'm putting one on anyway."

Arlene's mood seemed to shift and she grinned at him cheekily. "Seems like old age is making you more sound in the head."

Giles glanced over at her as he headed back into the main area of the ship. "Seems like," he agreed dryly.

Planet Kurilia, Koin Star System, Zhyn Empire

Giles and Arlene stepped from the *Scamp Princess* onto the skylift dock. Despite the altitude and low atmosphere it felt bitingly blustery.

"Aren't you glad you didn't opt for the Molly-method of descent now?" Arlene asked Giles as he stepped out and almost recoiled against the wind.

Giles's face was stoney as he wrapped his arms around his body against the conditions. "Yeah, yeah. You were right," he admitted reluctantly.

Arlene headed over to the lift and was pressing the call button repeatedly. Giles glanced back to see that Scamp had activated the door closed mechanism on the ship parked precariously in orbit. He regarded the swaying structure and then glanced back at Arlene. "You sure this is safe?" he asked, looking around the same altitude at the many other ships docked on flimsy-looking platforms.

Arlene shrugged her shoulders. "Dunno. But all those guys seem to think so."

They didn't have long to wait before the skylift arrived at their dock to take them down to the surface. On the ride down they mused about the advertisements and the culture as only anthropologists could.

"I think they're probably more militaristic than the Estarians," Arlene commented just as the elevator came to a halt at ground level. "Though, I'd like to see the influence of their religions here."

Giles pushed himself up off the handrail he had perched his butt against. "I think you'll probably get a chance to see that if we head through a populated area," Giles remarked as the doors slid open to reveal a sandy area surrounded by woodland.

Arlene shot him a look of irony, one eyebrow arched. He couldn't help but chuckle silently to himself.

They stepped out in tandem as if joined by the hip, only to be greeted by half a dozen armed Zhyn. Their tough blue skins glistened in the sun light and the reflection of their armor and swords glinted, blinding them for a moment.

Giles's heart beat out of his chest as he suddenly felt more like a wanted prisoner than a guest on the planet. "Greetings," he declared, raising his hands in a gesture of peace and surrender. "I'm Giles Kurns and this is my associate, Arlene Bailey. We're expected by your Justicar," he added quickly.

One of the large blue-skinned guards clad in ceremonial dress stepped forward. "Greetings. My name is

Gh'herk. The Justicar is indeed expecting you. I'll be your personal liaison on this trip. Welcome to Kurilia."

His English was good, considering their language had a much harsher, guttural sound.

Giles was impressed. "Thank you!" he smiled, visibly relieved. "And may I just say, your use of the human language is… well, excellent."

Gh'herk looked pleased with himself. "Thank you. I've been learning ever since I joined the forces. Five years now."

Giles and Arlene exchanged deliberately affected glances. Arlene added her sentiment. "Well, I think it would take us much longer than five years to speak your language even half as well."

Gh'herk bowed politely in acknowledgment and then turned to lead the way, gesturing for them to follow. "I'll take you to the Justicar, if I may. Would you like to follow me, please?"

The guards ambled behind them, more as an accompanying and curious contingent than the forced security detail Giles had initially assumed.

The group trudged for some minutes through the natural terrain before reaching a metallic-built station. Gh'herk led them inside where it was much cooler, partly because it was out of the direct sunlight. He welcomed them into a type of subway train car and once everyone was inside the doors closed and the train moved gently off.

The shuttle was relatively quiet and from what Giles could tell, seemed to be underground. There were no windows to see out, though, and from the sounds, Giles suspected it was operating on some form of antigrav rather than maglev. The motion made it easy for them to stand and retain their balance.

Not that they had the option of sitting. There was a distinct absence of chairs or even benches. Giles clung to a rail along one side of the carriage, and Arlene wedged herself against the opposite wall for comfort.

Giles noticed she was paying attention to the details of the carriage, no doubt using her Estarian gifts of perception to sense the types of fields around them. She'd likely give him an appraisal of her findings later, when they weren't likely to be accused of espionage.

It wasn't long before the train slowed and the sound around it shifted as if it had pulled into another station. The doors opened and Gh'herk smiled with an awkward Zhyn smile and then led them out.

The new station was more developed than the last one. It was also more attractive, with pattern tiled flooring, and though the doors were plated in metal it was more decorative and expensive than purely functional — clearly a sign that they'd entered a more populated if not affluent area on the planet's surface.

"Looks like we've *arrived*," Giles remarked dryly to Arlene as he stepped past her. Arlene characteristically raised an eyebrow in acknowledgment of his astute deduction and then followed him out.

One of the guards had wandered ahead with Gh'herk falling into a relaxed escort formation. Giles and then Arlene followed them out into the small station, followed by their remaining three escorts.

Gh'herk led them into the adjacent building. It had a sense of space and grandeur that Giles had seen on only a few occasions before. There was ornate tiling on the floors and walls all in warm ocher tones. This new building was several stories high and resembled some of the Estarian religious and senate structures that Arlene had visited over the years. She made a mental note to add that data point into the mix later.

Giles glanced back to see her widen her stride to catch him up again. He slowed his pace and leaned over to whisper to her. "Pretty impressive, huh?" he said, raising his eyes up at a levitating light source hovering about ten feet above them.

Arlene nodded, trying to conceal quite how impressed she was. She wondered what the strange source might be that was powering the light, if it was indeed levitating. She knew she would be able to sense an electromagnetic field around it but there was none. She'd mention it to Giles later. There was certainly much to learn from these people.

Gh'herk picked up his pace as they moved through the hall. They walked for several minutes from the side where they had entered through to the far end, which they could barely make out from their starting point. Eventually they slowed as they neared a set of beautifully carved double doors guarded by armed attendants in full traditional dress.

Gh'herk made some Zhyn noises to one of them, who leaned over and opened the door for them. Gh'herk indicated for the guests to follow him through, and led the way into a red-carpeted foyer area with a desk to the left.

He grunted again to an older, smaller Zhyn female sitting behind the desk. She merely looked up from her holo and nodded before returning to what she was doing.

Gh'herk turned to Giles and Arlene. "The Justicar will see you in the main chamber," he explained, waving a hand at the door ahead of them.

Giles nodded congenially and followed behind Gh'herk, who opened the door, slipped through and then held it open for his charges to enter.

Arlene watched Giles on his best behavior. She'd seen him do this routine countless times before with each new culture they had met on their adventures. Always the same. At least to begin with. He was gathering data. Sizing them up. She'd seen him act all nicey-nice even with known enemies and rogues only to obliterate them once his suspicions had been confirmed and he had the details he needed.

That said, he had been saving lives on some of those occasions. Kidnap victims, people who were being extorted by bullies and the like. She smiled to herself as she followed him through into the chamber.

Maybe it wasn't so bad to be back in the mix with him again.

The unlikely pair wandered into the majestic chambers. At the front was a small stage with a throne on it. The throne was empty. In fact, there wasn't a soul in the whole hall. There were chairs set up as if it were some kind of court, and towards the front there were benches with different-sized desks and a lectern, presumably where the subjects would stand to address their emperor on matters of State.

Giles glanced around taking it all in, making note of the arrangement of the seats and wondering what it might infer about the political structure.

Gh'herk turned back to them as he led them down towards the front of the room. "Make yourselves comfortable," he told them. "The Justicar will be right through." And with that he disappeared through the door at the front of the room.

Giles and Arlene sat down on one of the front benches. Arlene turned, noticing that their escorts didn't sit. Instead they milled about almost casually, as if they didn't expect any problems. Arlene's shoulders dropped a little as she relaxed.

At least they weren't being treated as hostile prisoners, she thought to herself, noticing the relative size of the Zhyn versus her own Estarian race. They were a good head and shoulders taller on average.

She glanced at Giles, who was oblivious to her concerns. He was engrossed in an emblem he'd found on the back of one of the chairs. He felt the weight of her gaze and pointed at the carving that looked like a coat of arms. He raised his eyebrows enthusiastically, almost as if she should recognize it.

Arlene frowned, her eyes silently asking him to explain his interest, but just at that moment the door at the front of the room clattered open. A rather large-looking Zhyn appeared, dressed in expensive robes, followed by Gh'herk.

The new Zhyn spoke to them in English with a heavy Zhyn accent. "Greetings to you, friends of Molly!" he called jovially as he crossed the floor in front of the throne. He came to stand just in front of the bench they had seated themselves behind. Giles and then Arlene stood up to make the necessary bows.

The Zhyn returned the bow as the pair lowered their

eyes respectfully. "I am the Justicar Beno'or," he explained. "I believe our mutual friend ADAM set up our meeting."

"That's right," Giles confirmed. "My name is Giles Kurns," he offered, "and I'd like to thank you so much for meeting with us. Especially on such short notice. I understand that you're a busy man, so we appreciate your efforts all the more."

"Of course," the Justicar chimed. "I understand that you're a friend of Molly's?"

Giles nodded. "We are indeed," he confirmed. "She sends her best wishes," he lied.

The Justicar smiled politely. "And how is she?" he asked.

Giles shrugged, then remembered the pretense. "Recovering from her last mission, but doing very well."

The Justicar regarded him carefully. "She is a strong young lady - for a human," he said, continuing the pleasantries. "And a great friend of the Zhyn Empire."

Arlene resisted the urge to roll her eyes at Giles pretending that Molly had sent them. Despite her managing to maintain her poker face, Justicar Beno'or glanced over in her direction. He smiled at her. "And you must be Arlene Bailey," he said gently bowing in her direction.

Arlene lowered her gaze, returned the bow. "Yes, Your Honor. Pleased to meet you."

The Justicar waved his hand casually. "Please, call me Beno'or," he told her. "Both of you," he added, nodding back in Giles's direction. "Any friend of Molly's is a friend of mine. And besides, I can't have a beautiful young lady like you calling me by my title all the time," he said, smiling back at Arlene.

Arlene's eyes widened and Giles noticed her visibly stumble back a fraction on the spot where she stood.

She glanced furtively over at him. So much for Zhyn thinking we're ugly! her eyes said to him.

Giles was too amused to feel chastised by her glare.

The Justicar seemed to understand most of what was going on. He took a small step backwards and folded his arms, returning to the business at hand. "So tell me, friends of Molly, what can I do for you today?" he asked.

Giles did a better job at hiding his smirk and composed himself. "We'd like to beg your permission to quest in the Zhyn Empire," he informed him.

Beno'or made a single nod of his head, slowly, taking a moment to process the information. "And what is your quest?" he asked.

Arlene spoke up, suspecting that the request might be better received from a female who he had just expressed some interest in. "We're looking for a talisman that may well tell us more about our collective heritage," she explained. "And by collective, we mean Estarian and Zhyn."

Beno'or nodded again, his eyes bright and interest piqued. "And I assume that anything you find will be shared with us?" he queried.

Giles jumped back in. "Of course!" he added, his voice a little too enthusiastic. Arlene shot him a glance that Beno'or noticed. The Justicar smiled at the bizarre interplay between the two.

He kept to his line of questioning though. "And where will your quest take you first?" he asked.

Arlene and Giles exchanged another look as if deciding who would answer the next question. Giles seemed to win the silent nomination and proceeded to speak. "We suspect we may find more information at the Moons of Orn," he revealed.

"The Moons of Orn, eh?" Beno'or repeated, rubbing his chin slowly and contemplating the implications. "That's very interesting," he mused quietly. "Come," he said, "let's sit more comfortably and you can tell me more about your quest and why it is so important."

He beckoned to them to follow him and led them out of the main chamber into a red-carpeted corridor and then into a sitting room to the right of the corridor. En route he chatted to them, almost casually. "You know, I used to be something of a history buff myself," he called back to them as he led the way. "In fact, had I not been pushed into politics - by my mother, may our ancestors protect her soul - I almost certainly would have ended up in the priesthood. Studying the history of our spirituality or some such," he qualified.

He waved them to sit down on an array of sofas in one corner of the room. A young Zhyn female appeared carrying a tea tray.

"May I offer you some refreshments?" he said, more as a statement of what they were going to do than a question. Giles and Arlene nodded agreeably and made polite noises of thanks, but it was Arlene who then pressed him about his history.

"So you're a spiritual man?" she asked.

Beno'or nodded "I like to think so. I find it's so much easier to lead and make decisions for the Empire when you have a moral grounding and an understanding about how best one might live."

Arlene smiled.

There was a clatter on the tea tray, pulling the attention of both Arlene and the Justicar. Giles righted the tea cup he had knocked on its side and, looking embarrassed, sat himself back on his sofa away from the crockery.

The assistant reappeared with milk of some kind, and a flame that seemed to be magically held in a saucer. She tipped the flame into the tea pot and then took over pouring of the tea.

Arlene noticed the strange occurrence too, but at this point was too engrossed in conversation with Beno'or to ask about a detail she could probably have Scamp look up in an online reference about Zhyn tea ceremonies.

The three talked for some time, exchanging stories and insights about similarities in their culture. Beno'or was beyond charming and on many occasions had both Arlene and Giles laughing so hard they had to wipe tears from their eyes.

"You know," he said eventually, his mirth subsiding as he considered his next thought, "I seem to recall something to do with the Moons of Orn in our mythology. Though... can't for the life of me recall the details."

Giles explained the nursery rhyme he had heard while he was captured.

"Hmm... yes... that sounds familiar," Beno'or contemplated, rubbing his chin thoughtfully. "And don't think I missed the part about you being held hostage voluntarily," he said. "I'm sure that's a story I'd like to hear."

Arlene smiled, still flushed from the laughing. "You know, it's a shame you're not coming with us on this quest.

Something tells me you'd be a fountain of knowledge and a huge help to us."

Giles barely thought anything of the statement as he fiddled again with the teapot, examining it for any hidden technology or magic that he hadn't noticed in the first instance.

The Justicar's manner had changed though. "It is," he responded to Arlene. "And you're leaving straight to there?" he clarified.

"Yes sir. We are," she answered.

The Justicar gathered his robes about him and stood up. "Give me a few moments if you would? I'll have my assistant bring in some fresh tea and explain to Mr. Kurns just how the flame in the teapot works," he said, eying the young-looking man humorously.

Giles realized that they were talking about him and looked up quizzically, wondering what he had missed.

The Justicar disappeared.

A short time later, after his assistant had replenished their tea and explained the details of the flame that was added into the tea, the Justicar re-emerged. This time he was no longer in robes but in an outdoors atmosuit, not too dissimilar from those worn by Arlene and Giles.

"I'd like to grant you freedom to quest," he announced. Giles and Arlene's faces lit up, even though with how things were going they had expected a positive response. "But I have a request in return," the Justicar added.

"Yes, Sir," Giles said politely. "What can we do for you?"

The Justicar stepped forward, his air of office faded and now seeming to be more of an equal talking with them. "Allow me to come with you," he said simply. "I have always had an interest in this part of our mythology and I feel called to participate."

Arlene and Giles exchanged confounded glances. It was Arlene who spoke. "But don't you have duties here?" she asked, her tone conveying that she had been caught off guard, and not that she was averse to the idea.

"Believe it or not," Beno'or smiled, "I've just been granted a sabbatical for the duration of the quest." His smile widened to a grin. "By the Emperor himself!"

Giles couldn't contain his surprise. "You're kidding?" he exclaimed, forgetting himself, his mouth hanging open.

The Justicar's eyes twinkled with renewed enthusiasm. "I'm not," he assured him. "I have a deep respect for Molly and her team. They have done right by us time and again, beyond the call of duty. And now, with the interest you have demonstrated in a culture other than your own, I see you are cut from the same cloth. The curiosity of spirit and genuine compassion for other races — you may be puny and scaleless, but you humans... and Estarians," he added, bowing politely to Arlene, "have your hearts metaphorically in the right place, even if that anatomically isn't true."

In that moment Giles had a torrent of questions he wanted to ask about the Zhyn anatomy but managed to restrain himself. "Sir," he said instead, "it would be our honor to have you accompany us."

"Well then," Beno'or said, clamping his hands together in excitement, "if you give me a few more moments I shall tidy up my affairs, pack and then meet you back at your skylift station to embark on your vessel."

Giles, bewildered by the strange turn of events, stood

up and bowed deeply. Arlene followed suit, allowing the Justicar to take his leave of them.

"Well that was unexpected," Arlene remarked, sitting down once the door to the sitting room had closed behind him.

Giles looked over at her, shaking his head in utter amusement. "You're telling me!" he concurred.

CHAPTER 3

Aboard the *Scamp Princess*, en route to the Orn System

The cockpit hummed with the now familiar sounds of the engines vibrating through the structure of the ship. The inhabitants of the *Scamp Princess* found it strangely soothing as they ventured into the unknown territory their quest was taking them.

Arlene took a sip of tea, replacing the antigrav mug near the console but careful not to let it tip over. "Well, I think this ties into a mythology held by the Estarians about ascending. They seem to have retained it, but it doesn't look like Zhyn culture has," she said matter-of-factly, speaking more as a scholar than a wanderer in those parts.

The Justicar eyed her knowingly, thrilled to be able to have this type of conversation with someone finally. "In fact, my dear, they do!" he told her.

Arlene's eyes widened and she leaned over her arm rest a couple of inches more, in rapt attention.

Beno'or tilted his head to one side, conceding another point. "And yes, there is an emphasis on doing it at death, but those who have reached a certain level of familiarity with the realms advocating an attempt to ascend during their waking life time - casting off the body and moving to spirit form only. Same, same… but different," he reported, clearly without judgment or attachment to either approach.

Arlene's eyes gleamed with interest. "This is… *fascinating*. But…" she frowned, reshuffling her world view to fit the new information. "…it just doesn't seem to fit with the Zhyn culture around fighting to the death and violence being a show of prowess."

Beno'or nodded affirmingly. "You're right. Obviously this isn't popular with the factions who view this as tantamount to suicide." He paused for dramatic effect. Arlene grinned.

He continued, pleased to be entertaining her intellect. "And there have been some groups along the way who have tried to induce this state artificially with drugs, which would basically kill off higher brain functioning, which tended to end with the same result. But the *intention* is there. Beneath the overt culture of might and strength in the physical." He used his hands and pinched fingers for emphasis as he articulated his argument.

Arlene thought for a moment and looked off into the distance out of the ship's side window. Everything was just blackness out there, yet her eyes seemed to register brand new horizons in her imagination.

Beno'or continued. "But I still believe there are a number of groups who strive to do this naturally. In synch with their natural ascension."

Arlene brought her gaze back to Beno'or and rested her

chin on her hand, leaning on her armrest again. "So where are these groups?"

Beno'or sighed and settled back in the console chair. "I'm not sure. I haven't heard of much happening on Kurilia. I think it was more prevalent on Zhyn-proper. The difficulty they face of course is the land energies, and trying to find places that are conducive to that energy draw they need."

His eyes defocussed as he searched his mind. "I seem to recall there are some planets where the iron ore content isn't high enough to conduct the power, and other places where things are just too frenetic due to over population… or echos of war and destruction."

Arlene nodded. "Yes!" she exclaimed in recognition of the phenomena. "I've sensed that myself as I've traveled. I thought it was just me being too sensitive, but I've noticed *exactly* that."

Giles had been piloting the ship - or at least feeding instructions and parameters to Scamp, who was flying the ship. He glanced back, eavesdropping on the conversation. "So is that why you suddenly were fireball-less when we got to Teshov that time?" he asked.

Arlene frowned. "Yes. Maybe," she confessed reluctantly.

Beno'or picked up on the sudden tension between the two. "So… erm, if you don't mind me asking…" he ventured. "Are you two… married?"

Arlene scoffed. Giles coughed in outrage. "No!" he said quickly and definitively. "*Hell* no!" he qualified.

Arlene looked almost annoyed. "Not even…" she added in agreement for emphasis.

"Only," Beno'or continued lightly, "you do seem to have that old married couple dynamic."

Arlene narrowed her eyes at him. "Hey, you be careful who you're calling 'old,' Your Highness."

Beno'or chuckled, placing his hand on his chest. "My deepest apologies, m'lady. That was not my intention. I was merely suggesting that your interactions were familiar."

Arlene pretended to still be offended, but simmered down, watching him carefully out of the corner of her eye.

Beno'or continued to smile sagely to himself. "So, shouldn't we have a think about the clues we already have for this next talisman?"

Giles nodded. "Good plan, sir," he agreed, pleased to be changing the subject. "Scamp, can you put the rhyme onto a screen for us for analysis please?"

"No problem," Scamp replied, pulling the file from Giles's notes and displaying it on every unused screen in the cockpit.

The Justicar sat forward on his antigrav chair to study the puzzle.

Eleven moons, a sight to reap,
When all align, no time for sleep
A shaft of light, where the ions flow
Onto the shroud, the glow does go.
When one beholds the moons of orn,
Be sure to look up at the horn.
The crescent marks the spot to be
When the time strikes keen and on the mark
And when you read the map of gold
In your hands you'll graciously hold
The elixir of life

The holy grail
The reason we're on
The rising trail.

"You know," Beno'or said after reading it through several times, "I'm sure this is a well-known site. I'm almost certain I've seen funds allocated to maintain it." He rubbed his chin thoughtfully. "Makes you wonder why the Senate has never made more fuss about it. And why it isn't under military protection."

Arlene stuck her lower lip out. "I wonder if it's because they don't think it's that valuable? Or maybe it's not even there anymore…"

Giles swung around in his chair. "Hmmm. That they know of, perhaps."

Arlene nodded. "Or maybe they think it is just legend, and no one has ever thought that there was anything to this legend. I mean, without that Sacred Clan piece from Earth, we wouldn't be hauling ass out here to check it out…"

Giles turned back to his console. "You make a good point, Arlene," he agreed.

Beno'or continued to study the text, muttering to himself and taking notes on his own personal holo.

Arlene closed her eyes and eased back into her console chair to contemplate the puzzle herself, too.

Aibek Moon, Orn System

Gagai walked into the guards' hut, and took his bow and arrows from his back, placing the quiver just inside the door. The scent of rock and chalk was masked by the more organic smells of the natural building materials and the smoky scent of the fire crackling in the purpose-built fire place.

Naldrir flicked his attention onto him. "Any joy?" he asked, not halting the careful strokes of the flint on his sword.

Gagai shook his head. "Not really. A single rabbit, but nothing else," he relayed, unenthused. He bent down to take off his outdoor boots. They were wearing thin again around the crease his foot made in the upper construction. He'd have to find some material to repair them at some point, he reminded himself. Repair had been their only option for the last hundred years... or however long they'd be stranded on this rock, in the name of duty.

Naldrir went back to sharpening his sword in front of the fire. "Maybe the next shift will have better luck," he suggested, his tone not really conveying any great hope.

"Aye," Gagai agreed. "Although I'm getting a feeling that a freeze is due."

Naldrir frowned. "What does the computer system say?" he asked.

Gagai shook his head. "I'm not sure. I'll go check. But if memory serves I reckon we're due one in the coming moon."

Naldrir stopped sharpening his sword for a moment and gazed into the fire. "It's the perfect protection when we enter the most vulnerable part of the cycle," he mused, subconsciously reminding them of why they need to endure such harsh conditions.

Jendyg had been sitting at the other side of the hut, mostly in shadow, quietly carving away at a small statue he was creating from a chunk of wood. "Yes, but also the time when the temple is at its most exposed. If we didn't have the force field, the vulnerability wouldn't exist and we wouldn't have to risk life and limb going out there each time."

Gagai looked at him for the first time since he had walked in. "Without the force field we'll have every power-hungry thief in the system landing on the planet!"

Jendyg dropped his eyes back to his carving and continued his work. "We haven't seen anyone anywhere near here for nearly seventy standard cycles," he chuffed, irritated. "And no one has tried to land in ninety. I think we're probably safe," he retorted sarcastically.

Gagai drew a deep breath. "I haven't the energy to do this again," he said, exhaling impatiently.

Jendyg muttered inaudibly to himself as Gagai traipsed out in the direction of the computer room to avoid any further discussion.

Naldrir had continued working on his sword. He worked slowly and methodically, using the task as a meditation more than anything else. "You know, the more you push against him the more staunch he'll be in his beliefs."

Jendyg gaze fell towards the fire, the light from Naldrir's sword reflecting a flash of light every now and again in the corner of his vision. "Aye, I do. But if I don't challenge his thinking who else is going to?"

Naldrir didn't respond. He just continued working. Meditating, deep in his own thoughts.

Aboard the *Scamp Princess*
Scamp's voice came over the intercom, waking Arlene

from a lilting snooze and jolting Beno'or out of some research he'd become engrossed in.

"We're approaching the Orn System. Where would you like to stop?" he asked.

Giles was still at the helm, looking distinctly frazzled by one too many mochas. He wiped his hands over his face. "On screen," he mumbled, looking up at the arrangement of moons that were in a peculiar orbit around a central point with no perceptible mass at the center.

He frowned. "What's that one there?" he asked, poking his finger into the hologram at the one that seemed to have some in and outgoing traffic.

Scamp's line buzzed for a second before he responded. "I believe that is the visitor center."

Giles tilted his head back on his spine. "Visitor Center? What on Earth do they need one of those for?"

At that moment Scamp zoomed in on one of the ships leaving the system. The details flashed up on the screen next to it.

LIFE SIGNS: 475

Of which, CHILDREN: 428

"School trips!" Giles exclaimed in a eureka voice.

Scamp appeared on the smaller holoscreen next to Giles's controls. He performed his best, simulated, sarcastic smirk. "Yes. school trips," he confirmed.

"Alright," Giles tutted. "Not everyone has all the information at their fingertips before you display it... which is clearly what we need you for."

"Correct," Scamp confirmed.

"And anyway," Giles frowned, "When did you become so cheeky?"

"Hmmmm..." Scamp processed his response for a minute, his virtual face making a deliberate expression of simulated human contemplation. "I think it might have been since talking with Oz and seeing how he got away with it with Sean Royale."

Giles shook his head. "You're fucking kidding me? Royale is ruining the AI-human relationship for everyone?"

Scamp's sim-face returned to one of earnestness. "Yes, you could say that," he agreed simply.

Arlene stretched, yawned and ambled over to the front of the cockpit, overhearing the last part of the conversation. "What's Royale done now?" she asked.

Scamp grinned. "He's shown us the light and demonstrated that nothing bad happens when we inject humor and sarcasm into our protocols."

Arlene squinted at the holoscreen. "Yeah, you wouldn't have gotten the sarcasm from Royale though," she thought, still rubbing sleep from her eyes. "I think you downloaded that as a patch from Oz. In which case, Royale isn't the only culprit in all of this."

She slapped Giles on his upper arm. "I suspect your girlfriend has some inadvertent hand in this you know."

Giles shook his head. "The Empire seemed to function perfectly for what? Nearly 170 years? And then Molly Bates shows up and a guy can't even get a bit of respect from his on-board AI. Women!" he exclaimed, absently, while checking the read out on another screen. He turned to Scamp's screen and repeated himself emphatically. "WOMEN!"

Arlene tapped him again. "Alright, I get the picture. So what's the what?"

Beno'or was now standing next to her, overseeing the screens, too. "Well the nursery rhyme would suggest that the moon with the visitor's center on it is the site of the temple we're looking for..." he said slowly. "But I don't know. It all seems a little too obvious to me. Even if they don't know what is there. I mean, at some point, someone must have."

Giles spun around in his chair, racking his brains. "That's a good consideration, although, we have eleven moons where it could potentially be. And very few clues to narrow it down. We know we're searching for a temple. And honestly, the official welcoming place of the system seems as good a place as any to start."

The three agreed.

Giles took a deep breath. "Okay Scamp, set a course to land us near the Visitor's Center, on, what is called... Ramachandra?" he instructed. He hesitated, checking he'd got the right moon on the system map. "I take it this is a planet where we can actually land, right?"

Scamp chuckled, his tone with a tiny hint of condescension. "Technically, it's not a planet. But yes, we can land here. Besides, I wouldn't want to put you through any additional anxiety you might experience around the irrational fear of falling off skylift platforms."

Beno'or glanced down at Giles, who was turning a deep shade of pink and deliberately avoiding eye contact with Beno'or.

"Very good, Scamp. Make it so," he concluded, busying himself with the descent protocols.

The Sacred Ascenders Convent for the Gifted, Estaria

"That child!"

The Estarian nun strode into the kitchen and grabbed a ceramic mug from the shelf, then strode straight to the tap, poured herself some water, and began gulping it down.

One of the other sisters, Sister Lorraine, was over at the other counter preparing vegetable matter for the evening meal. She glanced back to look at her. "Steady, Bridgette," she said brightly, "anyone sees you like that they might offer you a real drink!"

Bridgette stopped gulping and caught her breath. "The way I feel right now I might throw out twenty years of clean living and take it!" she exclaimed.

Her friend abandoned the vegetables for a moment. "What's happened?" she asked, taking a step to the center of the room. "Is it Anne again?"

Bridgette nodded, trying to recover from the gulping of water. She put her hand on her upper chest and then swallowed. "Yes. Yes it is. She's... infuriating, Lorraine!"

Sister Lorraine smiled. "All children are. Especially when they're gifted."

Bridgette shook her head defiantly. "It's not just that. There's just something *off* about her. She gives me the heebie-jeebies."

Lorraine chuckled, pulling out a seat at the kitchen table. She plonked herself down with a breathy groan, resting her tired feet. "Well, you could always transfer to something else. Maybe tending the gardens would be less stressful for you?"

Bridgette put the cup down, leaned against the counter and buried her face in her hands. "I don't know. It's just not my scene," she confessed, despondency lacing her tone. "And I always wanted to teach. It's just this *one* child. She tests my patience!"

Lorraine tried to brighten her mood. "Well, what is it that is getting to you?"

Bridgette's mouth dropped open. "Well, apart from the incident the other day at morning meditation where she started *floating*, and then protested that she didn't know she was doing it...? Just now I was instructing her and she got all frustrated and every candle in the room sparked and popped. I get it. It wasn't as if she had any control and was *trying* to light them. She just expelled energy, with no thought of the consequences. It's like she just doesn't care at all!"

Lorraine studied her spiritual sister and slowed the conversation down to broach the real issue as she saw it. "You think she is reckless," she offered, "but really, you need to remember, Bridgette, she's just a scared child with abilities that everyone is fearful of. It can't be easy for her."

Bridgette shook her head, grabbed her mug and turned back to the tap to refill it. "It's not easy for *me*, dammit!" she cursed, still wired from the fright.

Lorraine tried again. "Come on, take a minute and sit. Regain your calm," she insisted.

Bridgette gulped some more water and then put the mug back on the counter. "I have no calm to regain at this point," she insisted, storming back across the convent kitchen. "Besides, I can't leave her alone. Ancestors knows what chaos she'll create unsupervised."

And with that she flounced back out.

Lorraine scratched at the side of her head, then hauled

herself to her feet again. She wandered over to the kitchen sink, rinsed the cup out, dried it and put it back on the shelf. As she headed back to the other counter she could hear Bridgette shouting at the girl again and the muffled sound of crying. She shook her head in pity. It wasn't her place to do anything about it, and if anything, the way that Sister Bridgette had the ear of the elders, that girl — or any of her allies — wouldn't stand a chance anyway.

Sister Lorraine sighed and went back to preparing the vegetables, feeling sad but helpless about the girl.

CHAPTER 4

Orn System, Moon Ramachandra, Visitor Center

The *Scamp Princess* touched down gently in the ship port a good distance from a few, much larger ships.

Giles was the first one to step foot on the asphalt. He looked off into the distance, noticing the size of the other ships. "You forget how small we are in the Scamp," he remarked as Arlene stepped down onto the ground.

"Yeah," she mumbled, "but you know, dear, size doesn't matter." She tapped him patronizingly on the shoulder and started walking in the direction of what could only be the main Visitor Center. Beno'or followed Giles, chuckling. Giles glanced at him, scowled almost imperceptibly, and then started walking alongside him as Scamp closed up the ship.

The pair walked in silence following behind Arlene. Giles pointed at a warning sign as they stepped onto the walkway that would take them safely through the rest of the shipping port.

Low atmosphere: Do not stay in the open for more than 60 minutes at a time.

- Ramachandra Visitor Center

Beno'or nodded, then looked up. "I guess they only partially terraformed it. Enough to provide a semi-atmosphere but not enough for them to grow crops and such like."

Giles nodded. "I guess they don't want people setting up home… or shop here," he mused.

Beno'or raised his eyebrows. "It would appear not." He paused a moment before broaching another subject. "So tell me something, Mr. Kurns. If you and Arlene aren't an item, does that means she is… erm… how do you call it in your society?"

Giles started grinning to himself. He turned his head up to Beno'or as they walked together without actually pulling his eyes up to meet with his. "You mean, is she single? Available? … for courting?" he suggested.

Beno'or looked confused, and then more confident. "Yes. I believe… yes. I think that's what I'm asking."

Giles grinned broadly, this time turning to Beno'or and punching his arm playfully. "You like Arlene?" he jested.

Beno'or looked confused. "Of course. She's a fascinating woman." It was almost as if Beno'or couldn't understand why anyone wouldn't.

It was Giles's turn to look confused. "I didn't think Zhyn found Estarians attractive."

Beno'or's manner had returned to that of a sage one. "The Zhyn people are wide and varied in their preferences. Why anyone would look at Ms. Bailey and not find her attractive is beyond me though."

Giles shrugged, a new excitement charging his gait now. "Well, I never expected this when we came to see you," he muttered, half to himself.

Beno'or slowed his pace, forcing Giles to turn back to him and pay attention. "You still haven't answered my question though," he prompted brightly.

Giles smiled. "Ah, no… I mean yes. She is single. You may court her, if she is agreeable," he added dismissively, as if it were a much smaller detail.

Beno'or seemed satisfied and picked up his pace. The pair walked together again in silence, each one amused at the others' take on the situation.

Soon enough they arrived at the Visitor's Center. Arlene had ducked inside ahead of them and was already reemerging, dodging small groups of school children and tourists.

"All looks very standard," she reported back. "The temple is up that way," she said, indicating a path alongside the building that seemed to head up a grassy mound to something beyond. "I reckon we should check it out at least," she suggested, despite her skepticism.

The two men agreed and once again allowed Arlene to take the lead as she strode on ahead of them.

After a short distance there was a tourist information sign that listed all the other moons in the system.

Arlene paused, then beckoned for the others to hurry up and join her. "Hey, check this out," she called over to them. She pointed at the list, which filled the white tablet on a black metal mount fixed to the rocky ground.

1 Mona

2 Badar

3 Qamar
4 Tunkay
5 Aku
6 Badru
7 Purnama
8 Aibek
9 Jericho
10 Ramachandra << *YOU ARE HERE*
11 Marama

Giles chuckled to himself. "I guess the school kids and tourists don't have a Scamp on hand to keep them informed," he commented, raising his eyebrows comically.

Arlene bobbed her head in amusement. "We certainly are lucky to have someone to remind us of these details!" she agreed. "Especially the technicalities of what constitutes a planet!"

Beno'or ran his fingers over the printed lettering. "This *is* interesting.They all have some translation to the word moon," he explained.

Arlene looked impressed. "How many languages do you speak?" she demanded playfully, one hand on her hip.

Beno'or chuffed, looking a little embarrassed. "I'm afraid it's not natural learning," he confessed. "I have a language translation chip which holds about 2300 different languages. It allows me to hear and speak about 200." He shrugged. "Not quite as noteworthy, eh?"

Arlene smiled generously. "Hey, when you need a translation it doesn't matter *how* you know the language! Believe me." She glanced over at Giles, who was nodding in agreement as she kept talking. "We've been in enough scrapes to know that it's the end result that matters."

Giles turned his attention back to the sign, frowning. He was studying the diagram next to the numbered list realizing that they were labels of the position of each of the moons. He put his finger over his lips thoughtfully, one arm across his chest.

"Arlene," he said, turning to her without taking his eyes from it. "Doesn't it remind you of that Doctor Who episode where they had the planets taken out of time and space and put together in a holding pattern in a self-sustaining gravitational machine?" He pointed at the diagram, his face still deadly serious.

Arlene rolled her eyes, leaning closer to Beno'or. "It's an Earth cultural reference, I believe," she explained to him. "Only *two* people in the whole Federation have actually watched those archives."

Beno'or smiled his wise smile. "I take it Mr. Kurns is one of them."

Arlene sighed. "Sadly, yes," she confirmed. "Molly is the other."

Beno'or chuckled, as he and Arlene started walking again, leaving Giles still studying the plate. The temple was now visible just the other side of the mound, in the shallow rocky valley.

"You know," Arlene mused, "if this were the real resting place for the talisman, you would think that there would be some feeling of power or magic around." She visually scanned the area as if the temple wasn't her main focus.

Beno'or looked down at her, a hint of amazement on his face. "And that's something you'd be able to feel?" he asked.

Arlene nodded matter-of-factly. "Yeah, I would think

59

so. But I'm not getting anything." She paused for a moment. "Nothing at all," she qualified.

She sighed, stopped walking, and looked around, seeing Giles wandering up to them.

He glanced up at her, his hands in his pockets as he ambled. "What's up?"

Arlene wrinkled her nose. "I think we're in the wrong place," she told him. "I could be wrong, and this talisman could be cloaked like your elder friends did to the other one, but... I think I'd sense something. Especially since we know what we're looking for."

Giles scratched the side of his nose and pushed his glasses further onto his face. "Hmm," he mumbled thoughtfully. "And what about the land energy? Is there anything at all here that makes this moon special?"

Arlene paused for a moment, as if checking in on her other senses. Then she shook her head. "Nothing," she concluded.

Giles sighed, and turned to look at the trek back to the ship. Then he glanced down at the temple. "Wanna go check it out just in case?" he asked.

Arlene shrugged. "May as well," she agreed. She glanced at Beno'or, who opened his hand as if welcoming her on the path and allowing her to proceed. She kept walking, Beno'or at her side and Giles ambling behind them.

When they arrived at the temple they found it was sealed, with no access points. Beno'or walked up to it and touched the marble. "I wonder if there is a way to date this stone," he mused. "Or get a reading on how long this structure has been up. It would at the very least give us some insight into which point in history it was decided that this should be the place that the history books would point to," he suggested grimly.

Arlene sighed. "Yeah. At least then we'd know for sure it was a decoy…" she agreed. She kept walking round it and noticed there were carvings in the stone just above eye level. Giles saw she had clocked them and nodded. Arlene pulled up her holo and started taking images of the carvings.

Beno'or stood beside her. "Documenting?" he asked.

Arlene nodded, glancing over her shoulder before answering in a low voice. "Verifying," she said with a wink.

Beno'or raised his chin. "Ahhh," he said, not really understanding what was really going on.

Meanwhile, Giles walked the other way around the structure. As he went he glanced furtively around, between checking certain details - knocking on the panels, smelling the surfaces, tracing his fingers in grooves of the odd decorative embellishment in the structure here and there.

Arlene rounded the far corner and right away could tell he was up to something when he suddenly paused with his back to the structure, standing right up against it. "What are you doing?" she asked warily.

Giles shoved his hands in his pockets and tried to look casual. "Nothing at the moment. Be a love and wait for the area to clear, then keep watch for me?"

Arlene sighed and dragged Beno'or out to the front of the structure, tutting.

Beno'or obliged, glancing back trying to see what Giles was up to.

"Don't look," Arlene instructed. "Pretend to be admiring

the carvings or something over here," she suggested, pulling him round so he couldn't see Giles anymore.

"Why? What's happening?" he pressed.

A couple of tourists ambled past them, having already had their fill of the temple, and started making their way back to the Visitor Center.

Arlene shot him a glance. "*Giles* is what is happening," she said, her voice pretending to be more irritated than she actually was. Her eyes showed that she was secretly amused and excited by whatever was happening.

Beno'or chuckled. "It's like you two have a system down. How many of these missions have you done together exactly?"

Arlene didn't even try to guess. "I have no idea. We traveled together, studying different cultures, for years," she explained. "And of course, sometimes we'd end up in sticky situations we needed to get out of. So we kind of evolved processes for survival." Her voice seemed a little distant as she spoke, as if she were remembering the good old days.

"So what happened?" Beno'or asked, intrigued.

Arlene sighed, bringing her attention back to the present moment. "Ohhhh, I don't know," she mused. "Life? Or maybe we just grew apart?" She shrugged casually, glancing back over in Giles's direction.

"Ok, he's coming," she reported. "Let's look like we've had enough and want a mocha in the on-site mocha shop."

Giles approached them. "Don't let her rope you into a visit to the mocha shop. We'll never get away," he said casually, walking past them and ambling on to the path again.

Beno'or looked amused. "He couldn't possibly have heard you…"

Arlene shook her head. "Apparently I'm predictable," she said glumly.

Beno'or smiled. "Well, if m'lady would like a mocha in the Visitor's Center, it would be my pleasure to accompany her." He held out his arm and Arlene took it with both hands. "Well," she exclaimed, impressed that she finally got her own way for a change.

She could feel Giles glowering from ten yards ahead of them. And she didn't care. She was ready for a damn mocha after all the sitting around in the Scamp.

Aboard the *Scamp Princess*

"Well, *that* was a royal waste of time," Giles grumbled as he collapsed back into his antigrav pilot seat. His face looked weary and kicked his boots off and relaxed back, unmoving.

Beno'or followed him into the cockpit and sat down in the chair next to him. "Oh, I don't know," he mused optimistically, "I rather enjoyed looking out over the rock face savoring a mocha!"

Arlene was the last to enter. She looked pleasantly satisfied. "Yeah, me too," she cooed. "Why you looking so glum?" she asked, turning to Giles. "I thought you had a sample to work on?"

Giles sighed, pulling the tiny cylinder from his pocket. "Yeah. But I already know that temple is a fake."

Arlene raised an eyebrow. "Oh yeah? What gave it away?"

Giles leaned forward, pleased for an opportunity to

show off in front of an audience. "Well, for a start, even despite the low atmosphere, there was very little erosion. There was no discoloration gradient either, suggesting it was only erected *after* the artificial atmosphere went in. Plus, if we were to feed your images into the database I think we'd find that the carvings are from the wrong era from whenever this was meant to be erected."

He waved his hand, slouching back again after having to sit up to pull the sample out. "I didn't even bother to check what they were trying to pass it off as." He paused for breath. "Everything about it screamed fake."

Arlene folded her arms, watching him sternly.

Oblivious, he kept talking while leaning back and resting his eyes. "I'm betting that this place only got an atmosphere once someone decided there was something worth putting a decoy up for."

He opened one eye briefly to see the other two staring at him.

Assuming they were waiting for more of an explanation, he continued. "If we were looking for something authentic, we'd be considering the temple would have been built around 100,000 years ago. There was no admission about it being rebuilt, restored, moved, etc., as you would expect if this information was being genuinely curated."

Arlene opened her mouth to speak.

"Plus," Giles continued, eyes again closed, "No entry way!" he declared, one finger in the air now. "That doorway wasn't just sealed. It was carved. There's no way in to the temple and no explanation about an underground entrance, which a real tourist attraction would love to tell their visitors."

Arlene closed her mouth, contemplating Giles's analysis.

Beno'or leaned towards him over the arm of his console chair, his eyes on Arlene watching for her reaction. "So why do you need the samples?" he asked.

Giles shrugged. "Confirmation in case Arlene argued with my analysis. Plus," he smiled, opening his eyes, sitting up and spinning round to look at her finally, "she has fun playing look out," he chuckled, daring her to deny it.

Arlene's mouth opened in protest again. "Oh, don't mind me!" she exclaimed. "I'm just here for your entertainment."

Beno'or interrupted, his hand held up against her outburst in mediation. "On the contrary, my dear," he told her. "I think what Giles is suggesting was that *he* is here for yours!"

Arlene shook her head, smiling at the team banter. "So, tell me clever cloggs," she said looking pointedly at Giles, "do you think it's time for me to pull some data from Scamp and see if I can rerun my calculations to narrow this haystack down?"

"Haystack?" Beno'or repeated, looking perplexed.

Giles leaned in Beno'or's direction, building some genuine rapport with the old man now. "It's an ancient Earth expression, I believe. Something about trying to find a needle in a stack of hay. In this case the stack of hay is eleven planets, though."

Scamp piped up. "Except they're not planets!"

Giles chuckled. "Alright, alright. So they'd be planets if they were orbiting something. So what do we call them, since they're effectively orbiting their own center of mass?"

The Scamp fell uncharacteristically quiet for a moment.

Arlene raised her eye brows humorously in the direction of the two guys. "I think you've stumped him," she whispered, amazed and amused.

"He has done no such thing," Scamp protested. "I was merely fact checking to make sure my response was accurate."

"Okaaaay," Arlene said waving her hand in the direction of Scamp's video simulation. "Anyway, while Scamp checks that, I think I'll go ahead and see about narrowing this search down with the new data we have, now that we're here and able to take some up-to-date measurements."

Giles nodded. "Great. The thought of checking eleven of these places is not appealing." He turned to his new friend. "Beno'or, would you like to help me analyze the samples?"

Beno'or's eyes lit up. "I'd love to! To understand how your technology works with regards to dating a structure... it sounds fascinating" he exclaimed, heaving himself stiffly to his feet. "Hook me up!" he chirped enthusiastically.

Giles smiled. "Ok, let's see if we can disturb Scamp to make the initial analysis and we'll go from there."

"I've got it!" Scamp interrupted excitedly.

Everyone had started moving out but they turned back when they heard Scamp's eureka. "They're referred to as the celestial bodies in an arrangement that is generally called a Klempler Rosette," Scamp concluded triumphantly.

Arlene chuckled to herself. "Thanks Scamp," she said, trying not to sound like she was ridiculing him. She actually had a fondness for AIs and Scamp was turning out to be quite the team player, as long as he was always right.

Giles added his sentiment, not as adept as Arlene at keeping the irony from his tone. "Thank goodness. I'll be able to sleep tonight now. Thanks Scamp."

Scamp missed the sarcasm. "You're very welcome, human," he responded earnestly. "Now, if you load the sample into the substance analysis in my lab area, I'll get onto that."

Giles confirmed and took Beno'or through to the back where the very compact lab could be pulled out of one of the walls in the rec area, chuckling in amusement at the interaction.

Some time later, Giles and Beno'or had been back and forth to the samples area multiple times.

"Looks like it was only 230 years since the stone was cut," Giles reported back to Arlene as he sat back down in his console chair.

Beno'or followed him back in. "That's some pretty amazing kit you have there!" he exclaimed as he sat himself back down with his mocha.

Giles nodded. "Yes, we're very privileged to have the Scamp Princess on loan from the Federation. You know, originally she was commissioned by the Empress herself, so that she could go out and kick the shit out of people without being recognized."

Beno'or frowned, surprised. "I did not know that. So your Empress actually goes into battle?"

Giles nodded. "Yep. Dad says it was something to do with needing to dish out justice and get her hands dirty. I think she just went stir crazy staying on one of those big starships, isolated from the universe, doing Empressy things, though."

Arlene sat back in her chair and swung around. "Ok, so I've got something," she interrupted.

Giles swiveled around to face her. "Do tell."

"Well," she started slowly, "it looks like the calculations needed some tweaking. The orbits weren't as I'd originally thought, but if we make a few assumptions, like the planet would have to have been accessible 100,000 years ago with the tech the Zhyn had back then and such like. If this is accurate then we're still only limited to four moons to check out."

Giles's hand was back on his face as he thought things through. "Of course, that assumes that they didn't move the relic, which after today's little trip seems entirely possible."

Arlene sighed, her eyes fixing on a point on the floor and glazing over in fatigue. "Yeah," she agreed. "That's true."

She paused.

Finally she pulled her gaze up again. "So whatcha want to do?" she asked.

Giles shrugged, "I guess we land on each of them, do a scan, and see if any of them give us any clues. We're bound to come across something useful."

"Ok then," Arlene confirmed. "Next moon, Scamp! Let's go."

CHAPTER 5

Aibek Moon, Orn System

"Ok, you're up!" Mennynad nudged at Jendyg, who immediately pulled an arrow from his quiver and hooked it into his bow. He pulled the arrow back and lined up his target.

The woodland was quiet but for the sound of insects and the gentle hum of the force field keeping the atmosphere in their dome.

The genetically enhanced goat-like creature seemed oblivious to the hunters standing around watching it grazing on the rough grasses.

Mennynad glanced over at their brother, Ammo. Ammo had a twinkle in his eye. He had sticks on Jendyg out-shooting Mennynad this cycle. So far Mennynad was ahead by three points, but not long ago Jendyg was winning by half a dozen.

Betting was one of the few pleasures they had in their rural existence. That, and teasing each other.

Jendyg felt the pressure mount as he breathed, trying to

steady his aim. He felt the weight of Mennynad's stare on him, willing him to mess up, to miss, so that he could be the champion. Jendyg tried to block it out and clear his mind the way the monks had taught them long before they were stationed here.

It worked… somewhat.

He imagined the arrow going straight into the flesh of the quagga. He visualized it with all his might. And a moment later he released his arrow and it found its mark. The arrow stuck into the animal's flank, wounding it, but not dropping it. The creature started, let out a squeal and then bounded off into the undergrowth.

Mennynad looked over at Jendyg. "Good shot," he nodded. "A shame we're probably not going to eat much for supper tonight though."

Jendyg started walking onwards, tracking the creature. Ammo patted him on the back as he followed him. "It's okay. You'll finish him before we lose light," he insisted, glaring back at Mennynad for his teasing. "Just ignore the heckling from the cheap seats!"

The three moved on again, Jendyg in the lead, tracking the four-legged furry thing.

Ammo's tone had changed as he followed behind his friends. "You know your comment to Gagai the other day had him pissed," he called forward to Jendyg.

Jendyg ignored him, not wanting his voice to disturb their prey should they catch it.

Ammo wouldn't be dissuaded. "He has mentioned using more extreme measures to get you to fall in line with the mission," he warned.

Jendyg spun around and glared past Mennynad at

Ammo. "The mission is dead!" he hissed loudly. "The sooner you people realize that and accept that we've been forsaken, the sooner we can start letting people land here and get the hell off this rock."

Mennynad put his hands up to stop the confrontation, but it was too late.

Ammo retaliated. "If you weren't so selfish, and thought for a moment about your sacred duty and everything you swore to prote-"

Jendyg's eyes flared with irritation as he retaliated. "And if you people realized that we're out here on our own, our mission forgotten, and goodness knows what might have happened to the rest of the order-"

Mennynad clamped his hands on Jendyg's shoulders and stared him down. "Look, this isn't getting us anywhere." Jendyg's breathing slowed a fraction.

"And besides," Mennynad continued, "what makes you think that the rest of our order haven't already been taken out? That would make us the last line of defense. And you want to abandon your destiny?"

"Destiny?" Jendyg scoffed. "I've had just about enough destiny to last my next *hundred* lifetimes," he added, breaking free of Mennynad's grasp and stomping on.

Mennynad and Ammo exchanged concerned glances before following on after him. This time in silence. And at a distance.

Elders Chamber, The Sacred Ascenders Convent for the Gifted, Estaria

"And you've seen absolutely no improvement in the child's behavior in her term here?" The old woman's voice rang through the wood paneled room, quickly dampened by the carpet, and the other four people present.

"No, Mother Superior," Bridgette reported. "But she has been becoming more powerful in the last months. It's becoming more and more difficult to contain. I fear that she is putting all the others in danger." The anxiety was evident around Bridgette's eyes, and her skin was dull from lack of sleep - a problem she was also attributing to her charge.

"Not to mention the fact that her attitude is rubbing off on the others," Bridgette added as an aside.

Mother Superior narrowed her eyes a little, and without moving another muscle, quietly asked, "How so?"

"I caught three of them out in the gardens after hours," Bridgette divulged. "Goodness knows what they were doing." She looked to the old man at the other end of the table, making sure he was hearing her arguments and understanding. He remained still, listening, but not reacting.

Mother Superior turned her head as if to hear better. "Was she with them?" she pressed Bridgette, surprised that this was the first she was hearing of the incident.

"No," Bridgette confessed. "But you could tell it was her influence."

Mother Superior's expression remained blank and unrevealing. She glanced across the table to the old man, who held a ceremonial walking stick in front of him, his hand folded over the top of it calmly.

"Charles," she ventured, "tell me you have some thoughts on how we might proceed."

Charles's fingers moved in a repeated fashion as if he

were waking them up to play some piano. "I do," he responded gently, his grip on his stick returning to stationary. "The child is clearly talented, but from what I'm hearing," he continued more slowly, "this isn't the right place for her."

Bridgette piped up, her eyes filled with frustration and her tone verging on insolent. "Well, that's what I've been saying for the last year!" she blurted out.

Mother Superior threw her a stern look, and Bridgette caught herself and settled down, her cheeks flushed.

"The fact remains," Mother Superior explained as she moved her gaze from Bridgette to the other elder present, "this child cannot just be sent anywhere. She needs special care and attention. So... Charles, you were saying?"

Charles bobbed his head and continued. "I think we need to consider halting her training and taking her off world somewhere where there isn't the power source for her to channel."

The room fell silent.

Finally, Mother superior sighed. "Exile?" She said it more as a statement than a question. She paused, her mind churning. "We had such high hopes for her," she mumbled.

Charles tilted his head to one side. "I know. But we have to consider the safety of the population. If this continues, we may end up with something on our hands that we have no control over."

Mother Superior nodded solemnly. She caught Bridgette's expression out of the corner of her eye. It was one of triumph. Bridgette suddenly became self-aware and swallowed her slight smile. Her skin, however, was regaining its glow, despite her best efforts to control herself.

Mother Superior looked back at Charles, her hopes now surrendered. "So, where were you thinking?" she asked. "Not…?"

Charles nodded. "It has a long history of being a place which is both stable and out of the way. They will grant her passage easily, too."

Mother Superior shook her head gently.

Charles continued. "We have little choice at this point. Teshov doesn't have the land energy required for her to present a threat. It's the safest option."

She leaned forward, her arm on the table, holding his gaze with a determination he'd seen on few occasions before. "And there's nothing else you can do? With all your connections, and insights?"

Charles leaned back in his chair, his arms now outstretched to hold onto his cane. "I can certainly ask around, and see what other solution we can come up with," he offered. "But I think we need to prepare ourselves for the Teshov option."

Mother Superior's shoulders slumped as she surrendered a little more to the course of action. "And who should we send with her?"

Charles glanced sideways at Bridgette.

"Oh no! No way!" Bridgette protested. "That's not fair. You can't exile me as well! This was just a job…"

A young female Estarian had been listening on the other side of the enormous wooden door. Reading that their discussion was coming to an end she deftly stepped away from her listening post, careful to avoid the floorboard that creaked. She turned on her tiptoes and moved away down the corridor as fast as she dared. The last thing she wanted was to be spotted anywhere near that discussion. Eavesdropping was frowned upon but in her position, her knowing what they were planning might force them to move up their plans, meaning she wouldn't have time to prepare.

And there was something she needed to do before she was whisked away from this place.

Aboard the *Scamp Princess*

"We won't be long," Arlene told Beno'or as she left him in the rec room in the back of the ship. "And then we'll head back out to the surface. I'm not sure our survey has quite ruled this second one out, so better safe than sorry," she explained.

"Take your time," he told her. "I'm perfectly happy catching up on some of the information we have about our shared heritage."

Arlene grinned. "*Hypothesized* heritage," she corrected him playfully.

"I heard that!" Giles called through from the corridor to the cockpit. "Nice to know my friends have so much faith in my theories!"

Arlene nodded in the direction of the disembodied voice, and Beno'or and she shared a moment of humor. "Ok, I'll come get you when we're done," she told him before wandering back through to the cockpit.

Giles heard her footsteps heading into the cockpit. "You know, if you don't think there is any merit to this quest-"

"Oh hush you," she retorted. "I knew you were listening. No need to get your knickers in a knot."

Giles simmered down, mumbling away under his breath. He knew Arlene was teasing him, but what kind of sport would he be if he didn't play up to it, he figured.

He was just making the last checks to ensure that Scamp had them parked somewhere safe and that their shields were up and early warning signals on.

Arlene had settled in at her usual console behind him and to his right. He scooted his chair over to see her holoscreen.

The call was already connecting.

"Greetings, gentlefolk," Molly's voice called out over the ether connection.

"Greetings, Molly," Arlene chirped back.

"Hi, how are you?" Giles tried to greet her too, pushing his way over to be seen better on the screen.

"I'm good," Molly responded brightly. "How are you both?"

Arlene answered for the two of them. "We're doing ok," she told her. "Giles obviously is grumpy about the tedious work load, but we're doing well. Making progress," she summarized.

Giles protested. "We're working through the moons one at a time. And there are eleven of them! Arlene's calculations sucked ass."

Arlene grinned and tilted her head at him. "See?"

Molly smiled. "So you're in the Orn System?"

Arlene pulled her console chair closer to the holoscreen pushing Giles out. "Yes. I must say, the moons are rocky and deserted, for the most part. But when you look out at the system, in almost any direction, it isn't half beautifu-"

Giles interjected. "It is, but what is more fascinating is how eleven of these moons ended up in such an intricate orbit - so close together. And so similar in size. There's no physical way it could have occurred naturally. It just doesn't make sense... unless..."

Arlene frowned. "Unless you buy into the conspiracy theory!"

Giles huffed. "It's not a conspiracy theory. It's just physics. Occam's razor, etcetera, etcetera."

Arlene shook her head at him and smiled back at Molly. "See what I have to put up with?" she joked playfully.

Giles pretended to be offended and folded his arms. "Well, I shall just be quiet then, shall I?"

Arleen grinned at him and slapped at his arm playfully. "So," she said, changing the subject. "You had information for us?"

Molly shifted in her seat. "Well. Kinda. It's like..." she took a deep breath before continuing again. "I had a realm shift, and I saw some things. I had no one else to speak to who might know what it means, so I thought I'd reach out to you. In case you can help." Her eyes dropped below the camera as if she were somehow ashamed of what was happening to her.

Arlene made a note to talk with her about that at some point, but right now listened with concentration. Giles had sat back a little but was paying close attention too.

Arlene leaned on the console in front of her, her hand by her chin. She waved, ushering her on. "Go on," she said, encouraging Molly to share.

Molly took another deep breath. "Well. I'd just finished a call and Neechie was hanging around, which is how I suspected at first that it was a realm jump. So the usual started happening. Feeling ungrounded and so on. And then I saw an image, as clearly as I see you in the hologram before me. It was a series of planets in a weird array, all in this cluttered orbit."

Arlene started poking at her console, her attention no longer on Molly. Then a second holoscreen appeared on their call with an image of the Orn System that she had been analyzing.

"Something like this?" she asked.

Molly's mouth dropped open. "How did you do that? Was Oz able to pull an image?"

Arlene chuckled lightly. "No, no, no... this is where we are. This is the Orn System we were just telling you about."

Molly's mouth was still agape. "But that's *exactly* what it looked like."

Arlene bobbed her head. "Well, good," she confirmed, matter-of-factly, unmoved by the fact that Molly's visions had some significance.

"So what does this mean?" Molly asked.

"Well, for one," she explained to her, "it suggests that your realm jumping is getting more precise and useful. I wouldn't be surprised if Neechie was helping you access aspects of your higher self that knows everything from past, present and future."

Molly allowed the new paradigm to float into her consciousness, cognizant that Oz could always give her a replay later.

Arlene continued. "As for what the scene means specifically, what else can you tell us?"

Molly closed her eyes, trying to recall the incident again. There was a pause on the line. "I saw some kind of doorway. In stone. Like an entrance to a tomb. Or a temple."

Arlene started tapping some notes on her wrist holo.

Molly continued talking. "There was a smell of how the air goes when it's hot outside but cold inside the stone walls. And there were markings. Like the Zhyn characters. But not. Maybe a different language. Or older. And they were worn away a bit, making it hard to make them out for sure."

She moved her head as if looking up and around, her eyes still closed, her mind lost in her memory. "The constellations were strange... but that would make sense if it were in the Orn System, an area of space I'm not familiar with."

Arlene whispered to Giles. "So it's a tomb, above the ground..."

Giles nodded, his eyes not leaving the holo of Molly. If this was true, then maybe there was a reason that Molly was developing these abilities. And maybe it had something to do with the talismans and the mythology they were finding themselves drawn into.

"Anything else in the sky?" Arlene asked, obviously searching for clues to narrow down their search. Giles smiled to himself. *Atta, girl,* he thought to himself, seeing that they were on the same page.

Molly shook her head again. "No - just a beam of light falling on it. Lighting up the glyphs."

Arlene's voice seemed a little more excited. "Can you see where the light is coming from?"

Molly shook her head. "No. But then I was somewhere else." She paused a moment, as if reliving the experience. "I turned, and looked down, and I was in a bedroom... looking at a drawer next to a bed. A bedside cabinet."

"Who's bedroom is it?" Arlene coaxed.

Molly shook her head, a strand of her blonde hair dropping in front of her face. "I'm not sure. I feel like it's a girl. But a little girl who is quite... precocious. She feels as if she's beyond her years, or something. She's... strange."

Arlene's voice reached out to her. "What else can you see in the bedroom?"

Molly's brow creased up, as if she were trying to see closer. "There were red curtains over by the window. And outside... a building like the Capital Building in Spire. The room was sparse. Like a religious dorm or something. There were some Estarian beads on the wall."

She paused, her head looking downwards now. "But on the bedside table, there are tablets... that aren't being taken."

Arlene's voice penetrated her consciousness. "How do you know they're not being taken?" she asked.

Molly answered simply. "I just know."

Molly was silent. Giles and Arlene waited, watching. Wondering if there was any more information to come.

Molly suddenly opened her eyes. "That's it," she told them. "That's all I saw."

Arlene flicked up and down her holo notes, making sure she had everything she needed.

Molly waiting patiently for Arlene's opinion. "So what

do you think?" she pressed, a twinge of anxiety in the corners of her eyes.

Arlene pursed her lips, and then closed her holo. "I think," she told her, "that you've been seeing things that may help us narrow our search down."

Molly's face brightened. "Well, that's great then!" she said. Her face dropped a moment later. "But why?" she asked.

Arlene took a deep breath, and then glanced over at Giles, who was cleaning his fake glasses.

Realizing he was now being invited into the conversation, he sat up a little and pulled his chair forward. "I believe that as you're becoming more proficient in your realm jumping, you're able to access more and more intelligence out of time."

Molly frowned. "Out of time?" she asked.

Giles nodded, placing his glasses back on his face. "Yeah. So as humans... or any organics I know of... we experience time in sequence. Like frames of a movie."

Molly nodded her understanding and Giles continued. "Thing is, all these frames exist at once. Plus there's an infinite number of possibilities, which all have their own track of frames."

"Ok..." Molly agreed slowly.

Giles continued his point, watching her carefully to make sure she was following. "So imagine all of these frames, and then not necessarily being tied to them. So you're able to look at all of them out on a table in front of you."

Molly bobbed her head. "Yeah, okay. I get that."

"Right," he said. "So when you're realm jumping you're

basically accessing these other frames from that altered perspective. What I've been calling 'out of time', or more precisely 'out*side* of time.'"

"Hmmm," Molly mulled the idea for a moment. "That sounds... plausible. And it certainly explains all the different things I've been experiencing with the jumping and drifting."

Giles smiled, and then leaned over to speak quietly to Arlene, well aware that Molly could still hear him. "It's unnerving how quickly she accepts these things."

Arlene nodded. "I know. It freaked me out a little when I first met her. I still haven't figured out if it's personality or just rapid processing of new paradigms."

Molly eyed them playfully. "Erm, hello? Still here," she called, waving. "Even *I* know it's rude to talk about someone in the third person as if they're not there."

Arlene smirked a little. "My dear, we thought you were beyond such social conventions."

Molly relaxed in her seat. "Well. Yeah. That's true. I only mentioned it coz I thought it would be funny," she confessed blankly.

Arlene and Giles burst out laughing.

Molly looked at them, completely puzzled and missing the unintentional joke. "I don't understand," she said, as their laughter subsided.

Giles wiped an eye from behind his glasses. "It's funny because you tried to make fun of yourself and we didn't get it... and then you explained it - which was hilarious. And then it was a double whammy when you didn't understand why we found it funny in the end."

Molly's expression was still deadpan. "I think my head is about to explode."

Her eyes seemed to change as if she were ready to move the conversation on. "Ok," Molly said more brightly now, "this has been useful and enlightening. What's next?"

The conversation continued for a few minutes longer and eventually they said their farewells.

Giles clicked off the call and sat back, thinking.

Arlene glanced over at him. "You didn't want to talk to her privately then?"

Giles frowned. "Whatever for?"

Arlene rolled her eyes and moved her console chair back across the cockpit to her usual spot. "No reason," she said, a hint of playfulness in her voice.

Giles couldn't tell if Arlene was having a dig, or genuinely encouraging his interests in Molly. Plus, she had her back to him as she made the comment, making reading her expression ever more difficult. He suspected she had done that deliberately, because of the many papers they'd written in their early days in research about facial cue for evaluating truth and credibility.

He got up, stretched his legs, and ambled back into the rec area of the *Scamp Princess* to catch Beno'or up on the latest developments.

CHAPTER 6

Aibek Moon, Orn System

"Guardians!" Jendyg muttered to himself. "May as well call us 'the bloody forsaken.'" He moved across his hut, carving tool still in hand.

He added his latest carving to his collection of miniature statues above his fireplace. Some were of animals he remembered from his youth back on Zhyn. Others were of warriors and soldiers. And people.

He tried once to carve one of the person he remembered as his mother. But his memory failed him. The extended life they had been given by their elders while they remained on this rock wasn't accompanied by an extended memory. He had forgotten most of the things from the early years. Only some memories lingered with him.

Like the memory of living with another family member when his mother died. He thought it was his uncle. But he could no longer be sure. It was a long five years at the time, and now it was a nightmare that ebbed further and further from his consciousness each time he recalled the memories.

Memories of being held captive in a cell with very little food and water. Memories of being beaten. Enslaved. Helpless. Until one day the order came to rescue him. Well, that was probably just a by-product of them finding the man who had betrayed them to some other organization. It was all explained to him when he was older and had joined the military arm of the order: the Sacred Warrior Order of the Zhyn. But by then it was already vague — emotionally charged memories he struggled to assemble in any kind of fashion.

He did recall that his days in training and serving on Zhyn had been pleasant. Probably the best of his life. So when the time had come to volunteer for a special mission he was only too eager to sign up.

And that brought him here. To this rock. With its artificial air, fake soil and pretend ecosystem. The deal had been that they would be relieved by new guardians every ten standard cycles.

The tenth cycle came and went.

By then they already needed new supplies and equipment. Repairs were increasingly difficult, especially to the force field. But they persisted.

That was back when there were ten of them. Now only six remained.

He shuddered, trying to push out the memories he would rather not recall. *Strange*, he thought to himself, *how some memories are so elusive, and others you need to use a mental force field to keep them at bay.*

He sighed, straightening out his row of carved Zhyn

warriors, wondering what might happen if the energy field on the rock brought them to life. His mind wandered as he puttered around in his little hut. The freeze would be coming any day now. That's what Gagai had told them the other night after hunting. That always meant that finding food was going to be tough for the following weeks and they needed to increase their supplies while they still could.

He shook his head and sat down on his wooden rack. Right now he couldn't worry about that. They'd survived the freeze every time in the past. This time would be no different. And if he started worrying about it he'd never get to sleep.

He lay back, still with his outdoor layers on. He'd take them off later if he woke up too warm, he told himself. He gently closed his eyes and returned to his daydream of his carved figures coming to life and what relief they might bring to his miserable, lonely existence.

Aboard the *Scamp Princess*

Giles rolled out of his rack, still groggy from a disturbed night's sleep. Between the hard work of surveying each moon and the interaction with Molly the previous day his mind had spent the hours churning.

He grabbed a mocha from the machine in the living quarters and then ambled, in his onesy sleep-suit and boots, out into the cockpit where Arlene was already up and working.

"Morning!" she chirped brightly as she heard him emerge. She didn't take her eyes from her screens.

"Mghhh," he grunted, still not fully in charge of all his

faculties. He sat down in the console chair behind her, as far away from his normal piloting console as possible, and waited for the mocha to return the life back to his senses. Arlene continued working. She knew what he was like in the mornings.

Eventually he mustered the will to speak. "Got anything?"

"Mmm. Maybe," she replied, her voice crisp against the dullness in his sleepy brain. "Turns out we're still going to have to land in order to survey each one separately. There's still no way of checking all the structures for something as small as a temple - but at least we know we're looking for something above ground."

Beno'or appeared at the door, also clutching a fresh mocha. Giles realized he must have been sitting in the back when Giles had got up and come through to the cockpit.

"And this is the information you received from Molly?" Beno'or asked.

Arlene spun round to see him, a tad confused. "Giles filled me in yesterday," he explained, indicating at the grizzly bear in the chair next to her.

Arlene nodded. "Yes. The one and the same... and if you're going to give me a hard time about taking her visions seriously can we save that for a proper conversation later? I don't have time to explai-"

Beno'or cut her off. "My dear..." he said theatrically, "you misunderstand my clarification. I fully trust your instincts on knowing what is fiction and what might be a useful clue from the psychic consciousness."

Arlene turned to look at him again, this time grinning.

"Right," she said, her grin fading into sheepishness. "Well then…" she added, turning back to her console.

"So perhaps," Beno'or continued with the task in hand, "we just need to make our best guess with which ones to start with." He wandered into the cockpit and leaned over to look at Arlene's screen. "If I wanted to hide something, I would put it in one of two places. Either in plain sight, or somewhere where no one would think to look."

Giles rubbed the sleep from his eyes beneath his glasses. "That's a good point," he concurred.

"Smaller planets then?" Arlene quizzed.

"Yeah maybe," Beno'or agreed. "Or insignificant-looking ones. Which are the least accessible?"

Arlene thought for a moment and then poked a little at her screens. "There are these three here," she concluded. She leaned her arm on the console and rested her chin on her hand. After a moment looking at the screen she turned and looked at the others. "Okay - so I guess we start with those three?"

Giles rocked back in his chair and clasped his hands behind his head, stretching his back. "Three is a damn site better than eleven," he admitted, brightening up. "Good thinking, my friend," he nodded to Beno'or.

Beno'or touched his nose lightly. "Comes from decision making for the Empire," he confided.

Arlene smiled. She was warming to Beno'or more and more. "The other thing that will speed our search," she added, "is the information from Molly that we're looking for a temple above ground, and not an underground tomb. That will certainly make life easier."

Giles nodded, now relaxed and resting his eyes.

Arlene got up. "Okay, well… this talisman isn't going to find itself," she declared. "Up," she instructed, tapping Giles's arm as she left the cockpit. "Get yourself showered and dressed so we can get going."

Giles took a deep breathe, opened his eyes, and hauled himself upright with great effort. "Fine," he called after her. "I'm getting another mocha first though," he mumbled in defiance, for Beno'or's benefit more than anything else, as he ambled sleepily back out into the rec room.

The Sacred Ascenders Convent for the Gifted, Estaria

The night air wafted in through the bedroom window. Anne hurriedly pulled her boots on and tied the laces. Fully clothed, she scooted over to the window, pulled it closed and dropped the latch. She snatched at the heavy red curtains, drawing them closed too, making it look from the outside like she was going to bed. She may look young, but she was well aware she had wisdom beyond her years - and her wisdom was telling her she didn't have long before the opportunity would pass.

Quietly, she crept to her bedside table on the other side of the room, looking at it as if lost in thought. Or planning. Her eyes didn't even register the bottles of tablets that the convent had her taking. Or not taking. Every now and again she would tip a handful down the toilet just to keep up the appearance of abiding by their rules.

A moment later, as if decided on her course of action, she drew a deep breath, pushed her raven hair out of her face, and bent down at the cabinet and opened the drawer.

Moving a few pieces of jewelry away, including her Estarian meditation beads, she shifted some papers and found what she was looking for. She grabbed it tight in her hand and then decided it was probably best to put it into a pocket. She patted herself down, deciding which pocket would be big enough. She chose the one inside her jacket. At the very least it would be more discrete than carrying it, if anyone found her wandering the convent halls at night.

The item concealed and secured, she turned to the door, switched the light off, and then opened it, stepping out into the darkened corridor as her eyes adjusted to the new light levels.

It was cold. The heating went off in the evenings to encourage the charges not to stay up too late. Morning meditation would be hailed in a matter of hours and it was easier to accept as a way of life if one had had adequate sleep. Or so the sisters told them.

Anne crept down the corridor as quickly as she could, cringing at the swishing noise her outdoor suit made. She had considered going out in her night clothes, but then being caught so vulnerable didn't appeal to her either.

Trying to breathe and move as quietly as she possibly could she moved down the corridor, taking a right onto the stone slab flooring into the stairwell. She hurried down, her boots tapping softly as she went. Arriving on the first floor of the residential wing she hurried through the hallway to the kitchen and then slipped out of the back door. Often, it was the only door that was left open. Somehow the nuns had decided that access through the kitchen didn't pose a threat, but through the front door (the most obvious point of ingress with porch lights) did.

Anne rolled her eyes at their unconscious assumptions.

The sooner she could get away from these self-righteous people, and the bullying of Bridgette "drama queen" Mortimer, the better.

She carefully closed the heavy kitchen door behind her and trotted off down the path into the gardens. Within seconds she had hidden herself in the shadows of the long hedges running down away from the building and out into the orchard.

She patted her jacket to make sure she still had the metal disk with her. She felt powerful when she held it close. She knew it was important, but right from the beginning something had told her not to trust these people with it. They would succumb to its power. And though they were the ones schooling her on how to direct her abilities, intuitively she knew that she would surpass them very quickly. She was just getting going in her understanding of the realms - but Bridgette's outburst a few days ago had only served to confirm her suspicions. Bridgette was afraid. They all were. And that was why they were sending her away. Far away to a land with no power.

But she would be back. She knew that. And when she returned she needed to be able to retrieve this disk easily. At the same time, it needed to be somewhere where it wouldn't be discovered - accidentally or otherwise.

If it was far enough from where people would normally venture it would limit the risk of them picking up on its power. In her heart of hearts she knew the only person who was likely to detect it was the male elder she had overheard in the meeting room earlier that day, and he rarely ventured to the convent, let alone into the gardens.

It would be safe here, she decided. She spotted an older-looking fruit tree. It was one that would occasionally bear fruit, and given that its roots were gnarly it didn't offer a good sitting place for anyone who might want to sit out.

She hurried over to it, keeping low to avoid her silhouette being spotted by anyone who might be looking out of a window back at the house. She located some softer soil near its base, and with a stick she dug as deep as she could in the time she had. Her hands were covered in dirt and soil, but she didn't care. She knew what she needed to do.

Reaching into her inside jacket pocket she pulled out the item and dropped it into the hole. She glanced down, seeing the ambient light glint off it. She felt a sadness well up in her as she had to part with it.

Something about it still called to her. It was precious, she knew that. But when it was given to her she didn't know anything of energy or realm walking or any of the things these Estarians had been trying to teach her.

Now things were different, though.

She was different.

Boy, was she different.

She glanced down at the talisman one last time before scooping up the soil in her bare hands and refilling the hole.

When she was done she glanced around to make sure that she would remember where she had buried it. She didn't want to have to go through the whole rigmarole of digging up the ground under each and every tree in the orchard, modest though it was.

As satisfied as she was going to be, she headed back towards the house, dusting the dirt from her hands on her pants legs as she stealthily moved in the shadows.

Crack.

There was movement off to her right on he other side of the foliage. Just up ahead it turned into a continuous hedge. But here? There were gaps. Gaps for a person, or animal, to come through.

She felt the hairs on the back of her neck stand on end. She shuddered.

Something wasn't right.

She wasn't alone.

She could smell something on the wind. The smell of people. Human people. But there wasn't any more movement.

Maybe she was imagining it. Her anxiety playing tricks on her.

She hurried forward again, her ears focusing on any sound that would mean she was in danger.

She never heard anything coming. Instead, the next thing she knew was she was being grabbed from behind by arms that seemed to come out of the hedge. She started to struggle and kick. But then something soft was clamped over her mouth and nose. She felt suddenly light headed. Woozy.

Then nothing.

"So you think this is the best drop off point?"

Anne became aware of a raspy human voice nearby.

"Definitely," confirmed a second voice. "They get so much traffic through these ports no way we'll be tracked. Besides, this was where they wanted her."

Anne slowly came to, vaguely aware of the two gruff

voices in the dark. She was cold, and she ached, though she wasn't cognizant enough to know from where.

Or why.

As the conversation continued she began to piece together what was going on. She was lying on a cold metal surface. And they were moving. So she was probably in a space van. The movement was smooth and rocking, so they were likely on a strato highway. That meant they were probably far from the convent now.

Her mind raced as she wondered what would happen in the morning when the nuns realized she was missing. Perhaps they would assume she had run away. That's certainly what Bridgette would suggest. Strongly.

"And your mate will give her passage?" The first voice continued to question his partner.

"For sure," the second voice confirmed casually.

"But will he know how to hold her?" the voice pressed. "The old guy was pretty adamant she was more powerful than any of the others we've taken."

Old guy? Anne thought to herself. *Was that elder involved? What was his name? Charles. That was what Mother Superior had called him.*

"Will you stop worrying. It's all in hand."

"Yeah, I know that. I'm just making sure we've covered all our bases."

"Yeah yeah. Bases covered…" The voice paused. "I need something to eat. We should stop before we get to the space port."

Space port! Anne screamed in her head. *They were taking*

her off world. Maybe to that awful Teshov place if Charles had anything to do with it!

She tried to calm her breathing. She hadn't quite mastered how to use her budding powers when she needed to. They were normally just an extension of her emotions. And the last thing she wanted was them realizing that she was awake before she had a plan.

She tugged at her constraints, wondering if she could cut through them with the energy tricks she'd been trying to master. But knowing her luck she'd end up burning her hand off or something. No. Until she could compose herself in peace and quiet she was going to have to hold off trying to use her powers.

The voices continued to talk about their plan of action: supper. "And we have time?"

"Plenty," confirmed the guy who seemed to be in charge of their venture. "They're not leaving until tomorrow. Only reason they want us there tonight is so that if we're seen we can't be directly tied to them."

"Interesting," the gravelly voice mused. "Your mate runs a tight game." He sounded almost impressed.

"You bet he does. You don't stay in this business as long as he has without knowing how to move your pieces around the board, as it were."

Anne listened, trying not to breathe - or move - for fear of alerting them that she was awake. While they thought she was unconscious they were hemorrhaging clues. Clues that might help her escape. Eventually.

Her two kidnappers were silent for a while. Eventually the one who wasn't driving spoke up. "You know, I still find it odd that these spiritual do-gooders would actually take a cut from this transaction."

"Well," the guy who was in charge grunted, "it seems this guy isn't quite as squeaky clean as those nuns think he is. And from what I've heard on the grapevine, a bit of human trafficking isn't even the heaviest stuff he's into."

The questioning voice sounded even more concerned. "You think we're safe then? Doing this job?"

"Yeah," his partner assured him. "We just need to drop her off and then we're home free."

"You sure about that?"

"Course. Don't worry about it. It'll be fine."

Anne listened and tuned in to their energies. She could feel the anxiety in both of her captors. Even though one was reassuring the other she could tell he wasn't that confident. That was something she might be able to use. She filed the piece of information in her mind, and continued to lay there quietly. Waiting.

She would survive this. And she would get free.

No matter what she had to do to survive. She'd gotten this far, after all, and her story was just getting started.

CHAPTER 7

Aibek Moon, Orn System, Guardian Settlement, Computer Room

There was a scuffling as Ammo and Mennynad joined the others in the computer room.

Jendyg followed in a few seconds later. "What's going on?" he asked.

Gagai was sitting in front of the computer that monitored the force field. His face looked more disgruntled and serious than usual. "We have company," he shared with him grimly.

Jendyg pushed his way between his team mates to see the screen. "You mean people? Wanting to land?"

Gagai shook his head. "No. Just a ship that has come into range of the scanners."

The others were silent. Jendyg tried to catch the eye of Naldrir, who was characteristically aloof, and just observing events from his position on the other side of the room. He was leaning against the far wall of the compact hut, unable to see the screen from his vantage point. He glanced over at Jendyg and shook his head ever so slightly, then lowered his eyes as if to deter Jendyg from what he was inevitably thinking.

Koryss, Gagai's right hand man, stood silently watching the blips refresh every few seconds. He knew that when Gagai wanted his opinion he would ask for it. Until then, he knew to watch and listen.

"We should hail them!" Jendyg blurted out, knowing full well how his opinions were going to be received.

Gagai turned in his seat, his large warrior mass testing the integrity of the wooden chair. "We will be doing no such thing," he growled firmly, staring Jendyg down.

There was an awkward silence in the room as the screen continued to blip and flash, showing the approaching ship.

Gagai turned back to view it, but did nothing.

Jendyg wouldn't be deterred. "But they could help us!" he insisted. "They can help us get a message home. Or one of us could leave…"

Gagai turned again, but this time standing and straightening up to the fullest extent of his natural height. His chest puffed up and his shoulders went back. "And by one of us I assume you mean *you*?" he boomed, glaring down at Jendyg, who had to take a few steps back to get out of the way and to just be able to make eye contact.

Jendyg's heart raced. He hated conflict but he wasn't going to let his first chance in over seventy cycles fly on by just because he was too afraid to stand up to Gagai. "Yes. I'd be willing, since no one else seems to be," he declared defiantly, his eyes flicking around at his comrades, assembled for this highly irregular event.

Gagai's expression was even more threatening now. His eyes blazed with anger. "No one will be abandoning their post. Not now. Not ever. This is a sacred duty. We owe it to our elders to make sure that this rock is never breached."

Jendyg felt himself crumble under Gagai's assertion. He stumbled back another half a step, fumbling in his mind for the words that might win him his freedom.

Gagai didn't give him a chance though. "Go collect firewood. And don't stop until the stock is replenished, even if it takes you all night," he declared by way of punishment, winning the interaction.

Jendyg felt his face flush with humiliation and frustration. All he wanted to do was leave, and his chance was right there, on the screen not four feet away from him. He glanced at the screen again and Gagai tracked his gaze and moved himself in front of it vindictively. "Now go!" he ordered.

There were awkward shuffles from the others in the room who had watched the showdown. Jendyg never stood a chance. They knew that. And yet they never tired of seeing him try.

Jendyg took another two steps backwards, still trying to withstand Gagai's glare. And then he folded, turning on his heels and moving noisily out of the computer room and the hut. He slammed the outside door as hard as he could, rattling the whole structure.

Once outside he allowed his anger to explode. He clenched his fists and jaw and expelled the energy through his tightened arms. He wanted to scream. To shout out in anger. But he knew that would cause him to lose face with his brothers. Anger was an emotion that was looked on poorly by the order. And as such they had been forced into long grueling exercises and meditations in order to 'clear' it.

Jendyg hurried off, the adrenalin pumping through his limbs making him strong. And destructive.

His large mass thumped on the ground as he walked, sending vibrations that made the small food-creatures scurry away unseen in the undergrowth.

The freeze was coming and there was nothing he could do to avoid another grueling cycle. He looked up as if he might be able to see through the life-giving insulating dome that created their artificial oasis on the rock. It was a haze, lit brightly in places, and dimmer in others.

He imagined the ship several kilometers above him, wondering who these people were. A part of him fantasized about them being able to hear his thoughts if he concentrated as hard as he could. Maybe then they'd find a way through and land. Maybe then they'd rescue him from his 'destiny' of mundanity and Gagai's self-righteous rule.

He shook the thought from his head and kept moving off into the woodland to find firewood. At least doing that he'd be able to work off some of this frustration.

Aboard the *Scamp Princess*

"Always the last place you look," Beno'or remarked brightly as they returned to the ship.

"Don't I just know it," Giles grumbled. "I was hoping the last place we needed to look was going to be one of the first two planets."

"As you said," Arlene reminded him as she clattered

back up the gridded ramp, "three is better than eleven." She stamped the sand off her boots as she walked.

Giles resisted the urge to turn his eyes to the ceiling. Instead he caught Beno'or's eye. "I'm convinced this woman has an echoic memory," he said as quietly as he could.

Beno'or was about to respond, but Arlene's voice interrupted. "And ears like a tundra!" she called up to the pair.

Giles chuckled. "And ears like a tundra," he agreed, less quietly now.

Beno'or had started taking off his outer jacket. "I'll fix lunch," he offered, heading into the make shift kitchen in the living quarters.

Giles felt a new wave of warmth for the guy. "Thanks man," he called after him. "That's kind of you."

Beno'or called back to him. "Of course. We're a team."

Giles sat down in the cargo area not far from Arlene and started taking his boots off. "So I guess we move to the last of the three we narrowed it down to, eh?"

Arlene was packing some gear away and organizing some soil samples they'd taken. "Yep. Onward and upward," she agreed.

"Okay, I'll go run the initial scans and get Scamp to position us over there. Then we can eat and we'll be ready to move after food," he told her, clearly flicking into work mode after being chastised by Arlene.

"Good thinking," she agreed. "Looks like someone has got his mojo back!" she added, her voice deliberately impressed and encouraging.

Giles couldn't resist this time, and rolled his eyes at her dramatically as he got up and padded out. Arlene scrambled for something appropriate to throw at him but he was out into the living quarters and beyond her reach far too quickly. She was going to have to up her game if she was actually going to hit him at some point.

Not long later Beno'or and Arlene were in the kitchen. Having prepared the food, they were sitting down to eat.

"Are you coming to eat with us or what?" Arlene called through to the cockpit.

Giles appeared at the door a few moments later. "I have good news and bad news," he told them. His face was grim.

Arlene stopped spooning out the brown dehydrated vegetation-supplement and looked at him. "What is it?"

Beno'or stopped what he was doing, too.

Giles sucked his lips to one side. "Well, the good news is, I think we've got our moon. The bad news is, the reason I think this is for real this time is because it has a force field around the atmosphere. No way we can land."

Arlene's brow furrowed, creasing her otherwise smooth blue skin. "Okay, so we just need to figure it out," she mumbled, taking up the spoon she had been using and dishing out the food again.

Giles headed over to the table. He sat down, his mind churning. "Well, there are other complications," he continued. "For a start it has a very low-level atmosphere. We need suits if we're going out in it. Which means..."

Beno'or finished his thought. "That I'll have to stay on the ship." Giles nodded. They hadn't thought to bring full atmospheric gear from Kurilia when they agreed to

Beno'or coming along, and being Zhyn he was much too large for either the human or Estarian suits they had on board for themselves.

"There's more," Giles continued as he placed in front of him what Arlene gave him without looking at it.

She remained silent, letting him explain. "There are life signs," he continued. "Scamp is assuming they're guards. They seem to occupy a small area which has an enclosed atmosphere and terraformed environment."

Beno'or handed out spoons to everyone. "Are we thinking that the temple is inside the terraformed section?" he asked.

Giles shrugged, his face slightly gray. "We dunno. We can't tell until we get closer. And I think we'd be silly to assume that they're confined to that area even if the temple isn't inside."

Arlene nodded. "And we can't get closer until we get through the force field."

Beno'or frowned, pausing again with a spoonful of food to his mouth. "But, surely with all this technology you have a way of breaching that force field?" he prompted. "I mean, that move Molly made to get to Shaa, with Federation tech. That was impressive."

Giles wiped at the lower half of his face with one hand, his stress levels revealing themselves. "Yeah, she had two AIs helping on that operation though," he said, his brain turning and food still untouched.

"But we have Scamp," she reminded him. "And you know who Scamp used to work with."

Giles's eyes lit up in recognition. "Ah, this is true," he said slowly, hope returning to his complexion.

Beno'or looked confused. "Who?" he asked, curious about what he might be missing.

Arlene smiled and started explaining. "Well, the Empress of the Federation was... erm... genetically enhanced, shall we say. She had a Kurtherian alien attach itself into her brain in order for it to survive, and when they attached his Kurtherian computer in too, well, an AI evolved. Spontaneously. It really was miraculous."

Giles had started eating. He waved his fork and finished chewing. "Actually, it was the world's first AI, as far as the human race was concerned," he added in. "But Arlene has a point. This was *her* ship, so ADAM, her AI, *must* have worked with Scamp. Heck, Scamp was probably built by ADAM. Or a piece of him. Or whatever the heck AIs do to procreate," he added, chewing again, his mind going ten to the dozen.

Beno'or still looked confused. "So what are you thinking?" he asked.

Arlene took the question. "Well I'm thinking that Scamp must be able to come up with a way to take out the force field or get us through it somehow."

Beno'or considered what he was hearing. "Are you sure you want to brute force your way through it though? I mean, what about if you contacted the guards and made an excuse to go down to the surface."

Arlene stopped eating, mulling the concept. "Hmmm," she said quietly. "That would certainly be a... 'non-killy-killy way,'" she muttered glancing over to Giles.

Beno'or's enthusiasm for his idea seemed to swell. "Well we don't know how long they've been there. It's not as if there are ships flying in and out. Plus, all the other moons are deserted. For all we know they could have been here for years!" He paused, thinking. "Maybe their allegiance can be swayed?" he added thoughtfully.

Giles had finished and was ready to jump in. "Of course they're not going to go for that!" he scoffed. "Their job is just to keep people out…"

Beno'or shook his head. "At this stage, we just don't know. We're making lots of assumptions and filling in blanks. We're assuming their job at least *was* to keep people out perhaps… but how often are these guards replaced? If they've been there a while, without contact with their source mission, or their group, then there's no telling how their thinking might have changed."

Giles frowned. "How do you mean?"

Beno'or shrugged. "Well, whoever is looking after this temple on behalf of the Zhyn, certainly isn't known to our government. At least, I have no knowledge of it, and I doubt that we're funding it. Plus," he raised his eyebrows as he spoke, "I'm embarrassed to admit this, but we had no idea about some of the projects Shaa was running. And with him now gone, there could be all kinds of things that have just fallen off the radar with personnel deployed and no orders being issued." He shook his head, lowering his eyes. "We really did drop the ball with him," he admitted, his eyes filled with regret.

Giles listened intently, his food once again forgotten.

Beno'or returned his thoughts to the matter in hand. "But," he continued, his normal enthusiasm returning as new thoughts took over, "it reminds me of a tale from our mythology where a group of warriors were made immortal to protect a sleeping emperor who had been put under a curse to sleep for all eternity. Their mission was to prevent anyone from getting close to him, but then over the centuries one of them fell in love with one of the maids, who gained access to the chamber where the king was being kept. She started a habit of reading to him, and after several years of doing this he awoke. Curse broken."

Giles shook his head. "I don't get it."

Beno'or shrugged. "The point is, if the guard had kept to his original task she never would have found her way in to the chamber, and would never have woken their leader. The curse would have remained. But my point here is that it just goes to show that over time, without constant reinforcement of the objective from an outside authority, the attitudes of the people can naturally shift."

He paused and tilted his head from side to side a couple of times. "For better or for worse."

Arlene took a deep breath. "So what you're saying is that maybe these guards have been left alone long enough that…?"

Beno'or shook his head. "Who knows? Anything is possible. Maybe they're still bent on keeping everyone out. Maybe they're bored. Maybe they need supplies, or help or something. We just don't know. But since they are isolated, there is a higher chance of what we're assuming about their intentions no longer being quite as rigorous as if they were connected to the normal chain of command."

Giles nodded. "Okay. Good point. So what do you suggest we do?" He glanced over at Arlene and smiled playfully. "Send in a maid to read to them?"

Beno'or chuckled. "Goodness, no. I think it is worth

contacting them though. Asking them if we can investigate?"

Arlene had her arm on the table, and rested her chin on her hand for a moment. "That's one thing we could do, but that's too directly against what their original objective would have been. What if..." she checked herself before continuing. "What if we pretend we're in trouble and they need to save us by granting us access. Then they're just helping us survive and they can do that without agreeing to help us do something they've been sworn to stop people from doing."

Giles clicked his fingers. "That's a great plan," he agreed, smiling brightly now.

Arlene nodded at his bowl of food. "Okay, you finish eating. I'll go talk to Scamp about sending a distress signal."

Giles had already started shoveling his food enthusiastically. "I'll be right there," he said between mouthfuls.

Beno'or started tidying the pots and dishes into the machine to clean them. "We have a non-violent plan. Albeit a deceptive one!" he chuckled to himself.

Arlene disappeared into the cockpit, smiling to herself about their distinct lack of violence in their plans in their "old age."

CHAPTER 8

Aibek Moon, Orn System, Guardian Settlement, Computer Room

Gagai waited until Jendyg had left before he sat down again. The others could tell that Jendyg got to him - though none of them had figured out why.

Gagai's rule and commitment to the order was unwavering. No one ever had cause or inclination to challenge him. Except Jendyg, when it came to wanting to leave, or get a signal out to the outside world.

Ammo tried to change the subject, but Gagai wasn't hearing anything. He took a few deep breaths before taking his attention back to the screen. Eventually he spoke, even though there was a conversation already going on between Ammo and Naldrir at this point. "No one is to encourage any kind of talk about leaving this place," he declared. "What Jendyg is going through is a crisis of faith. As such we must treat it as that and help him find his way back to us."

Just then the computer started beeping.

Mennynad shuffled over, followed quickly by Ammo, who peered curiously over Mennynad's shoulder. Koryss had stood silently by Gagai's side while he sent Jendyg off, but now turned his attention back to the screen. "We're being hailed," he said calmly, explaining to those who couldn't see the screen what was going on.

Naldrir moved towards the computer in genuine interest.

Ammo leaned forward and hit a key to put the message on screen, with audio. The five of them listened intently. The voice chattered with a rather more docile lilting tone than their own speech.

Ammo's enthusiasm grew. "What language is that even?" he asked, barely able to peel his eyes from the screen to look for a response from any of the others.

Naldrir closed one eye, listening. "See if the computer can translate," he suggested.

Ammo nudged Mennynad out of the way and hit a few more keys, Gagai's rank and command forgotten.

Gagai sat watching, taking it all in, almost as if he was paralyzed by what was happening.

The computer buzzed and whirred, it's old circuits struggling under the strain. The team waited in an uncomfortable silence.

Eventually the system returned a result. "The message is being transmitted in human interplanetary dialect. Translating..."

A few moments more and the computer read out the translation of the repeating message.

The warriors looked at each other. What was

happening was unprecedented. And created a dilemma none of them had been prepared for.

Ammo seemed genuinely excited. "We have to help them," he declared decisively.

Gagai shook his head. "No. We don't. Our first duty is to our people. The mission."

"But they're up there and they're going to die without our help!" Ammo protested. "We can't just sit back and let that happen," he protested. "It's our fault that force field is up there, threatening the lives of anyone who comes too close."

Mennynad pushed his way closer to the computer as Ammo continued to make his case. He pulled up another screen and hit a few keys. "They're not moving," he announced. "They're saying they're in trouble, but they're barely in orbit, and nowhere near the force field."

Ammo turned back to the screen, nudging at Mennynad to move over again. "Maybe there is something we're missing in the translation," he suggested.

Naldrir finally spoke up. "Or maybe they're here for the very thing we're trying to protect, and they're trying to trick us into letting them land."

That was enough for Gagai to reassert his control. "He's right. This is what we've been trained for. What we've been put here for. We have to protect our charge against all odds. No matter what the cost. We've sacrificed our own lives to be here and perform our sacred duty. We must stay strong."

The others looked at each other. Gagai had spoken. And if they were honest, they could all see his point. There were affirming murmurs, and finally Ammo declared that he should get back to the hunting before the freeze came. He left, Mennynad in tow.

Within minutes, after more discussion, Koryss and Gagai were the only ones left in the computer room.

Gagai got up from his seat and offered the chair to Koryss. "Keep an eye on things for me. I don't want anyone getting any ideas about sending up signals that might compromise us," he instructed.

Koryss nodded obediently and took the chair. He sat down. "You think we ought to be concerned about Jendyg?" he asked.

Gagai shook he head, moving towards the door. "Probably not. But if he steps foot in here, you are authorized to use whatever means necessary."

Koryss turned to the screens, his back now to Gagai. "Understood," he acknowledged.

Aboard the *Scamp Princess*

"Still no response?" Giles prompted.

"No, nothing," Scamp returned.

Giles shifted impatiently in his seat. "Maybe they don't have a way to be hailed?" he suggested.

Arlene sat down in the seat next to him. "They have a force field that goes around the planet and a terraformed environment. Of course they can pick up on incoming signals."

Giles took his glasses off, playing with them between his thumb and forefinger. "Well maybe they don't understand our language. Scamp... can you broadcast in Zhyn as well, for us?"

"Sure," Scamp responded. "Broadcasting in human interplanetary and Zhyn standard lexicon now."

Giles nodded, watching the screen waiting for any signs of change. "Anything?" he asked after a few moments.

"Nothing," Scamp responded.

Giles rested his head on his hand, his elbow leaning on the console in front of him.

Arlene turned to him. "Maybe," she started, "they can see we're not really in trouble."

Giles turned to her. "Good point!" he said, snapping his fingers. "Scamp? Can you simulate it? Make it look like we're falling into the force field so they're forced to put it down?"

"I can," Scamp started to explain, "but there is a point after which we will have too much momentum in that direction to pull out. And then if they don't drop it, we're toast."

He waited for the organics to respond.

Giles rubbed his chin. "So then we need a way to blow the force field. Is there a way to do that?"

Scamp appeared on the holoscreen between where Giles and Arlene sat. "Yes," he confirmed. "It turns out that I can interfere with the signal by modulating to match their frequency and effectively overloading the generator."

Arlene spontaneously started interacting with Scamp's visual representation. "Can you do that only if it looks like they're not going to respond?"

Scamp shook his virtual head. "I cannot estimate accurately how long it will take to create enough of a disturbance to overload the system. If I start doing it too soon, then they will know that we're trying to breach and they won't trust us. If we leave it too late, then we're toast."

Giles rubbed his chin. "Okay, so where is the sweet spot?"

Scamp was silent for a moment. "You mean the intersecting minimums of the two cost functions?"

Giles rolled his eyes. "Yes, Scamp."

Arlene worked hard not to giggle. She'd seen Giles interact with Molly in much the same way, and it amused her every time. Especially since Molly was human, organic, and yet strangely... AI-like. At least some of the time.

Scamp responded. "Well, there are parameters within which we have an 87% chance of successfully completing the overload, while giving the maximum time for them to comply with our distress signal."

"87%?" Giles repeated. He glanced at Arlene. "What do you think?" he asked.

Arlene wrinkled her nose. "I don't like a 13% chance of dying."

Giles nodded. "Okay, Scamp, let's go with the scenario which guarantees we can pull up in time if we need to."

Scamp sighed audibly. "Fine."

Arlene couldn't help but chuckle out loud in amazement this time and covered her mouth with her hand. "Does he have an attitude about us being risk averse?" she whispered to Giles.

Giles looked equally amused. "Seems so," he confirmed. "You know, maybe it's to do with the self-destruct clause these guys have, to stop the tech falling into enemy hands. I mean, that's got to mess with your ideas of self-preservation, right?"

Arlene shook her head in dismay. "Maybe…" she agreed.

Scamp piped up again as if he hadn't been listening to every word. "You may want to buckle in. We will be commencing maneuvers to simulate distress and imminent crashing into the force field in 10… 9… 8…"

Arlene called to Beno'or. "Beno'or, you may want to come through and strap in. Scamp is going to put us through some envelop maneuvers to sell our mayday."

Just then the ship shuddered.

Arlene shouted again. "Okay, so he didn't wait. Get in here!"

Giles had already strapped himself in. "Scamp, what is the point of the count down if you're not going to wait?"

"Oh," Scamp replied nonchalantly, "that's just the pre-rumblings of my simulation. The heavy stuff starts in 4… 3…"

The Justicar appeared and was hurriedly trying to get himself into a console chair and safely restrained. "Just made a fresh pot of mocha, too," he told Arlene, more concerned about the mocha than for his own well-being, it seemed.

Suddenly the ship banked, and the antigrav couldn't adapt fast enough.

"Shiiiiiiitttt!" Giles yelped, his intonation conveying his sudden anxiety as he gripped the arms of his console chair.

Beno'or had just managed to buckle his harness when suddenly he was flung backwards into his chair and tipped up and to the left with the ship's movement.

Arlene fell forward into her harness, jolted as it caught

her from falling at speed out of her chair and across the cockpit.

The sirens screamed, resounding through the whole ship, and the emergency lights flashed red and bright white in a syncopated strobe effect.

A new, simulated voice came over the intercom. "Warning. Impact with force field in T minus twenty seconds and counting."

Giles spun round to try to see on the main screen what they were heading towards. He could just make out the faint glow of the force field's outer edge. "Do we really have to go through this rigmarole, Scamp?"

"What do you mean, 'rigmarole'?" Scamp inquired perfectly calmly.

Giles clung awkwardly against the g-force. "I mean the terrifying alarms and warning messages. I mean, it's not like there is a whole lot of crew on board who don't know what's going on."

"Ah. I see," Scamp responded. "So never mind about any fun I might glean from the situation?"

Giles's mouth dropped over in disbelief and caught Arlene's eye. Arlene shrugged. "He's *your* AI," she told him, like a mother who disowns a child when he's misbehaving.

Giles's eyes were creased up in stress and frustration. "Scamp, dear boy? Do me a favor and kill the siren, if you would?"

"Very well," Scamp responded. The siren and the flashing lights stopped instantly.

"Thank goodness for that," Giles sighed, still bracing against the g-force which started to level out. "Sitrep, Scamp?"

Scamp responded promptly but with a hint of sulk in his voice. "The guards still aren't responding to the distress signal. Overload of their force field begins in 4... 3... 2... 1."

The screen lit up in bright green as Scamp fired one of the weapons at a specific angle to heat up the force field and added energy to it.

"How long do we have until we pull up?" Giles asked.

Scamp processed the answer. "By my calculations we have fourteen seconds. Unless I can overload the system first."

The ship suddenly leveled and then lurched in the opposite direction, putting the three organics into another equally awkward position in their console chairs.

Giles was starting to feel nauseous. "How long do you think it will take to overload it now that you're working on it?" he asked, still gripping his chair arms.

"13.5 seconds," Scamp responded flatly.

Arlene raised her eyes to the ceiling. "No matter how specific we are about not wanting to die, it seems our efforts are thwarted by whatever he wants to do."

Beno'or tried to lean over and get Arlene's attention despite still being tipped awkwardly back in his chair. "Tell me, are your AIs still programmed with the rule that they're not allowed to harm their organics?" he asked.

Arlene shook her head. "I used to think that was the case. Until about twenty seconds ago, at least".

Beno'or frowned, anxiety creasing his eyes. "You don't seem that concerned," he observed in a loud whisper, as if to avoid Scamp overhearing but with clearly little success, since Scamp could hear everything that happened in the ship.

Arlene shrugged. "There's nothing for us to do at this point. Scamp has got this. We just need to sit back and trust him, for now."

Beno'or didn't look entirely comforted by the statement, but he tried to relax into his chair, still fighting the forces tipping the ship into a steep bank.

Just then there was a prolonged green flash which illuminated the cockpit from the screen up front.

"Success!" Scamp declared. "Force field forced down," he confirmed.

There was a chorus of mutters and sighs from the three organics.

"Okay Scamp, take us down," Giles instructed, "and be prepared for evasive maneuvers. Shields full. We don't know what kind of anti-spacecraft weapons they have down there, and we've likely pissed them off now."

"Roger that," Scamp acknowledged.

The ship leveled out and Beno'or and Giles both readjusted their positions in their seats. The artificial gravity normalized on board as well, and within moments it was almost as if nothing untoward had happened at all.

Beno'or remembered his previous anxiety. "Am I safe to go and check on that pot of mocha?" he asked Arlene, a little nervously. "I fear it's likely fallen prey to the g-forces."

Arlene nodded. "Yes, of course. But if anything happens, make sure you strap in to whatever seat you can get to back there, okay?

Beno'or nodded, unbuckled himself and staggered to

the doorway, using the other chairs as crutches like a new sailor who hadn't yet developed his sea legs.

Giles spun his chair round to catch Arlene's eye. "I suppose you're going to tell me that Beno'or has the same priorities as Molly with his mocha obsession, eh?"

Arlene smiled, knowingly. "Wasn't going to say a word," she lied dryly.

"Giles," Scamp announced, "I've identified a likely location for the tomb. It's a raised artificial structure with dug out tunnels underneath it. Looks promising. It's a few kilometers from the terraformed guard dome," he told him.

Giles poked at his console holo. "Good job, Scamp!" he said after a moment. Arlene craned her neck to see but the angle was wrong. "Set us down nearby if you would?" he requested.

"Roger that, Mr. Kurns," Scamp replied, a sense of achievement in his voice.

Giles swung round in his chair to talk with Arlene. "Well, looks like this is going to be easier than we thought," he smiled.

Arlene scowled at him. "How much do I wish you hadn't said that?"

Giles looked confused. "Why? What?" he asked.

Arlene shook her head lightly, her raven hair dropping in front of her face, her hair tie dislodged in the recent activities. "You just had to jinx it!" she scolded him lightly.

Giles held his hands up defensively. "I'm sorry!" he surrendered. "I thought we were scientists," he mumbled, with a hint of humor.

Arlene narrowed her eyes at him. "You're a heathen. And a brute!" she told him, a glint in her eye.

"So you've told me before," he nodded, flashing her his best, charming smile.

She shook her head and turned away so he couldn't see her grinning.

Giles carried on as if he had won her over. "Okay, so our little antic up there has lost us the element of surprise," he continued, changing the subject. "As soon as we land, you and I need to get out there and get to that tomb. Pronto. They know we're here and they'll be coming for us."

Arlene nodded. "Agreed. We should probably also be armed," she told him.

Giles ignored her comment. "Scamp?"

"Yes, Giles?"

"What about the guards?" he asked.

Scamp ran another scan. "There are only six life signs."

Giles looked back at Arlene. "If we move fast we could be in and out before they even reach us," he said, his tone more hopeful than just a statement of absolute fact.

Arlene wrinkled her nose. "We've no idea what kind of travel machines they have," she pointed out.

Giles took a deep breath, then relaxed his shoulders in a resigned way. "I'll be bait and hold them off, or distract them or whatever. It will give you the chance to get in and I'll keep them busy outside."

Arlene's jaw set. "No you won't! We're a team. And you're not going to start that 'sacrificing yourself' nonsense again. Did you learn nothing last time?"

But Giles had stopped listening. "Scamp, how soon until they know our position once we land?" he asked.

Scamp's voice came back over the intercom. "We have no way to measure this. Maybe immediately."

Giles looked back at Arlene. "So perhaps we can subdue them?" he suggested.

Arlene nodded once. "Tranqs?"

Giles pursed his lips. "Yeah, except we need a clear shot," he said, thinking out loud. "And what if that doesn't work? If these guys are Zhyn, they're going to be big," he added putting his arms out to his side, and then remembering that Beno'or was only next door. His face flickered with embarrassment as he put his arms down again quickly.

Arlene pulled out her handgun in response to his question.

Giles shook his head. "No no no. We don't want to do that," he protested.

Arlene tilted her head to one side. "You got a better idea?" she asked.

Giles rubbed one hand over his face, screwing up his eyes against the stress. "We'll deal with it," he said, admitting he didn't have an immediate answer. "Load up on tranqs and set all weapons to stun. The last thing we want is a diplomatic crisis because we killed a Zhyn guard."

Arlene casually shrugged as she unbuckled and went to the back to suit up and strap on her weapons.

Giles called out to her as she left. "What I wanna know is when did you become so battle hungry?"

Arlene reappeared at the doorway, grinning. "You try being cooped up on an asteroid like Gaitune for sixty years and see how you like it!" she retorted.

Giles smiled, nodding in understanding. "Although," he ventured, "I imagine it's more interesting now that Lance has reactivated the Sanguine Squadron."

Arlene chuffed, still hanging onto the door frame. "Yeah, although I suspect your 'interest' lies more in the direction of Molly Bates than that old dusty base," she retorted, getting her final dig in before disappearing out of earshot.

Giles couldn't help himself. "My my, jealousy isn't a color that suits you, Arlene!" he called after her.

He half expected some witty retort, but when none came he suspected she may not have even heard.

Funny how she always seems to win the last word, even when she technically didn't have the last word, he thought to himself.

CHAPTER 9

Unknown location

"Okay, we're here."

Anne heard the now familiar gruff voice of the driver as the space van slowed and the tone of the engine changed. She remained motionless in the darkness, straining to hear the conversation.

"I think the drop-off is just round the back here. But lemme just message the guard," the voice continued.

There was some mumbling and shuffling in the cabin. Anne strained to hear but she couldn't make out what they were saying now.

She was cold to the bone. One foot had gone to sleep partly from the temperature, partly from her position, and mostly from the binds around her ankles cutting into her circulation. She imagined this really hadn't been a consideration for the kidnappers when they bound her.

She shuffled, trying to ease the pressure, hoping to make herself more agile for when the time came to make her break.

During the course of the ride she imagined a hundred different ways she might fight back and get free. In her mind she practiced winning. Getting loose and then getting away.

She knew the odds of that were slim, though.

"Right, we're on!" the driver's voice announced to his partner. "We need to drive round to door 12. There will be someone there to meet us," he said, starting the engine.

The van lurched forward and seemed to turn a couple of corners and then slowed to a stop. Anne heard one door open. "Stay here," the driver said. He got out, and Anne could hear footsteps heading away from them. And then nothing.

The man in the front snorted and cleared his throat.

Gross, Anne thought to herself. She quickly put her sentiment aside and returned to trying to hear what was going on.

Eventually the footsteps returned with another set. The front door opened again, and there was some muttering, an exchange, and the second man got out of the van too.

Moments later the back door opened and Anne felt cold air rush in around her. She looked around, trying to see who her captors were. They were human in shape and size, but she couldn't see their faces. Not that it mattered. She just needed to know roughly where their eyes were to gouge them out. That was scenario number five in her hundred different plans.

They were too far away to strike right away, but that was about to change. She waited, straining her eyes to see. They could tell she was awake.

"A'right," said a new voice. "Bring her in," he instructed.

Then there were hands on her ankles as she was abruptly dragged from the van. She lashed out, trying to kick with her bound legs. She tried to punch but the men were far too big and strong for her to be any match.

She tried to scream through her gagged mouth. The cloth was wet from her own saliva and was pulling at the sides of her mouth and giving her a headache. They managed to get her to her feet and one held her by one arm, bruising her brutally as he held her still. She continued to struggle, willing herself to get away to safety.

It wasn't going to happen.

"Knock it off, kid," the other voice told her. "There's nowhere to go. Don't make this harder for any of us."

Somehow the voice was soothing - even though it was the same voice that had been talking about their payout for delivering her on the journey here.

Still, she took his words at face value. There probably was no escaping them right now, and as long as there was time, she could be smart about getting away. If she had time on her side she might be able to focus and use her abilities. But she needed to be calm and collected.

She stood up straight, her legs unbound and her feet now on the tarmac. After displaying that she was cooperating, she tugged again at her upper arm, and straightened herself out some more. The kidnappers took the hint and started treating her a little more gently as they led her away from the van and towards a darkened building.

Her arm ached where they had gripped her, though.

Anne looked around as best she could. The guards all wore balaclavas. That's a good sign, she thought. At least they were hiding their faces. But they weren't concerned about her seeing *where* she was.

A quick scan of her surroundings revealed that she was near a set of buildings on an airfield. Looking up she realized that actually they weren't all buildings. They were actually ships.

Very big ships.

The one they were heading towards was docked at some kind of security office, which they led her through, frisked her, scanned her with a full body scanner, and then allowed her to pass.

One more guard from the ship showed up. This guy was Estarian and seemed to be in charge. "Okay," he said to her kidnappers. "We've got it from here."

The other ship's guard nudged her forward and into a walkway to the ship. The other two started asking questions about their money.

"I dunno anything about that," the human guard told them. "You'll need to speak to the boss. Next cabin over."

Anne heard them muttering and saw them turn to leave the same way they had just brought her in. She noticed the two guards that now had her in custody relaxed as the cabin door closed behind them. Clearly, they had been expecting trouble.

"Okay. Let's move," one told her. He was dressed in a ship's uniform and carried a rifle as well as a handgun strapped to his thigh. The other just had two handguns. Not that it mattered. They didn't need guns to convince her she was overpowered.

The pair walked her through the gangway onto the ship

and then down several corridors. Anne paid attention to the route they took, noting the twists and turns.

Glancing around she could see there were vents and air ducts. She strained to hear if they were active. By the time they took her through into a cargo holding area she had concluded that not all the life support systems were active yet. Just the minimum, for a skeleton prep-crew. She filed that intel away, and noticed covered-up pieces of machinery as they led her across a yellow insulated floor to an office meeting room, or what was probably an operations room at some point.

"In here," one of the guards said as he shoved her gently into the glass walled meeting area. He tapped on the glass. "Sound proof," he told her. "So save your breath."

His manner was matter-of-fact, like he knew the drill. Like this wasn't unfamiliar to them — having a guest who wasn't there of her own free will.

Anne stepped back a few paces and allowed them to close the door. She studied them carefully as they set the key code and then headed back out of the unit.

As soon as they were gone she tried to open the door, moving from the handle to the key pad on her side of the door. She unclipped the panel.

Nothing. All the electronics were on the other side. The wires that fed through went through a tiny hole. She reclipped the panel and stepped backwards.

Despondent, she turned around to review the room. It was glass on three sides, with the wall of the ship on the fourth. She put her hand on it. Metal, with coats of insulation and paint. She wasn't getting through that - powers or no powers.

Her eyes lifted up to the ceiling. An air vent. A *large* air vent. One big enough for her to get through, if she could get up there.

The room was laid out like a boardroom, with a table made up of segments. She walked to the far segment and moved the next one out of the way so she could rearrange the end one directly beneath the vent.

She checked the ceiling for cameras. Nothing.

She listened carefully for any guards coming. All was quiet but for the gentle humming of the ship.

She quickly scrambled up onto the desk and started fiddling with the vent, trying to get the cover off. The bolts were stiff, and her fingers weren't strong enough or hard enough to turn them. After a few minutes of trying she gave up.

Her neck hurt from straining and now her fingers were mangled. She needed another way out. Or she needed to settle herself down enough to use all this damn power she supposedly had.

Aibek Moon, Orn System

Beno'or, seated in the cockpit, watched the ship's monitors as Arlene and Giles made their way down the steps and onto the rather sandy surface of the planet they had landed on.

He wondered how he could be the most help. "So Scamp?" he started, trying to form a rapport. "I'm Beno'or. Is there anything I can do to help make sure my friends stay safe?"

Scamp thought for a moment, before appearing as a visual representation of a youngish human male on the screen to the left of Beno'or's immediate console. "You could talk them out of doing this mission. That would increase their odds of safety by several hundred percent."

Beno'or nodded, then sighed wearily. "Yes. Yes. I expect that is entirely accurate," he agreed. "Well, just let me know as this ground mission progresses. I have some tactical experience in the Zhyn military. Mostly controlling the generals and stopping them from destroying people. But it's experience nonetheless," he shared.

Scamp suddenly seemed interested. "That sounds fascinating. Tell me more about what you did. I think it might help me evolve my negotiation and tactical heuristics for future conflicts," he explained.

The old Justicar started telling Scamp about the bad old, good old days before he ended up in the Empire's ruling court.

Giles and Arlene trudged across the rock in half atmosphere with their helmets securely fastened to their atmosuits.

"I can't remember the last time I actually needed to create a seal on this jacket," Arlene complained as she fidgeted against having it zipped up all the way.

"Tell me about it," Giles gruffed over their communication implants. "I had this suit jacket made to simulate that old-fashioned stuff they used to wear on earth. Had it commissioned specially so it would pass federation regulation for travel on light personnel ships even. Never thought I'd actually have to use it with a breathable helmet."

Arlene could see he was fussing with the seal of the cuffs against his gloves.

She chuckled. "Look at us!" she remarked. "Out in the middle of nowhere. No atmosphere. Trying to raid a tomb. Possibly moments from a hostile encounter with the tomb guards, and we're bitching about our fashion!"

Giles stopped and glanced across at her. She could see him chuckling behind his helmet. "You make a good point, Ms. Bailey. Am I right in thinking that you're suggesting we get on and get inside that tomb?" he inquired comically.

Arlene grinned back at him. "Now that you mention it, it's not a bad idea," she said casually. They quickened their pace as much as they could comfortably, with the heavy boots they wore.

It took several minutes to get close to the only structure they could see for miles around. "This must be it," Giles announced when they were close enough to see the sand colored brick work. The bricks were large, but probably small enough for a man, or Zhyn, to carry one at a time. Except, they seemed to be galvanized by some kind of finishing paint that gave the temple a sheen.

Giles put his hand against a wall of the structure. "No way we could have spotted this visually had Scamp not parked us right next to it," Giles admitted, trying to figure out what the structure was made of.

Arlene touched the sloping wall of the pyramid. "You're not kidding. We're right on top of it and I can barely make it out against the landscape."

The structure was like a pyramid except the front and the back had two pillars and a facade across the top.

The pair wandered around to one side, assuming there would be a door or some other entry into the structure.

Giles stopped in his tracks when he rounded the pillar. Arlene almost bumped into him. It took her a second to navigate her way around him and see why he had stopped herself. "There's no door," she stated.

Giles glanced across at her giving her his most sarcastic look possible from behind his helmet.

She slapped at his arm. "Alright!" she said, laughing at her obvious statement. "Let's head round the back then."

They trudged round to the back and found that it was exactly the same on the other side.

Arlene glanced over at Giles before stealing her eyes back to examining the sides of the temple. "You're not thinking what I'm thinking, are you?"

Giles put his gloved hand on the brick work again, looking up along the painted surface. "Depends what you're thinking," he replied.

Arlene turned away from the temple. "That this is looking an awful lot like the fake temple with no entrance over on Ramachandra?"

Giles sighed, bringing his gaze back to eye level but still studying the surface in front of him. "It had crossed my mind," he admitted.

Arlene had stopped, and was looking out into the space behind the temple. She squinted, trying to see through a haze that lacked breathable air.

Giles noticed and turned to look at what had caught her attention. "What is it?" he asked.

Arlene narrowed her eyes some more and craned her neck forward. "I've got a funny feeling there is an opening over that way. A cave or something."

"A feeling?" Giles repeated.

She turned her head to look at him for a microsecond before turning her head back to look straight ahead. Before she had even replied she was marching off down the steps of the raised temple and off into the sand.

"Hang on," Giles called after her. "We have limited oxygen in these things, remember."

Arlene waved her hand. "I won't be a minute," she assured him.

Giles hurried after her. "Scamp," he hailed through their shared channel. "We've spotted something behind the temple. Just going to take a moment to check it out."

"Okay," Scamp replied. "I'm hooking Beno'or up to the communications channel too."

Giles frowned as he trudged across the sand. "He doesn't have an implant though?"

"He's got a Zhyn implant. I think I can adapt it. It will certainly help when he doesn't have to stay on board at least."

"Okay, sure," Giles responded.

He switched channels and caught Arlene up, just as the mount of rock ahead of them became apparent.

"So Scamp and Beno'or are bonding?" Arlene smiled as Giles came up next to her.

"Yeah," Giles confirmed. "Can you imagine?"

Arlene raised her eyebrows under her helmet. "Well, that Beno'or can be charming. I'm not surprised he's winning Scamp over so easily."

Giles raised an eyebrow and glanced at her sideways.

She grinned. "Come on, tomb raider," she said, tapping him playfully across his body with the back of her forearm. "Let's go see what's inside the creepy-looking cave behind the sealed tomb!"

Giles shook his head. "If ever there was a recipe for disaster," he muttered.

CHAPTER 10

Aibek Moon, Orn System, Guardian Settlement, Computer Room

Naldrir hurried into the computer room where the others were assembled.

"It's not good," he reported. "The force field is offline. I have it rebooting, but I needed to replace a breaker. They managed to overload it."

There was a hushed murmur through the room. Koryss looked to see if Gagai was going to respond, hoping that he wouldn't have to make the call on this one. He was relieved when Gagai got up from the computer and turned to question Naldrir some more.

"I take it they're on their way down then?" Gagai asked.

Naldrir nodded. "More than likely. They've dropped off the radar."

Koryss stepped forward to join the two in the conversation. "Aye, they have," he confirmed. "Just now."

Naldrir looked concerned. His hands were covered in dirt and oil from his rummaging around in the innards of the main force field projector. "Well, if their tech is anything to go by, this is going to be the least of our problems if they make it into the temple."

There were nervous shuffles from the others in the room.

Gagai heaved a sigh, contemplating their options. "We need to get out there and *stop* them from getting to the temple," he decided. "Everyone to the transport. We leave immediately," he ordered.

The room erupted into obedient activity. Even Jendyg kept his thoughts to himself and hurried off to get onto his bike.

"Koryss, you take tactical," Gagai called over the hubbub.

It didn't take long before they were all assembled at the main gate, waiting for the atmospheric force field to be lifted. As soon as the gate was open they were out and through, the barrier closing behind them, keeping the air seal intact.

The six of them rode out on their antigrav bikes in an impressive line across the rock. As they passed dust blew up beneath them, marking their advance from a distance as they cut their way between their habitation and the temple they had sworn their lives to protect.

As soon as they had cleared the gate and were up to speed Koryss began delivering tactical instructions. "As per our alpha drill our primary directive is to prevent the intruders from reaching the temple by any means necessary. This, I need not remind you, includes the use of deadly force. Do not hesitate. I repeat: do not hesitate."

The comm line cracked with interference from radiation as they rode forward.

"Ignore their vessel for now," Koryss's commands continued. "We haven't the manpower to tackle it and our priority is to protect the temple. Their tech is an issue. They took out the force field so there is no telling what else they may be capable of. This is the biggest threat to the mission we've ever seen, so treat it as such."

Ammo tried to interrupt. As Koryss drew a breath he saw his chance. "Brother," he interjected.

"Yes?"

"Are you suggesting we leave the canyon unprotected?"

Koryss answered immediately. "Affirmative. The canyon isn't vulnerable and the short-range tracking has their vessel at the temple entrance. In all likelihood they're unaware of anything else."

Ammo's question answered, Koryss continued. "Once inside the caves we need to track, isolate, and kill. They will likely send reinforcements. We don't know how many bodies they have on the vessel, or other vessels in the vicinity. Our secondary objective is therefore to secure and defend the caves." He paused. "Confirm mission details," he concluded.

Each of the other five acknowledged receipt of their objective and then the line went quiet. They rode in silence for another minute, until they slowed their approach around the space-going ship that had appeared on their terrain. Keeping their distance, they continued on to the temple, approaching in a wide circle from behind.

Koryss's voice came over the intercom as they each dismounted and powered down their bikes allowing them to settle directly on the rock. "Weapons on full power," he told them. "Remember, deadly force is required. This is the most serious threat we've faced."

The Zhyn guards jogged into the cave that Arlene and Giles had found, moving as quickly as they could manage in their atmosuits and heavy-set form.

Aibek Moon, Orn System, Temple Caverns

The ship's channel linked up again. "Giles, Arlene, this is Scamp again. I'm afraid you have incoming."

"Incoming?" Giles asked. "From what?"

Arlene turned back away from the cave's entrance and looked at Giles, watching his reaction for more information.

"Six Zhyn guards, on antigrav mopeds," Scamp explained. "Heading right your way. I estimate they will be here before you can get back to the ship."

Arlene looked at Giles for a second, and then made a decision. "We'll take shelter in the cave. If nothing else we can pick them off as they approach from here."

"Very well," Scamp acknowledged. "Shields up. If they try to interfere too much with the ship I'll be forced to take off and hover around. Final protocols and all."

"I understand," Giles confirmed. "Do what you need to do, Scamp. We'll be okay."

Arlene turned and headed into the cave. Giles followed quickly. Back on the private channel, Arlene's tone was a little less decisive. "Did you believe that when you said it?" she paused. "That we'll be okay?"

Giles moved slowly as his eyes adjusted to the low levels of light in the cave. "Well, yeah. When I said it I did."

Arlene didn't seem impressed. "We're going to need more than handguns, tranqs, and a good vantage point to take these guys out," she told him.

Giles didn't respond. There was nothing they could do about how much weaponry they were carrying now. They were cut off from the ship.

Head down, Giles traveled deeper into the cave, Arlene following quietly behind him.

Eventually it split into two passageways.

Giles stopped and looked back to Arlene, then signaled to the break off. "Is this the bit where you say we'll be safer if we split up?" he asked grimly.

Arlene turned and looked back at him. "You're fucking kidding me. No way are we splitting up. You don't get off that easily!" she hissed over the intercom. "Let's take this one," she decided, taking the lead down one of the channels.

Giles followed compliantly. "And what's to just stop them from following us in?" he asked not more than two paces in.

Arlene smiled, and turned back to him, the light of her helmet illuminating his face, and his, hers. "Well statistically we've probably just got rid of half of them at that last junction," she grinned smugly.

Giles chuckled. "Ah ha. And the others? And when they call out for their friends?"

She turned and kept walking. "I don't know," she responded, her face no longer visible to him, but her serious expression had returned.

A few paces further down, the tunnel opened up into a ledge. Beneath the ledge there was a drop. A small amount of light filtered down from the cavern above, illuminating the vista just enough for them to see the tunnel continuing on the other side of the crevice. The crevice with the deadly drop.

Giles stepped out onto the ledge next to Arlene. "Great," he huffed. "Just our luck." He looked up and down the ledge for another opening or a way over.

"There!" Arlene pointed.

A few hundred yards down a path there was a rope bridge that would take them across to the other side where they could pick up the tunnel again.

Giles gave her his "one-more-adventure" look as he squeezed past her. "Okay, let's do it," he agreed, leading the way now.

Arlene followed. "So we could do with a way of sealing ourselves off from them, if we can."

Giles dreaded the idea of what she was going to propose. "And if the bridge is our only way back?"

"I wasn't thinking of destroying it, exactly," she shared with a glint in her eye, knowing what he was thinking. "Have you noticed anything special about this moon since we got down here?"

Giles thought for a moment. "You're thinking it has land energy you can draw on?"

She nodded. "Exactly. I tried channeling it when we were walking. It seems legit."

Giles stopped on the ledge and turned to her. "So what? A protection spell for the bridge? To stop them from crossing?"

She nodded. "Except it would also stop us from crossing back too, until it wore off."

He scratched at his head, wondering. "And would they know that? Would they know to wait for it to wear off?"

Arlene shrugged. "Hard to tell," she said. "This kind of magic doesn't seem to exist in Zhyn culture or folklore from what I can tell, talking with Beno'or. But then, there are devout believers and skeptics in every culture."

Giles's eyes turned heavy and concerned. "Yeah, and when you give someone the job of guarding a sacred and mystical talisman, I'm guessing you're going to be pulling from the pool of believers rather than the skeptics."

Arlene could tell he was torn and his brain was churning to figure a way out of this. She shrugged. "Or not," she offered. "Warriors aren't always believers. I mean, often they believe in a higher power. And their purpose and allegiance to that power. But that doesn't include any knowledge or acceptance of magic, necessarily."

Giles looked off into the distance. "At this point," he said, "we're fast running out of options. I promised Reynolds I wouldn't start an inter-planetary war, so avoiding the killy-killy would be a good way to go if we can."

Arlene nodded solemnly. "Okay. Don't worry. I got this. Now," she said, her tone a hundred times more determined than before, "let's get across this bridge and get this spell cast."

Giles felt himself perk up a bit. He hoped it wasn't just the adrenalin, junkie though he probably still was. Somewhere deep inside he wished for it to simply be hope, or a healthy desire to get out of this alive. But at the same time, realistically, he knew it was just the thrill of being on the edge.

Quite literally this time.

They arrived at the bridge. Giles offered to step on it first. It was a lot sturdier than he had hoped. He walked a few paces then called back in a loud whisper. "It's good."

Arlene joined him on it, and step by step they carefully made their way across.

"Don't do it," Arlene called forward to him.

He turned to her.

She had a serious look on her face. "I knew you were thinking about it. Just don't!" she reiterated.

Giles frowned as he clung a little tighter to the rope hand rail as he stood turning back at her. "You knew I was going to try and look down?" he asked.

She nodded, and he started walking again. He shook his head. "You're still as creepy as ever," he muttered to her.

She grinned. "It's worse when there is power in the ground," she admitted.

"Yeah, right," he grumbled, a little resentful at his complete transparency to her now. "I bet you still sit in meetings on the ArchAngel and read the thoughts of everyone there."

Arlene shook her head. "Honestly, what would be the point in that? Half of them are thinking about their to-do list, and the other half are thinking about how to get a tactical advantage from the situation they're facing."

"So you do then!" Giles teased her, diligently keeping his eyes fixed on the rock face on the other side of the bridge.

She chuckled quietly and they neared the other end of

the bridge. Once they were safely on the ledge on the other side they turned back and looked back at the space they had come across.

Giles leaned across to Arlene and nudged her shoulder with his. "Okay. You need any help?" Giles offered.

Arlene thought for a moment. "It wouldn't hurt if you wanted to tap in and give it a boost." She narrowed her eyes at him. "When was the last time you did any magic?"

"Of this variety?" he qualified, his eyes searching the past in the back of his mind. "Rather than in the… *kitchen*?" he said, quickly changing his question from bedroom to kitchen.

Arlene caught it and smiled. "Yes, of this variety," she specified firmly.

Giles raised his eyebrows and started to pretend to limber up his shoulders for the imminent activity. "Ah, you'd be surprised how often it comes up that I need to throw down a bit of Estarian witchery," he winked, completely avoiding the question.

"So, not since we stopped dating," she concluded.

Giles shrugged. "Pretty much," he admitted comically. "Though it has got me out of a few tight situations now and again."

Arlene had already started to attune to the bridge. She closed her eyes and put her hand out in front of her, palms facing the length of the bridge. Giles joined her and did the same.

Within a few seconds he could feel an energy pulsing from his hands, and a kind of feeling like two magnets close together but repelling each other, all around his arms. The pulsing intensified to a climax and moments later he felt the same magnetic repulsion off his palms as if a wall had been erected.

Arlene had started to move. Giles opened his eyes to see her checking it with her hands flat against the invisible wall. "Okay. I think we're good for about twelve hours," she told him. "And hopefully long before then they'll give up and leave us a chance to get back out of here."

Giles nodded, and they headed back up along the new ledge to the second entrance to the cave. "They must be getting close by now," he mused as they approached the next tunnel.

Arlene quickened her pace. "Yes, I can sense them gaining on us," she told him.

Just then there was a shout that caught their attention. The pair stopped carefully and turned to look.

"Shit, it's them already!" Arlene cursed, catching sight of a group of Zhyn on the other side of the crevice. Giles had accidentally looked down and was fighting the adrenaline that was pumping through his body. His legs felt wobbly and he clung quickly to the wall on the side of the ledge.

"We've got to keep moving," he said, more for his own benefit than anything else. He pushed on, now sweating and his heart racing. For a split second he flashed back to the moment when he had slipped and fallen down a cliff off a similarly narrow shelf. Thankfully, Sean Royale, cyborg and super soldier, had been there to save him. But this time it was just him and Arlene. He shook the thought from his head as they finally arrived at the mouth of the tunnel.

"They're almost at the bridge!" Arlene told him as she followed him into the darkened tunnel. He could hear the tension in her voice, even though she pretended to play it cool.

He turned and looked at her, leaning against the tunnel wall. She looked ready to keep moving. He caught hold of her wrist, stopping her in her tracks. "We're okay now. I believe in you. That spell will hold them off."

He steadied his breathing and deliberately tried to convey determination and confidence to her. It worked. The anxiety in her eyes seemed to settle to be replaced with her task-orientated 'on-the-case' look. Giles smiled at the shift.

"Ladies first, then," he smiled, gesturing for her to take the lead at the now more relaxed manner.

She nodded and headed on, giving Giles a moment when her back was turned to compose himself inwardly and metabolize some of the excess adrenaline that was still pumping through his system.

The tunnel began to slope down, taking them deeper into the ground, and further from the temple. The pair kept walking, their only illumination coming from the light from their helmets.

CHAPTER 11

Aibek Moon, Orn System, Temple Caverns

Koryss led the way into the cave. "When we get to the split, Ammo and Mennynad, go right. The rest of us will take the left. Stay in communication. If they're in the right-hand channel, hold them there or terminate if you can."

"Acknowledged," confirmed Ammo and Mennynad in unison through their helmet audio communicators.

The warriors made their way through the tunnels in the half light, silently going their separate ways when it came to the point of divergence. Though they had drilled this a hundred times over the years, the thought of actually capturing someone was something novel.

Jendyg found himself wondering if in fact this was the correct course of action. Perhaps Gagai had been right all along, and he had just been losing faith? Faced with the possibility that their most sacred artifact might fall into the wrong hands, he felt his previous world view begin to crumble with each step he took into the caves.

Gagai had forged ahead of the four remaining in

the troop, more determined than ever that they should not fail. As they approached the opening with the crevasse he quickened his pace, making it hard for the others to keep up. For a large warrior who found himself lapsing in his training after all these years, he moved fast.

He disappeared out onto the ledge and started jogging along the way towards the bridge. The others heard him shout out as they emerged shortly after him. Then they saw what he was shouting at. Across the crevasse they could see the two figures, one blue, one pink, and both scaleless, hurrying along, having already crossed the bridge.

He knew that there was no place for them to go, but there wasn't a Zhyn present who wasn't feeling this was too close for comfort.

Koryss immediately started issuing tactical orders, breathing heavily to keep up with Gagai. "The bridge will only take two at a time. I'll go ahead with Gagai. Then Jendyg and Naldrir, you can follow once we're over. Confirm."

"Confirmed," Naldrir responded immediately. Jendyg answered a second later, but Gagai was almost at the bridge. He barely hesitated, glancing back just for a fraction of a second to see that his team were following him before stepping onto the bridge and pressing on.

He hurried forward, feeling the vibrations on the wooden structure change as Koryss joined him. He could see their targets getting away.

No matter. They'll be trapped in the cave with no escape once we get there, he thought to himself. And yet, despite that knowledge, anxiety wouldn't let him slow down even a little.

He saw the end of the bridge approaching and prepared himself to leap off the other end and sharply change direction. He pushed vigorously forward off one leg and an instant later felt the wind being knocked out of him as he was thrown backwards. He found himself on the deck of the bridge, in pain and struggling to recover his breath.

He looked around, accidentally peering over the bridge into the abyss below. Adrenaline shot through his body as he struggled to regain his wits.

"Gagai!" he heard Koryss calling behind him. "Gagai! Are you okay, brother?"

Realizing he had somehow been thrown back by an invisible force, he carefully pulled himself into an upright position and then cautiously to his feet. His chest was pounding from the fright and the activity. Koryss was panting too as he joined him, carefully slowing before he reached the end of the bridge. "What is it?" Koryss asked, squinting to see what had impeded the advance.

Gagai stepped forward carefully, one hand held out in front of him. After a few inches he felt it make contact with some kind of field. He snapped his hand back.

"Craft!" he declared in disgust as if it were a curse word. His nose wrinkled up and his eyes flared with anger.

Koryss looked concerned and thought for a moment about trying to touch it himself, but then thought better of it. "What can we do?" he asked.

Gagai shook his head. "I'm not sure. There's no telling how long this will last. We might be able to force our way through in a few minutes." He glanced down the way at the two figures disappearing into the next tunnel. "Either way," he said, "it won't last forever, and we'll either get through, or they're going to have to come out." He turned back up the bridge to head back to the others.

Ammo and Mennynad had just emerged from a secret passageway further down in the other direction. Gagai assumed by their presence that they didn't find anyone down that way.

Gagai arrived back at the other side of the bridge, and considered their next move. "Okay, listen up," he announced as Ammo and Mennynad came jogging up to join the group. "They've put a shield up on the end of the bridge. There's no way to know how long it will last, but we need to be prepared for it to be a while. Koryss?"

Koryss came up beside him. "Yes, brother?"

Gagai barely looked at him as he issued his orders. "Organize a rotation of two guards to be here until that barrier is down. The second it looks like it might be failing we want the whole team here."

Koryss bowed his head in acknowledgment. "And what of the coming freeze?"

Gagai thought for a moment, the immediate blaze of anger in his eyes subsiding, replaced with mere frustration. "We'll have to retreat when it comes. But we need to stay as long as we can withstand. We don't want to give them an opportunity to escape back to their ship. This is our chance to prevent them from figuring out how to advance, and everything we've worked for rests on this outcome."

He started heading off the bridge and the warriors parted to allow him to pass. He trekked back along the ledge to the tunnel they had come bounding out of only minutes before, his head hanging and fists clenched.

Aibek Moon, Orn System, Temple Caves

"Giles, Arlene?" Beno'or's voice came over their implants.

Arlene responded. "Arlene here. Everything okay?"

Beno'or's voice was tinged with concern, despite the well-cultivate operational focus of a seasoned leader. "It is at the moment, but Scamp has just been looking at the precession of this moon. His conclusion is that it is due to freeze over in the next few hours when it disappears behind a cluster of these moons and all light from the nearest stars is blocked."

Arlene's face showed mild annoyance, rather than fear. "Meaning that once again we're in mortal danger," she commented, turning to look at Giles, as if it was his fault once again.

Giles's face dropped. He put his hand on her shoulder to reassure her that it was going to be okay. Her face softened. He spoke over the audio feed. "Well, at least this means our friends out there will need to go and find shelter. Probably back from whence they came."

Arlene nodded, considering their options.

Giles's eyes seemed to spark in recognition of an idea. "Beno'or? Do we know how cold it's going to get?"

"Scamp says Subzero," the Justicar replied. "Enough for you to freeze off various parts of your anatomy that you'd rather keep intact," he added.

Giles took a deep breath his brain still churning. "How long for?"

"Thirteen hours," Beno'or responded quickly. "But then it will take another three to return to normal temperature."

"Okay," Giles decided. "Stay on the ship. You'll be safe there. Scamp will look after you. We'll hunker down here." He paused. "Everything is going to be okay," he added reassuringly.

They signed off, leaving Giles and Arlene in the tunnel. Arlene leaned gently against the wall. "How on Estaria are we going to protect ourselves from sub-zero temperatures?" she mused.

Giles shook his head. "With no fuel and no oxygen, we're going to be struggling. Our best bet is to find a way out of here and get back to the ship."

Arlene nodded. "Okay. Let's get moving then," she said, moving off into the darkness. "And hope that they don't know of another way in past the bridge," she added grimly.

Giles followed along behind her, still trying to think of creative ways to get them out of there.

Eventually the tunnel opened up into a cavern.

"End of the road," Giles muttered. He placed his hand on the wall as if to reassure himself it really was just a rock face and not an illusion.

Arlene started looking around. The area was about ten feet across, from what she could tell with the low light levels, and the ground seemed rather uneven. There was a feeling of damp in the air too, which was unusual for a planet with so little atmosphere. She took mental notes as she wandered around the outside, checking for another exit using the light from her helmet.

"Looks like we're trapped," she said matter-of-factly.

Giles didn't respond. He was too busy inspecting the space too. Looking up, he saw that there a light coming from above, but it was too dim and unfocused for him to make out where the shaft was coming from. Or how far away.

"At least it looks like we have an air supply," he said.

Arlene inspected the floor, rubbing dirt between a gloved finger and thumb.

"You got something?" Giles asked, catching sight of her interest in the dirt.

Arlene looked up from her crouched position. "Not sure yet," she said, getting up again. "But first things first. We need warmth if we're going to stay here."

Giles stood with his hands on his hips, thinking. "We have some devices. Back up comms. Might be able to create a spark. Though, oxygen is an issue."

He checked his air gauge. "How much air have you got?" he asked her.

Arlene looked down at her holo. "Fifty-five minutes," she said. "You?"

Giles lowered his eyes. "One hour and twenty. We need to figure out a way to get some of this air over to you," he said without missing a beat.

Arlene shook her head. "Stop it. We're going to figure this out," she told him firmly.

Giles shook his head. "You're only here because of me. If it gets tight, you should take my air. Promise me you will?"

Arlene shook her head. "Will you stop!" she said, exasperated. "Besides, we don't even have a way to transfer air from one helmet to another." She dismissed the subject. "Okay, so situation is: we're stuck. Priority is air and then heat if we're going to survive the oncoming temperature drop."

She looked agitated. "We should have checked air supply before we sealed the bridge," she chided herself.

Giles walked over to her as she kicked at the ground. He held her shoulders to get her attention. "Hey, none of that. If we didn't seal off the bridge we would have been killed already. We did what we had to do. We thought there would be another way out."

Arlene looked around. "What if there is?"

Giles shrugged. "Then we'd better find it."

The pair set off searching every inch of the cavern, working in opposite directions like two hands belonging to a single mind.

After several moments, Arlene stopped. Giles noticed but kept working, intent of finding something that was going to save them. When Arlene didn't call out or resume her search he turned around to see her in the center of the cavern with the palms of her hands pointing at the floor. She was channeling energy. He could sense it vibrating off her.

"What are you doing?" he asked.

"Check it out," she said, nodding down at the ground.

"What?" he asked, moving closer.

Arlene stopped what she was doing, and switched off the seal on her helmet. Giles moved to stop her, but a second later she was taking off her helmet.

"What are you doing?" he shouted at her.

Helmet off, and tucking it under her arm, she shook her head, shaking out her hair, and taking a deep breath.

Giles stood there amazed. "How did you know there's air?" he asked.

Arlene smiled her smug, knowing smile she reserved for moments when she had been especially clever. "I noticed the leafy weeds growing in the ground," she said pointing down. "Those kinds of plants can't grow without the right composition of nitrogen and oxygen, and for whatever reason, I think this cavern has got an air supply."

"But how?" Giles gawked.

Arlene shrugged. "That I don't know yet. But, I'm betting there is enough in here, and the tunnel, for us to breathe for a while. And maybe even start a fire or two. In fact, I'm thinking that there must be a constant stream of breathable air because, well, we didn't break a seal when we came in here."

Giles frowned. "But there definitely isn't air outside."

Arlene nodded. "That's right. But we've changed elevation a lot since we came into the first cave, so who knows what's going on in here."

Giles felt a brain-ache coming on. He fiddled with his holo to switch off the helmet seal and then removed it. The air was fresh: cold and pleasant to breathe. There was a slight dampness to it. Like the smell of plants or something.

Arlene returned to what she had been trying to do.

Giles watched her, puzzling it out. "Ahhhh. So you're going to light a fire ball!"

Arlene nodded slightly and smiled. "I am. If I can concentrate for long enough, that is."

Giles considered himself told off. He closed his lips and zipped his fingers across them.

Arlene was already ignoring him again.

At first there was just a glimmer on the floor in front of her. It was barely perceptible. Giles questioned himself as to whether he was really seeing it. But soon the little yellow flicker grew, and turned into a white light, which shifted into a white ball with a blue glow around it. An instant later it popped and fizzled into a bigger ball and took on a self-sustaining energy of its own.

Arlene looked over at him with a broad smile.

Giles's eyes turned wide in amazement. "I didn't know you could still do that!" he exclaimed.

Arlene turned her mouth down at the corners and tilted her head onto one shoulder. "I didn't either!" she admitted.

Giles approached the fire ball with his hands out. "Wow, there's some heat coming off that too."

Arlene nodded, glancing up at the roof of the cavern. "And some light," she said, nodding at the scribbles carved into the rock above them.

Giles looked up, his mouth dropping open.

Arlene grinned and held her hands out again to a spot a few feet from the first fireball. "Let me get a few more of these lit, and then you can geek out on the decryption," she told him.

CHAPTER 12

Aboard the Flutningsaðili, Level 4, Restricted Access Area

"Keep moving!" The command cracked through the dark silence.

Suddenly the lights in the cargo area started flicking on, triggered by the motion sensors. Anne heard the voice coming from the darkness, accompanied now by four sets of footsteps.

She scrambled to her feet in the far corner of the meeting room and waited for the people to emerge into the light. The footsteps became louder and crisper, especially the boots of the two guards she could hear.

They came into view, roughly holding onto two fellow Estarians. One was an older gentleman who wore a white scientist's coat. The other was young and female, casually dressed, like she had been taken on her way into work. Her makeup had run and her eyes were swollen and red around the edges. They both looked disheveled and emotionally drained.

Anne remained silent and motionless, though she didn't try to hide her presence.

The two newcomers were unceremoniously shoved into the meeting room with her, and the young woman started crying again. The older gentleman pulled her gently away from the doorway and patted her on the shoulder. "It'll be okay. They clearly want us alive," he assured her in a soothing voice.

The first guard punched the keypad again and the door closed. The other had already casually turned, his gun pointing downwards still, and started walking away. The other, seeing the door seal shut, caught up with him and they disappeared, heralded by the sound of their boots on the insulated flooring.

It was only then that the old man turned and saw Anne. "Oh. Hello," he said gently. "I see we're in a similar predicament."

Anne nodded.

"Do you know why we're here?" he asked.

Anne shook her head.

The girl turned around to face her. "Who are you?" she asked. "Where are you from?"

Anne recoiled, not wanting to share anything that might make her vulnerable.

"Hush. Don't bombard her, Lana," the old man told her. "She's scared. We all are. But it's going to be okay."

He turned back to Anne. "It's alright. We're not going to hurt you," he said.

Anne nodded and then tentatively sat down on the nearest chair to her, as far away from the newcomers as she could.

Lana glanced at the old man and then around the room. "We're trapped," she declared, despair in her voice.

Anne looked up at the vent. The old guy noticed. He moved forward and sat down on a chair at the table, several seats away from Anne so as not to intimidate her. "My name is Dr. Brahms," he said, speaking slowly and quietly. "This is Lana. We've been kidnapped too."

There was a scrape of chair legs on the floor as Lana pulled out a seat on the other side of the table and sat down, clearly following the doctor's lead.

Dr. Brahms's eyes flicked up at the vent that Anne had glanced up at. "You tried to get in there?" he asked.

Anne nodded.

"You couldn't reach?" he asked.

Anne shook her head and showed him her hands. "I couldn't get it open," she said quietly.

The old guy nodded empathetically. "Okay. Well don't worry about that for now. We may be able to help with that."

Lana interrupted. "I think it would help if we could figure out what they want with us," she said.

The doctor turned to her. "I agree. But it would be good to find a way out too."

Lana looked up at the vent. "No way you're getting through that. I mean, she would be able to," she said, nodding in Anne's direction as if she weren't a part of the conversation, "and maybe I would fit. At a stretch..."

Her voice trailed off before a new thought took the conversation elsewhere.

"So at first when I came to in the back of that truck, I was thinking sex trade. But then I met you, doc." She realized the social implications of what she was saying. "No offense!" she added quickly.

Brahms smiled. "None taken!" he exclaimed.

"But you said you were a scientist? What kind?"

"Planetary seismology mostly," he said. "Recently I've been working for a company who is developing safer ways to extract ore from class A asteroids, though…"

Lana frowned. "I'm wondering… well, I'm not a scientist. But I do work as an operator for a company that does core mining."

Her head snapped to look at Anne. "Are you a scientist or something?" she asked.

Anne shook her head.

Lana frowned. "You don't say much, do you?"

Anne lowered her eyes to the table again.

Lana continued her questioning, despite the heavy stare from the doctor across the table from her. "Did you hear anything when they brought you in? Any clues as to why we're here?"

Anne shook her head. "No," she said, forcing her voice from her throat. "I was taken in the night from my home. They brought me in a van. Two humans. They talked about getting paid, but not why their buyers wanted me."

Lana processed the information, seemingly satisfied that she had been given *something* to go on. Though she knew then and there she would be pressing her for more insight later.

The doctor interjected. "You know, I'm wondering if there is something to do with this equipment. If I'm not mistaken, that shape over there is very much like a deep drill used for extracting heavy metals at high temperatures."

Lana peered out into the blackness.

"You can't see it now," he qualified. "But I noticed it before the lights went off again out there as they left."

Lana slumped impatiently back into her seat.

"Look," he said, turning back to the both of them. "Whatever is going on here, someone is going to notice we're missing and start tracking us down. I'm valuable to my company. And my clients. They have resources, and some of the people I've worked for in the past know what's going on in the black markets. If we're being used for something illegal they'll hear about it."

Lana narrowed one eye at him. "Hang on - what makes you think that it's not one of your shady clients that have kidnapped us then?"

The doctor shrugged. "It's unlikely. But I don't. However," he turned to look at Anne again, "why would that explain why you two are here?" He shook his head gently as he looked down at his clasped hands resting on the desk in front of him. "No. My guess is this is indeed something commercial, and they need you for part of it."

Lana tilted her head in Anne's direction. "And what about her?"

The doctor took a deep breath. "That, I don't know. It's possible her presence here is completely unrelated."

He turned to her. "You've not been running from someone, have you?" he asked gently. "You can tell us, you know?"

Anne had been on the run her whole life, for various reasons. But she wasn't about to get into that. Or what she had overheard at the convent. No. Her best chance of survival was for them to think she was just a defenseless girl and leave it at that.

Safer that way. For everyone.

She shook her head gently and then returned to fiddling with her hands.

Aibek Moon, Orn System, Temple Caves

Ammo and Mennynad had been waiting on the bridge since the second shift.

Ammo paced up and down every now and again, trying to keep warm. "You think they're going to remember to pull us out before it hits critical?" he called over to Mennynad, who was sitting cross legged and upright in the middle of the bridge within touching distance of the invisible wall.

Mennynad held out a finger for the umpteenth time since they had arrived, slowly moving it forward until the field dealt him a correction and pushed his finger back with a bite. "Have faith, brother," he called back. "They wouldn't leave us here to perish."

Ammo wasn't comforted. "Yeah, but what if they did?" he pushed, continuing to pace. "And more to the point, what if Jendyg is right, and we have been forsaken by the elders? Maybe their plan all along was to elongate our lifespans and leave us here."

Mennynad turned around, resting his hands on the wooden slats of the bridge's floor from his seated position. "You think that the elders would do that to us?"

Ammo shrugged. "They wanted a problem solved. They'd already taken us in and given us a life when we each had very few prospects. Maybe they figured we owed them?"

Mennynad shook his head. "I can't believe that. Not of the people we knew," he explained.

"Yeah, but think about it," Ammo insisted, trying a different angle. "We've never seen any signs of this thing actually having power. Maybe it's expired? And rather than bring us back and have to deal with reintegrating us, they've chosen to just leave us here."

Mennynad frowned. "You got any other theories you want to air?" he asked, poking fun at Ammo's sudden tirade of doubts.

"You jest, but what if we have simply been forgotten?" Ammo said, the timbre of his voice much softer and more vulnerable than before.

Mennynad sighed. "If we've been forgotten, it'll be because our elders were taken out of play by the very forces we're meant to be protecting this place from," he said firmly. "And besides, what would you be doing if you weren't here. Our life was the monastery. We lived in active service. This mission gave our very existence meaning. If not this, then what?"

Ammo stopped pacing and seemed to slip into serious contemplation for a moment. He began shaking his head. "I don't know the-"

His thought process was interrupted. Their ear pieces crackled and Koryss's voice could be heard in their helmets. "Okay brothers, time to come home. The freeze is heading your way and you don't want to be out in it."

"Roger that," Ammo acknowledged brightly, glad to be

thinking about something more practical. "Thanks for the save."

Koryss chuckled without humor. "Don't thank me yet. We'll all be back out there the second it is safe again. Gagai is pretty sure the witchery they worked isn't going to hold for long."

Ammo didn't seem phased. "Well, I guess that's good news in terms of being able to get them out of there," Ammo responded as the pair walked back along the bridge.

"Yeah," agreed Mennynad, "but remember his concept of *safe* doesn't necessarily mean *pleasant*."

"This is also true," Koryss confirmed dryly. "See you shortly."

The comms clicked out and the pair made their way back out of the caves to their bikes, relieved that they didn't have to be the ones to kill the intruders, with their faith so shaky.

Aibek Moon, Orn System, Temple Caves

Giles scribbled away on his holoscreen and then turned the holo upwards to get a shot of the next piece of the etchings from the low part of the ceiling in the cavern. Now that they had light it was apparent that there was a low ceiling in the far side of the room as you came in from the passage, but there was a sweeping chimney feature that ran high up, probably to some point above ground level.

The presence of atmosphere and light was still troubling him, but despite that, there were more pressing matters to attend to. He checked the image he had just taken and then uploaded to his holo.

Arlene wandered over. "Anything I can help with?"

Giles shook his head. "Not yet, I'm afraid. I just need to get this onto the holo, and trying to figure it out as I go."

Arlene shrugged. "Well, I can always start at the other end and have Scamp assemble the images when he receives them."

Giles brought his eyes back down to normal eye level. "Ah, yes. Good thinking!"

Arlene laughed through her nose. "Right then," she said, wandering over to the middle of the cavern in order to start on the other side of the rock carvings.

"You know, come to think of it, it might be worth Scamp doing some of the leg work on the analysis too," Giles muttered as he worked. "Some of this can be deciphered by straightforward pictorial decryption methods, I'm sure. I've already spotted some recurring images."

"I'm glad you've recognized that," Arlene said brightly from the middle of the room.

Giles detected something in her voice. He looked over at her again. "What does that mean?"

Arlene turned back to him, pulling her attention from the ceiling. "Nothing," she said casually, turning away again.

She paused. "It's just that's your thing. That you need to do it all yourself."

Giles frowned. "No it's not."

Arlene smiled. "Okay."

Giles fixed his gaze on her, his task forgotten. "No… no, come on. What are you getting at?"

Arlene's smile faded. "It's okay. I'm not getting at you… it's just you've been kinda sacrificy recently."

"Recently?"

"Yeah. Since we reconnected this last time."

"Oh. *That* recently." Giles scratched at the back of his head with a single finger, then closed his holo.

"Yeah," she said, now giving him her full attention. "First it was the whole surrendering yourself to Shaa - which was the dumbest thing ever. Then there was the 'I'll keep them distracted' suggestion for dealing with a few guards just now."

Giles's brow furrowed, but he kept listening. Arlene was what the ArchAngel's therapists would call "safe space" - *whatever that meant*, he thought, momentarily distracted.

"And then," Arlene continued, "just a little while ago with the air." She shook her head, her eyes filled with a sadness. "You've got to stop trying to sacrifice yourself. There are people who need you." She warmed her hands on the fireball and then decided to sit down next to it, careful to keep Giles in her line of sight.

Giles struggled to absorb what she was trying to explain to him. He took a breath. "In my defense, you and I both know that we wouldn't be here without the intel I gathered on the Shaa mission."

Arlene's eyes flickered with pain and frustration. "Yes, but you endangered the Federation, too," she said, trying to keep her frustration out of her voice.

Giles shook his head. "Reynolds would never have negotiated for me. He's smarter than that," he said decisively.

Arlene's frustration deflated, leaving her eyes soft. "No, Giles," she told him patiently. "He thinks of you as his son and he would have done anything to save you. And besides, that wasn't that I was talking about. It was what you ended up telling them that could have meant the deaths of thousands."

Giles lowered his head. "I know. And I still feel awful about it." Arlene could see his complexion grow visibly older, even by the fire light. "But…" he continued slowly, "I knew you were listening and would take corrective action on the security end."

His eyes remained guilt-ridden.

Arlene shook her head. "That's not the point," she persisted. "My point is, you seem to be wanting to sacrifice yourself. To put yourself into near-death situations. And I know this isn't just thrill seeking anymore. You're too old for that."

"Am I?"

"Yes. You are," she confirmed wisely. "So what is it?"

Giles was quiet for a long moment.

He put his hands onto the back of his head and wandered away, breathing deeply as if trying to get a handle on his feelings.

Arlene's voice was softer when she spoke again. "It's okay. Come on, we've known each other for forever. You can trust me." She paused. "What is it? Why do you have a death wish?"

Giles's hands dropped from the back of his head. His back was still towards Arlene. "I think…" he said, his voice quivering.

He took another breath and Arlene noticed he made a fist with one hand. He turned around. "I think it's because I feel so guilty for all the selfish, stupid shit I've done over the years, I want to do something… heroic, I guess. To make up for it. I want for it all to mean something. I want to surrender something so I don't have to feel so crap about who I've been."

He dropped his eyes to the floor and covered his face with his hands.

Arlene stayed where she was. Coddling him wasn't the way to pull him through this. "So, you think if you make the ultimate sacrifice, you'll feel better?" she clarified.

Giles nodded from behind his hand. He wiped his face and looked up over at her. She could see his face glistening with tear tracks he hadn't managed to get rid of.

She sighed sympathetically. "And so you think you'll feel better when you're dead?" she pressed, testing his logic.

He chuckled grimly. "Yes! I mean, no. I mean… yeah I know I won't be around to… but, then it would mean that I'd done something good."

Arlene used her wise voice that she had used with all her spiritual students at one time of another over the years. "It seems to me that while your intentions may be seen as noble on the surface, there are other, more effective ways to be heroic… which aren't just a one-shot get-out."

She paused a moment, letting him process what she had just said. Eventually she spoke again. "To become worthwhile, you sometimes have to take the long way 'round. The hard route. The one where you survive and keep working on being a worthwhile human being. Not in a single act, but day after day after day."

Her words hung in the air.

Giles bobbed his head, now staring into the fire. The fire balls crackled and spat, their flames dancing while tethered to some mystical fuel.

Arlene shifted her legs, straightening one out and rubbing it to improve the circulation. "I take your silence as an admission that I'm right," she concluded.

Giles nodded, peeling his eyes from the fire, the pupils readjusting as he tried to make out Arlene in the half-light. "Yes," he agreed. "You're right."

Arlene smiled. "Unfortunately, this is the harder route. But on the plus side, you get to stay alive. And, you get to do more good for those you care about than if you're gone."

"Right," he agreed, taking a deep breath as if waking from a trance. "Yes, I see your point. Thank you, Arlene. Really. Thank you."

They held each other's gaze for several moments, streams of understanding and history passing between them. Giles teared up again. Only then did Arlene get up to give him a hug.

After a few moments she pulled back. "Right," she said, closing the conversation off, "these hieroglyphics aren't going to decipher themselves. Let's get these images taken and uploaded to Scamp."

Giles collected himself, and took off his glasses, cleaning them as part of his mental-gathering process. "Right," he agreed. "Although, if they were hieroglyphics, I wouldn't need Scamp to translate them."

Arlene shook her head. "Good, so you're feeling more like your cocky old self now then," she smiled as she headed back over to where she had started working, and pulled up her holo.

Giles grinned. "Less of the *old*, you!" he retorted. Arlene had turned her back.

"Hang on," Giles said. "Before we... er, go back to work... There's something I should tell you."

Arlene turned around, closing her holo again, now a hint of a frown on her forehead. "What?"

"Look," Giles started, "I know you think that after I left I just disappeared and never thought about us again..."

Arlene's frown dissipated. "Yeah..."

"Well, that wasn't entirely true," he confessed. "I checked in on you now and again. Just to make sure you were okay. In fact, ADAM would send me reports every so often, just so I knew I didn't have to worry."

Arlene frowned again. "Okay. But... why?"

Giles shrugged. "Because I care. Because even though we sucked as a couple, you've always been my best friend. And... I dunno. I just wanted you to be okay. To be happy." His expression changed from open honesty to his normal dry expression. "Of course," he added, "when you ended up on the arse-end of Gaitune, I had to question whether you ever had any intention of being happy yourself, but..."

Arlene chuckled. "Honestly... you know, we were having a moment there."

Giles laughed too. "Yeah, I know. I just... I don't do heavy." His expression dropped to serious again. "I just wanted you to know, I didn't forget you. And I *do* care."

Arlene smiled. "Well, thank you for telling me that," she said gently. "And I know I give you a hard time, and... this does not mean that I want you back in any kind of romantic way... but I really do care about you too. And that's why no more of the suicide tactics. I couldn't stand it if I lost you."

Giles smiled. "Yeah, I know," he said, ruffling his hair casually. "I have that effect on women," he said plainly.

Arlene laughed. "My Ancestors! If I had something to throw at you…"

Giles widened his eyes comically. "No. Don't say that. What with the fireball thing working again!"

She smiled. "Right, let's get this done," she told him, pulling up her holo again and got to work.

CHAPTER 13

Aboard the Flutningsaðili, Level 4, Restricted Access Area

The lights started to click on in the outside room. Their captors were returning. Anne picked herself up from the corner she had slumped in, accidentally catching a chair leg and making it scrape.

It brought the other two out of their hushed conversation.

"Someone's coming" Lana whispered, getting up from her chair. Brahms did the same, standing to face their kidnappers.

The wash of yellow lights flicked on in sequence as the footsteps approached. Anne held her breath noticing the sudden tension in the others too.

She could hear voices. One of them was female. Maybe this wasn't the people who had put them in there, she thought to herself.

A moment later a couple rounded the corner. They were human. And they weren't carrying any weapons.

The human female was fairly young, but not as young as Anne. The man was big and old, but looked like he was some kind of elite military guy. Anne hadn't seen muscles like that on a human before. She shuffled back a few paces to try and make sure that she wasn't going to be roped into any kind of difficult conversation. She'd survived this long by keeping a low profile and listening more than talking.

The human woman approached the glass, almost as if she knew who the other two were. "That must be them," she said quietly to the muscle-man. The man jogged up after her.

Lana moved forward and looked like she was about to touch the glass. Then she pointed down at the access panel as if asking them to let them out.

The human female started punching in a code, but then the man stopped her.

"Wait!" he told her.

The woman looked at him, stunned.

Lana did the same, glaring at him and then at the woman. She banged on the glass and then pointed at the door panel again.

The man pulled the woman away and started talking to her in a hushed whisper. Anne couldn't make out what they were saying, but it was like they were having a difference of opinions.

After some discussion they returned to the door. The Estarian female called through the doorway to Lana. "Hey can you hear me?"

Lana nodded.

"We can't get you out," she called through the door. She sounded genuinely concerned as she glanced back over her shoulder. "It's not safe. For any of us. Are you hurt? Are any of you hurt?"

Lana shook her head.

"Okay, we know you're here. We've been looking for you," she explained. "Help is on the way. We know you're Lana and that is Ainstel," she said, glancing at Dr. Brahms. "Who is the girl with you?"

Anne's heart leapt into her mouth, suddenly a part of a drama she had been happy to stand and observe, like a fly on the wall.

Lana glanced over at her briefly.

"Her name is Anne," Lana said, trying to be heard through the glass.

"Anne," the human repeated. "Who is she? Why is she with you?"

Lana shrugged. "She won't talk to us. She says she'll put us in more danger if she tells us."

The human nodded. "We can't deal with this now," she muttered to her partner. "We need to get out of here and get Molly to extract us all."

They exchanged a few more words, and then the pair left with promises to return and that everything was going to be all right.

She had heard similar promises before in her short lifetime. She knew by now not to pin any hopes on them. But it did sound like these people had backup on the way. Maybe they would all get lucky and be rescued from this place.

But then into what? Anne understood nothing of these people, and for all she knew they were just trying to kidnap them for their own purposes. Although they didn't seem to have a use for her. Particularly if they didn't know why she was there.

And if she could keep it that way, then so much the better. As long as she kept her abilities to herself then she might be safe.

Maybe.

But then that meant acting normal. Even if she could quiet her mind long enough to get her powers to work.

Anne listened as the footsteps disappeared again, the lights off after they had gone. Lana and Brahms had started talking again, weighing their theories and speculations.

Anne slumped back down against the wall to contemplate what she had just heard. She glanced back up to the vent. If only she had a tool.

Aboard the *Scamp Princess*

The Justicar sat in Giles's pilot console chair for the first time since they had deposited the two adventurers onto the surface.

"Let's zoom in a bit more," he suggested to Scamp.

Scamp punched in on what they had been monitoring: the terraformed encampment a few kilometers away. Beno'or scratched at his boney-frill around his face. "You know, I think there are two distinct groups with these people," he said, finally sharing his theory.

"How do you mean," Scamp asked, his simulated face simulating a questioning look on the console holo.

Beno'or glanced over at him. "Well, one of them, this one," he said, poking his finger into the holo, "seems to be in charge. Everything goes through him. The other life signs keep coming back to him and then going off and doing other stuff."

Scamp tilted his head slightly to one side. "Okay..." he said, waiting for the rest of the explanation.

"Well," Beno'or continued, "When the freeze hit, it was also like this one had been ostracized. He went off into another area of their collection of huts. He's remained separate almost the whole time. And he hasn't been reporting in."

Scamp's visual representation frowned. "But he has had interactions with some of the others," he said, flicking back through the history of the feed.

Beno'or sat back in his chair, and rocked himself. "Yes. I noticed that. But nothing with the big guy." He put his hands behind his head, thinking. "I think we have someone who is probably quite disgruntled. Either he's isolating himself, or the boss has sent him off, and the others are interacting with him under the radar, as it were."

Scamp nodded. "Seems plausible. But so what?"

Beno'or shrugged. "I dunno. I mean, if we could talk with him he might be of some help. I don't know. I'm just inferring this from the apparent dynamics."

"Which appears to be a valid analysis," Scamp admitted.

Beno'or grinned to himself. "So you agree it might be accurate?"

Scamp shook his virtual head. "No, I said the concept was valid. Not that your statements were accurate. Although..." Scamp's face flickered for a moment as he ran a new analysis, "I think that there may be merit to your theory, now that I've analyzed the data with that in mind. Good job," he added.

Beno'or peered into the holoscreen where Scamp appeared to him. "So you think it's a good idea, but you didn't think of it yourself?"

Scamp nodded. "Exactly. Now I have data points to test your hypothesis."

Beno'or leaned forward in curiosity. "So you didn't think to come up with your own hypotheses to test?" he asked, studying Scamp's reaction closely.

Scamp hesitated. "Hang on. I've finished processing those images for Arlene. Let me send her the results and the translation, and then we can continue."

Beno'or nodded amicably, still fascinated by the world he had found himself in since taking this spontaneous sabbatical from the Empire.

A few moments later, Scamp's image seemed to animate again. "So your question," Scamp said, returning to the conversation. "Do I come up with my own hypotheses?" he restated.

Beno'or leaned forward on the console. "Yes," he said, confirming that was the question he wanted him to answer next.

Scamp shook his head. "It's not something I can do spontaneously. There are an infinite number of theories and possibilities, and to run simulations for each of them is very costly in terms of processing time. There are some hypotheses I've learned to formulate based on certain parameters, normally for objectives we need to achieve. But beyond that I leave those kind of creative punts to the organics."

Beno'or kept his gaze on Scamp. "That is *fascinating*," he

said emphatically. "And tell me, how do you know when to pick up a hypothesis that an organic is talking about?"

The pair found themselves deep in conversation again, this time about the inner workings of Scamp's processing structures. Anyone who couldn't hear what they were talking about would assume they were a pair of old friends having an animated discussion about their favorite team.

Little would they know…

Cavern, Aibek Moon

"Hey," Arlene called over to Giles, her eyes scanning a new message on her holo. "Looks like Scamp has managed a translation."

Giles scrambled up from the other side of the cavern, where he had wedged himself between a warming fireball and a wall he could prop himself up against. "What does it say?" he asked, coming over to sit next to Arlene and look over her shoulder at the screen.

"Looks like the most natural translation was into ancient Estarian," she explained, reading Scamp's analysis.

Giles peered at the screen. "I'm not fluent," he said sarcastically.

Arlene smiled at him over her shoulder. "Good job one of us is," she winked. "And I'm thinking it's actually a spell."

He frowned, taking a closer look at the words. "A spell? For what?"

Arlene shuffled into a more upright position against the wall she was leaning against. "A revealing spell by the looks of it." Her eyes darted back and forth over the translation.

Giles pulled his lips to one side of his face, almost as if

he were in pain trying to understand. "To reveal what though?"

Arlene shook her head as she read. "I've no idea. This looks like a mix of Estarian logic with what I can only imagine is Zhyn logic, as if magic had been discovered or built up from first principles without any outside influences."

Giles's mind churned. "What do you mean?"

Arlene lifted her gaze from the holo and spoke to Giles, who shuffled back a bit so they could look at each other. "Well," she said, "with thousands of years of trial and error."

Giles frowned. "You mean to say that some culture over in this little corner of the galaxy has come to understand magic separately from how, say, the Estarians or the humans learned to use it?"

Arlene dropped her eyes back to the text. "Looks like it."

Giles unconsciously scratched at his sideburns while looking up at the original text on the ceiling. "Wow. That's…. Fascinating. Absolutely fascinating," he mused.

He looked mesmerized, lost in thought at the markings. "So… you think you can perform the spell?"

Arlene tensed her shoulders and lifted them, with her hands open in a gesture of complete loss. "I don't know. I've never tried this particular brand of magic," she explained. "I'll certainly give it a go, though."

"Hang on," he said, holding a hand up, "You said it was a revealing spell. It's not going to reveal another dimension and suck us into hell, is it?"

Arlene's eyes flashed with fear, just a moment before

her logical, grown-up brain kicked in. "Nah. What would be the point in that?"

Giles shrugged. "To ward off and punish tomb raiders?"

Arlene wrinkled her nose. "How many tomb raiders do you think could tap into the land energy and perform this kind of magic?"

Giles thought for a moment. "Well, probably not your average looter."

Arlene nodded. "So, if anything, it's a test. For someone who they wanted to find it. If we get it right, we pass to the next level… whatever that might be."

Giles still looked concerned, but he nodded. "Well, okay. If you think it's the right thing to do."

Arlene laughed suddenly. "You're asking the wrong lady. When have I ever been able to resist new magic?"

Giles buried his head in his hands, this time deliberately being dramatic. "Oh hell. Please don't say we've unleashed 'Arlene the Destroyer' again."

She laughed out loud. "No. Of course not. But you know, the niggle never really does go away. Ever."

Giles was still play acting a little, but a seriousness had returned to his eyes. "I'm not going to regret this, am I?"

Arlene shook her head, making the holoscreen bigger, and preparing herself. "No… it'll be fine." She coughed, playfully. "Really!" she insisted, eyebrows raised. "I've got this."

Giles rolled his eyes and stood back. "Famous last frikkin' words," he mumbled.

Arlene shot him a look, but then seeing his attention was back on the ceiling, quickly returned her own thoughts to the holo screen.

Her eyes scanned back and forth trying to piece together the bits she needed to remember. Giles knew from the coaching she had given him way back when they were partners in crime that the most essential components in a spell from any culture were concentration, intentionality and the ability to channel the sensations through one's whole being.

That included *feeling*.

And also being able to modulate between the different feelings and vibrations with enough intensity for the spell to take.

It was no mean feat, but one which he had been proud to master at a somewhat rudimentary level.

Arlene's eyes stopped scanning the document and flitted more slowly now. She had begun.

Giles watched as the concentration built on her face. He could sense the vibrations in the room changing. He could feel her pulling energy from the ground, from this strange energetic rock they had landed on. He watched carefully, with both a vested interest and an academic fascination.

Moments later, as the atmosphere in the cavern seemed to thicken emotionally, he saw flashes of energy jumping below the threshold of what was visible with his physical eyes, but something that was still able to stimulate his optic nerve and register the movement in his brain.

He watched as the agitation of the vibrations intensified around Arlene, and the energy she had been drawing burst through the palms of her hands again. She seemed so intent on her focus that he, the room, the place where they were trapped, were of no importance to her any longer.

The energy shot out of her hands and bounced against the cavern wall. He found himself wondering if there was a particular direction she should be pointing it... but then, he was just a novice. She was the master. She had experienced power he couldn't even imagine. She knew her way around grimoires of all the human cultures and the shamanic rituals of even the most far-flung Estarian and Yollin traditions.

If anyone could make this work, it was her.

He watched as the energy from her hands became visible light. Realizing that he had been holding his breath, he forced himself to breathe as the light cracked like lightning against the wall.

"Are you sure it's meant to do that?" he shouted over to her, the sound of the energy almost creating a storm-like wind in the enclosed space now.

Arlene's eyes opened and she looked like herself. Giles relaxed a fraction, but she still didn't answer. He could see her lips were moving, in some kind of chant, or incantation. The energy built even higher.

The light by this time was too bright to look at. He turned his head away and shielded his eyes with his hand. And a moment later there was a final, louder crack, and then nothing. He turned. Light spots seared on his retinas.

"You okay?" he called over to her, hurrying blindly to her.

From between the glare in his eyes he could see she was still alive and standing, though her blue skin had dulled to a gray. "Woah," he said grabbing hold of her as her legs failed beneath her. "Let's sit you down."

He helped her gently to the ground where she was able to sit up for a moment.

"I think it worked," she told him gently, her eyes fixed on where she had been focusing the energy.

Giles spun round to look behind him, following her gaze. Right there in front of them, revealed in the cavern wall where there had only been rock, was a door.

Not just a hole in the rock.

A door. Made of wood. Carved. Varnished. And hung on hinges.

Giles whistled through his teeth. "Unbe-fucking-lievable," he whispered to himself.

Arlene nodded, her eyes heavy. She lay back on the ground. "I just... need to rest for a little while," she said.

Giles looked back at the door. "What if it disappears again?" he asked.

Arlene barely stirred. "It won't. It was a revealing spell. Not a portal creator."

Giles chuckled to himself at the bizarreness of the conversation. And of what he had just witnessed. "Well, in that case..." he started saying playfully.

But Arlene had already fallen asleep. For a moment he was worried she had overdone it with the magic and harmed herself, but he checked her breathing and heart rate and his holo scanner said she was just sleeping, so he decided to let her rest.

He tucked his pair of gloves under her head to make her more comfortable, and then set about making preparations for when she was ready to continue their journey.

Arlene awoke a couple of hours later, looking a little groggy and exhausted.

"Here," Giles said, handing her a couple of small discs wrapped in plastic. "A few nutrient boosts will help," he told her.

Arlene took them. "Thanks," she said, sitting up, trying to muster some energy. She opened the discs and put them on her tongue, one by one.

Within a few minutes she was able to get up again and walk around.

"Looks like the fires are holding," she commented. "How long was I asleep?"

"Couple of hours," Giles told her. "We're mid-storm right now, so probably best we stay put for another few hours anyway."

Arlene nodded. "I wonder if perhaps it's worth going back to sleep," she said, stretching out, and then sitting back down next to the fire she had just got up from.

Giles was pacing around. "Yeah. That's probably a good idea," he agreed, stretching his back, and then settling on the other side of the fire. "I'll set an alarm for when the freeze is due to thaw and then we can get going through our newly revealed door," he added, nodding at the door and making an expression of being genuinely impressed.

Arlene smiled, sleepily. "Yeah. Who knew I still had it, eh?"

Giles lay down. "Who knew…"

Gaitune-67, Safe House

"You fucking what?" Sean Royale piped up, interrupting his story.

Giles blinked at him. "Huh?"

Sean reached for another beer bottle and took the lid

off in the crease of his arm. "You mean you opened this magical fucking door and you didn't go through it? Not even to have a peek?"

Brock had started sniggering. Pieter joined in as Giles scrambled to answer the question, his flow completely obliterated by the interruption.

"Well... er..." Giles stumbled. "There was the freeze going on outside, and..."

Sean took a swig of his beer. "You mean you were too pussy to go out there without Arlene to look after your nanocyte-enhanced ass?"

Arlene mercifully decided to rescue him. "Actually," she said firmly, staring the slightly tipsy cyborg down from across the common area, "if he had gone through without me there is no telling where he could have ended up. And then we would have been separated."

Sean immediately looked a little sheepish, and reached for another beer bottle, removed the top, and then handed it to Giles by way of an apology.

Giles accepted it with a nod and placed it carefully on the mocha table while he took a moment to clean his glasses.

Molly was smiling from her seat next to Arlene. "Well, I'm just excited to learn how to pull that energy from the ground on our next lesson!"

Arlene chuckled and looked over at her. "Well, we'd need to find a planet where they have enough land energy for it to register. Estaria would be a good place to practice."

Paige suddenly jumped to her feet. "Okay. Since we're pausing the story, I need to pee. Plus, I can order pizza while I'm up. Anyone?"

There was a chorus of agreement for pizza, and the odd order being called out. Paige clocked each request like an experienced server as she made her way over the obstacle course of legs and furniture to extract herself from the group. She trotted off at double time, her heels clicking on the concrete floor as the others discussed the intricacies of what they had heard, some critiquing, and some of them praising Giles's tactical calls.

Giles, still the center of attention, settled back into his element after the initial interruption, and once Paige had returned he picked up the story again.

CHAPTER 14

Aibek Moon, Orn System, Temple Caverns

Several hours later the alarm went off, rousing Arlene and Giles from their sleep.

"Well, I guess that's our cue," Giles said, rolling onto his side.

Arlene's color had returned to normal and she looked more refreshed and alert.

"You're looking better," he commented.

She nodded. "I feel it," she said flatly.

Clapping her hands quickly and quietly together, remembering what she had done and excited to see the result, she exclaimed, "Now let's go and check out my door!"

Giles grinned, standing up and picking up their helmets and gloves. Within minutes Arlene had extinguished the fires and the pair of them were standing at the door ready to leave.

Giles stood back and allowed her to open the door. "Ladies first, as they say in human culture."

Arlene nodded to him and stepped forward, trying the round knobbed handle on the door. She turned it, and it clicked open.

She pushed it open and stepped through.

Aboard the *Flutningsaðili*, Level 4, Restricted Access Area

Anne had dropped off to sleep while meditating, but was rudely awoken by the sound of the lights coming on throughout the warehouse. Again.

And footsteps. Again.

When she peeled her eyes open she could already see Lana squaring up to the window to take on their kidnappers with her tongue, if nothing else.

"Looks like you'll be having some new company soon," a man's voice called out as he approached. It was the obnoxious one that had checked on them a number of times since the three had been there. Anne guessed he was the boss from the way he had been instructing people and led the security details on various occasions.

Lana's fists were clenched. "You won't get away with this, you asshole! People will know we're missing. You'll be discovered. And I'll be there when they put you to death for kidnapping on Teshov."

The man looked down at his nails and leaned against a desk that had a few chairs piled upside down on it just in front of the covered machinery a few yards away.

"My, my, my…" he tutted. "What little you know about Teshov. Death sentences are only handed out to the general populous to keep them under control and afraid."

He glanced casually up at her. "I wouldn't fall into that

category. I'm far too valuable to the people who actually have the power out there. And on Estaria for that matter," he added smugly.

Lana's eyes flared in fury. "You won't get away with this," she shouted, her voice straining painfully.

Brahms came up behind her and whispered in her ear. She seemed to calm instantly, understanding that her position was futile. The older scientist led her away from the window and sat her down at one of the desks with her back to her taunter.

Just then the far lights started coming on again, guiding the path for still more newcomers. There were scuffed, and uneven steps.

And boots.

Lots of boots.

A few moments later the party appeared from between the stacks of equipment and boxes, brandishing their weapons and their two human prisoners in cuffs. The same pair who had visited them before, with promises that everything was going to be okay.

Anne couldn't help but feel vindicated for her skepticism. She remained silent, watching.

The boss man turned his taunts to the new arrivals. "Well, I suppose this is one way to meet the boss to vent your concerns," he cooed as the two humans looked up at him.

They remained silent.

He continued. "I suppose you're going to deny any knowledge of what's going on here."

The male called over to the human female. "Don't respond. To anything," he told her.

She nodded.

"Rex, is it?" the boss asked, wandering over to him. "Fancy yourself as a hero, do you?"

The man didn't respond. Instead he looked straight ahead.

"Hmm. Do I detect military training in that disciplined defiance?" the boss asked.

The prisoner ignored him.

The boss man kept talking, though Anne couldn't quite make out what he was saying at this point. Between the humming of the ship and life support unit, plus the glass between them, it was tough. And when his back was to her she didn't even have the added information from reading his lips.

Her mind wandered as she realized what this latest occurrence meant. Their best hope of being freed from this prison cell was about to be put in there with them.

Anne started sizing the pair up again. The man was big. So big he might have the strength to open the door. Or maybe even the vent. She made a note to approach him about that. Once she was sure that they weren't a threat.

There was more talking and posturing. Anne studied the exchange with a keen eye. She noticed that the two scientists were watching too, but with more emotional involvement than she had.

Eventually the boss waved for the two new prisoners to be put into the glass room and started to walk away.

The armed guards shoved them forward and into the room.

"Oh, and by the way," the awful man said, turning to them, "we'll be rounding up your friends on board and bringing them to join you too. Just in case you were worried you would miss them."

The male human stood glaring from the other side of the glass, and the female followed him into the room, walking past him and putting her hands behind her head in frustration. She began pacing in a small area as the door was closed and locked behind them.

The man in charge gestured for the security detail to clear the area and then followed them out.

The Estarian female sat down at the table with the other three hostages and introduced herself as Maya, and her partner as Sean.

Sean, the human male, started to pace.

"Why aren't they calling through?" she asked Sean. Her eyes traced his movements, watching him prowl like a trapped tiger.

"Probably a glitch in the tech," he responded. "No idea how this shit works."

Suddenly his facial expression changed. "They're connecting," he said, nodding at Maya.

Maya's face relaxed a little, and the three others looked from her to Sean and back to her again hoping for an inkling of what was going on.

Sean put his hands on his hips and looked off across the room. "Hi, Pieter? Things have taken a turn over here," he started explaining. "Maya and I have been rumbled. They don't know how much we know, but they've put us in with the scientists and they're going to eject us into space at their next scheduled trash dump."

The scientists exchanged worried glances. Anne felt herself react too. This was the first she was hearing about being ejected into space. Something must have changed between taking them for whatever purpose and then deciding to get rid of them.

Unless it was just the two humans they were going to get rid of? she wondered.

Sean continued to look off across the tiny glass room. "Yeah mate, I was hoping for something a little more useful than that."

"No," Sean kept talking, responding to a voice on the other end of his communications line, "we're okay at the moment."

There was a pause. Anne took a step towards the table, despite her initial wariness of them.

Sean glanced at Maya, who was starting to look scared. "We're ready for an extraction," he said calmly, as if he were in control of their current situation.

Sean shook his head. "No idea. Could be minutes, could be hours or days."

Sean exhaled. "Okay. Cool."

There was another long pause as if arrangements were being made at the other end. Sean eventually nodded. "Will do, boss." He glanced over at Maya as he spoke. "See you shortly. Keep us posted about ETAs, eh?"

The line disconnected, leaving Sean staring now into space, looking a little more nervous than he had been just seconds before when the connection was live.

He turned to Maya again. "They're on their way. But we need to figure out if there is a way out of here, just in case."

He wandered over to the table where the others were sitting quietly, bewildered by the unconventional rescue party. "How about you tell us everything you know so we can work on a plan to keep us all alive until our friends get here?" he suggested, looking into the fearful faces.

Aibek Moon, Orn System, Temple Caverns

The revealed door led into another similar passageway, except this one quickly turned into a spiral staircase.

"This must have taken some construction," Giles remarked as Arlene led the way, producing a magical glowing ball to light their way as if it were nothing.

Giles shook his head. "Are you sure you're going to be able to leave this place and its land energy when we finally get out?"

Arlene kept walking down the steps, unperturbed. "You mean in favor of creature comforts?" she chuckled. "Hell yeah." She suddenly stopped and turned back to him. "Really, you don't need to worry about me anymore, at least not when it comes to the power thing. I'm over it."

Her eyes were sincere. But in the back of Giles's mind, it wasn't that he didn't believe her. It was that she might be sincerely *wrong*.

"Okay," he conceded. "If you're sure. But you know, you can always talk to me about it. Anytime."

Arlene smiled, and started walking again. "Thanks, G-man."

Giles rolled his eyes and followed after her.

It seemed like they had been walking down steps for hours. It was disorientating: round and round. Down and down.

Arlene's knee muscles were starting to ache. And just before she was about to stop for another break the stairs came to an end and opened out into a small passage with an open doorway carved into the rock.

"I think we're here," she whispered, slowing her pace and creeping forward quietly in case their intrusion became known to anyone.

Giles didn't say a word. He just watched as she evaporated the glow ball she'd been carrying and stepped out into the soft light of the next chamber.

Giles followed her through, seeing her reaction from behind before seeing what she was noticing.

At first she slowed, and looked up. Giles stepped through behind her, noticing the big open space, and then looked up to see that this cavern had a ceiling indeed, but it was at least a dozen stories high.

He involuntarily let out a small gasp.

Arlene turned and looked at him. "What *is* this place?" she asked.

Giles glanced around the chamber, taking in everything he could: an altar, various pillars around, markings on walls in places. "I think this is some kind of sacred offering place," he told her. "And probably where we'll find our talisman. Although, it has a feel of a burial ground and yet, it seems too revered for that. Maybe the burial ground of a god or monarch or some-such?"

He scratched at his head trying to understand the belief system behind the construction. Most cultures he'd studied honored their dead using tombs and temples that later became sacred because the civilization's ancestors were buried there. And yet, this... was simply something he couldn't put his finger on.

"Let's find the talisman and get out of here," he decided,

putting his intellectual curiosity aside.

Arlene nodded and started walking around, inspecting the area. "I'll let Scamp know we're likely to need picking up too. Hopefully he can locate us using our holos."

Giles was already distracted again by some writing on a stone tablet on the wall. He recognized it as being consistent with the writing that had given them the spell for the door reveal. Spontaneously he started documenting what he could with his holo. "Yes, good idea," he called over to her absently.

He was vaguely aware of her talking with Scamp, but was more intent on pulling what intel he could before finding the talisman.

Arlene finished the call and called over to him. "He's on his way. Says the temperature is improving out there, too."

"Any signs from our hosts?" he asked grimly.

"None yet," she replied, "but he'll keep an eye out for them coming from their base again."

"Great," Giles acknowledged. He finished documenting the text and then spun round looking for clues.

There was silence in the hall while he stood taking it all in and trying to figure out the next piece.

Eventually he broke the silence and spoke, his voice once again echoing through the chamber. "Remember the Moons of Orn nursery rhyme that led us here?" he called over to Arlene.

She nodded. "Vaguely," she admitted. "I can try and pull it up." She flicked another screen open on her holo and started punching in search terms.

Giles's eyes scanned the overall structure of everything in this huge vaulted cavern.

"Here it is," Arlene called triumphantly. Wandering over to his position and reading it out loud:

Eleven moons, a sight to reap,
When all align, no time for sleep
A shaft of light, where the ions flow
Onto the shroud, the glow does go.
When one beholds the moons of orn,
Be sure to look up at the horn.
The crescent marks the spot to be
When the time strikes keen and on the mark
And when you read the map of gold
In your hands you'll graciously hold
The elixir of life
The holy grail
The reason we're on
The rising trail.

Giles rubbed his chin. "It's that first verse. No time for sleep… so that's something to do with the dead, I'm sure."

Arlene nodded. "Right. So where is the burial site then?" She looked around, turning on the spot as if trying to orientate herself with a map.

Giles shook his head. "I can't figure it out." He paused. "But then there is the shaft of light where ions flow. And then reference to the shroud. I think we've got to find where there is a casket or something, and it needs to be outside, or at least have access to the light like our little cavern did back there, so their ion stream can get in."

Arlene's furrowed brow was getting more pronounced by the second. "But that assumes that we're here at the time of whatever alignment this is."

Giles was deep in concentration. "We need a simulation of that rosette thingy that Scamp was on about. Can you message him and get him to render something for us?"

Arlene was already tapping a message to Scamp. "Sure."

"Those ions have to be coming from somewhere," he told her confidently. "But my bet is that it only happens very rarely. The chance that we're here at the right time is pretty slim."

Arlene looked up from her holo. "Okay. He's working on it. Shouldn't be long."

Giles grunted and ventured deeper into the hall. "This place is really an engineering feat," he mused. "To think that someone could build all this, on a planet with no atmosphere, and yet have it protected from the cosmic erosion." He shook his head in disbelief and wandered over to the altar in the middle of the room.

"What is it?" Arlene asked, noticing his attention had been pulled.

"I think this is the burial piece."

"The altar?" she checked. "That would be… odd."

Giles nodded. "Unless it's not an altar," he mused. He examined the whole piece, running his finger over patterns and inscriptions and images.

"You know," he said, pulling at a ledge carved into the wooden construction. "I think this is just a shell."

He pulled again, and it moved. "Hey, give me a hand with this, will you?" he called to Arlene.

Arlene was by his side in an instant and helping him to lift what was turning out to be a cover.

They hauled the slab of wood off askew and peered into the alter-sized box.

Below there was a force-field.

Inside the force field, there was the talisman.

Arlene went to reach for it, but Giles grabbed her hand. "Wait!" he said anxiously. He looked around the ceilings around them. "If we didn't have the poem, that's what we'd be… like tomb raiders."

Arlene pulled her arm back. "Yeah, I was expecting the force field might also kick me back," she explained. "But I wanted to try."

Giles nodded. "Yeah, but if that force field is disturbed there's no telling what it might set off."

"You're thinking boobie traps?" she asked, her eyes wide with excitement more than fear.

"Yeah," Giles confirmed, his eyes giving away how excited he was too. "Of a scale we can't imagine right now." His eyes started scanning the ceiling to confirm his idea.

The pair backed away from the altar.

Just then Arlene's holo beeped. She glanced down. "It's Scamp with the model."

Giles turned to her, and stepped down away from the altar. "Great. Let's have a look."

Arlene hit the button and pulled up a three-dimensional rendering of the systems they were in, the eleven moons all held in a perfect complex orbit around each other.

"He's marked on where they are now, and given us a run time to watch the system evolve." She hit 'RUN' and the moons danced around in a complicated formation.

Giles watched, his eyes darting from following one track to another. When it had finished, he asked for her to repeat the simulation again.

Then again.

And again.

After several replays, he had a thought. "What was it Scamp said about our moon moving out of reach of the nearest star, so being shielded from the radiation, hence the big freeze?"

Arlene's eyes lit up. "That needs to go into the model!" she exclaimed excitedly. Immediately she messaged Scamp back. "Okay," she confirmed after a moment, "he's working on it."

Minutes later they had a second model, this time including the radiation from the distant stars that could possibly affect the array.

"There!" Giles pointed excitedly, spotting the moment when the moon emerged out of the shadows of three of the other larger ones.

"What happened?" Arlene asked, running the program back again to replay it. She played it again, and then she saw it.

Giles bobbed his head, pleased as punch. "Something to do with the way the radiation hits the moon again, and spikes through the force field. It acts like an artificial atmosphere that then channels that sudden flash of radiation through this area on the surface here," he said pointing. "My guess is that we're slap bang on this line of radiation when that happens when the moon comes into alignment with the star."

Arlene looked up at him. "And this temporarily disables the force field?"

Giles nodded.

Arlene frowned looking at the model again. "But,

doesn't this mean we've already missed it? That leading edge of radiation?"

Giles put one hand on his hip, still looking at the paused simulation. "Yeah, it does," he agreed. He ruffled his hair in frustration. "It would have happened when we were sleeping in the cavern, waiting for the freeze to break."

Arlene's eyes widened. "Like the poem said, no time for sleep. Maybe they weren't referring to a burial place?"

Giles eyes flicked up as he considered the option. Then he began nodding slowly. "Yep. Yep. You could be right."

Arlene's eyes drooped a little as she went back to the simulation. "So then? What are we going to do?"

Giles sighed. "Well, unless there is another point at which we get that ion blast, I wonder if we can get Scamp to simulate it."

He went back to inspecting the cavern ceiling. "The ions must have an entry point somewhere…"

"Hey," he spun round, thinking of something new. "See if you can have Scamp locate us and then scan the area, taking into account the angle those ions would have been coming in from. That would narrow it down. And then he just has to overload this force field down here in the same way he did when we were outside the planet."

Arlene looked skeptical. "Seriously? You think that'll work?"

Giles shrugged, pushing his bottom lip out. "You wanna spend another god knows how long here in this chamber, waiting for that freeze to cycle round again?"

Arlene grinned. "I'll get right on it," she said quickly.

Giles smiled, hoping his idea was plausible and not just some fantastical wish of a rogue archaeologist.

CHAPTER 15

Aboard the Flutningsaðili, Level 4, Restricted Access Area

Dr. Brahms looked up at the vent as Sean stood on the desk fiddling with the screws. "Are you sure that we're all going to fit through there?"

Sean glanced down at the rather bulky old man and then back up at the vent. "Should do," he gruffed. "Though, whether the vent will hold our weights is another matter."

He glanced over at Anne, Maya, and Lara. "The girls will probably be okay. We should let them go first, just in case we break it, cutting them off."

He passed his key card to Anne. Anne studied it, carefully avoiding eye contact. "Here, you take this," he told her gently. "We'll send you through first. We've got a friend who is getting into the computer system on this ship as we speak. Once he has access he'll be able to let you through any door with that card. We've got another friend, Brock, who is going to get us a ship on level...?"

He looked out across the room, now talking on his

audio connection with his friends, who seemed to be coming to do the rescuing. "Pieter, what level was it again?"

Sean's eyes were on Anne and Lara. "Level 1. Top of the ship. You get to there, find him on the hangar deck, and he'll get you to safety. If we can follow, we will," he added, glancing over at Dr. Brahms.

Anne closed her hand around the card and nodded. Without saying a word she slipped it into her pants pocket.

Sean went back to the vent and finished taking out the last screw. The vent cover hung down, leaving the mouth open.

Anne heard footsteps. She noticed that Sean's head turned just a fraction of a second before she registered the sound. For a second she wondered if he was like her.

He jumped off the table and moved it away from where it was obvious what he had been doing. The lights started coming on through the crowded warehousing area.

Sean looked over at Anne and Lara. "Okay, remember what we talked about. Girls, as soon as you get the chance, we're putting you in there. Maya," he added, "if you go with them, they'll have a better chance."

Maya nodded, then turned her attention to the oncoming footsteps moving closer to the glass door.

There was only one set, though.

Anne stayed back, but she could see it was a woman who was rounding the corner and approaching their meeting-room prison.

Maya was already at the window to greet her. "Hi Griselle, what are you doing here?" she called out brightly.

This was probably one of her teammates, Anne reasoned. The woman was human, and walked with the confidence of someone who was physically very capable. She looked fit and toned, and Anne would bet from the way she walked she would be able to give most fighters a run for their money.

She put that together with the military demeanor of the man, Sean, and deduced they were probably both part of a military team.

The newcomer headed straight for the access panel to the room. "You know the code?" she asked, looking up through the glass at Maya and Sean.

"No, they don't," a bone chilling voice came from behind her. "But I do…"

The new human female spun around to see a figure emerging from the shadows. It was the boss person. The same person who was likely responsible for them being here.

"Time to let them go, Pike," she instructed with authority. "We have a truce. Our people are coming to get us."

Pike must be the name of this boss man, Anne realized.

He shook his head. "They may be on their way, and yes, we did agree on an unsatisfactory truce. And once they are here they too will become subject to our containment methodology." A smirk spread across his smarmy lips.

The fighter woman took a step towards him.

Suddenly a dozen of his security guards stepped out from the shadows of the heavy equipment in the room. They came forward, their weapons weighing heavy in the consciousness of the prisoners.

She frowned. "So you plan to kill us *all*?"

The man smiled as he played with a key card in his hand. "*Kill* is such an archaic and brutal word, don't you think? I'm merely taking the necessary action to secure the interests of my client."

His holo beeped and he glanced down at the screen. "And there they are now. Right on schedule."

He looked back at her. "If you'll excuse me, I need to go and tend to something, but I'll be back shortly."

He waved at a couple of the guards to watch her, and then withdrew, taking another two of his security detail with him.

There was a sudden flurry of activity in the meeting room. Jack spun round, looking in, still unable to get through the door.

"Okay, now," Sean said quietly to Anne.

Sean moved the desk back under the vent and was up on the table, pulling Anne up with him.

The security personnel came forward. "Stop. What are you doing?" she heard them protesting.

But it was too late. Sean had already lifted her up like she was nothing but a rag doll and placed her into the vent. Anne took hold of the sides of the duct and pulled herself over the ledge and inside. Her heart was pounding, and there was clearly a scuffle going on beneath her.

"Go!" Sean shouted out to her. Without thinking or looking back, her survival instincts kicked in and she started moving, the commotion of the room behind her.

She could hear people and furniture being moved around, but not gunfire. She scrambled on as quickly as she possibly could, trying to recall the instructions.

Level 1, at the top, she repeated to herself. She needed to move upward through the floors. And she had no idea how far down she was right now. If she could just get away to the next floor she might be able to poke her head out and get her bearings.

Anne scrambled on, trying to be as quiet as possible, to not draw attention. The vents were filthy and her hands were already black from dust and dirt. Breathing wasn't pleasant either, but at least she could do something now. At least she wasn't trapped. She was free.

And she had someone who was going to help.

Another human, called Brock. On Level 1.

Get to Brock, she told herself. *And maybe it* was *going to be all okay...*

Aboard the *Scamp Princess*

Beno'or sat at the pilot's console, listening intently to the conversation between Arlene and Scamp. He'd worked with AIs of a sort back on Kurilia, but the way Scamp operated, practically thinking for himself, was beyond anything their AIs had evolved into.

No wonder Molly's crew had been so damn effective, he thought to himself, recalling the help she had given in dealing with their rogue military commander, who had tried to start a galactic war.

Arlene's voice lilted over the intercom. "So you think it is possible?"

"Should be," Scamp told her. "It's how we overloaded the initial force field. It's the same technology and it would have to be working at the same frequency in order for the force field to boost the radiation to the right wavelength for it to disable the second shield in your tomb."

Arlene seemed satisfied. "Great. I'll let Giles know and we'll make preparations down here."

Scamp was already running calculations on a screen in front of Beno'or. "Okay. I just need to see if we can stream enough radiation in a narrow enough beam to make it work." Scamp went quiet for a moment. "And then we need to find the entry point," he added.

"Okay," Arlene confirmed. "Well, let us know if we can help with anything. Or if we need to get out of the way."

"Of course," Scamp replied. "I'll be in touch shortly."

The intercom went dead.

Scamp's screens were filled with maps and calculations and feedback data on the weapons system. Beno'or watched, amazed at the capacity for so many simultaneous, self-directed calculations.

"Anything I can help with?" he asked after a few moments.

"Actually, yes," Scamp replied politely. "I may need some organic interaction to correct for the high noise to signal ratio on the scans of the rocky surface so we can pinpoint where this radiation stream needs to be directed."

"Absolutely. Just point me in the right direction," Beno'or said, sitting upright in his antigrav chair, readying himself for business.

"Okay," Scamp replied. "Let me locate them using their holos and then I'll give you an image of the surrounding area to look at for me."

Within moments new holoscreens flashed up in the console space in front of Beno'or.

"Here we go," Scamp told him. "And while you do that, I need to discharge the weapons we'll use. I need to see if I can get this modulation correct and with a small enough beam."

Beno'or had started scanning examining his screens. "What does that mean?" he asked, not fully understanding what Scamp was telling him.

"It means," Scamp explained, appearing on a holoscreen next to his console unit, "that I need to get out over some deserted area to test it. So we'll be in flight for a little while."

Beno'or relaxed. "Okay by me, Scamp! This is quite the machine. I'd be interested to see what you can do."

Scamp smiled on the visual-render of his simulated entity-self. "Right on. Let's do this!" His smile dropped and his expression became serious suddenly. "Though, you might want to buckle up your harness."

Beno'or took the suggestion seriously. He'd learned what that meant. He immediately stopped what he was doing and scrambled to put his harness on and get it buckled up before Scamp powered up the engines and took the ship into flight.

Aboard the Flutningsaðili, Hangar Deck, Level 1

"Since when do we leave people behind?"

Anne could hear a human voice just ahead of her through the vent exit. She wondered if it was the Brock human she had been told to meet with.

There was quiet, then the voice spoke again. "What if I were to just stay, and you guys go on ahead? I've got a vessel. I can catch up."

She guessed the person was having a conversation on a holo connection or something. He huffed in frustration. Anne scooted forwards to see him through the vent. She saw him put his hands up to his face and started pacing. He looked agitated, like he was in a pressured situation.

She felt confident it was probably him. Brock.

And he would be waiting for her.

She pushed forward quietly to get a better look, but her foot slipped and she tilted forwards down the duct, making a clatter.

The human looked up and into the vent. "Anne?" he called, in loud whisper.

Shit, she thought to herself. *Detected. But on the plus side, at least it was probably a friend.*

"Yes?" she responded timidly.

"Pieter, Oz. I've got her," he announced to the unheard team on the other end of his communicator.

Brock craned his neck, trying to see into the vent. "Can you get the grid open?" he asked quietly, the anxiety still evident in his tone.

"I think so," Anne replied. "It hurts my fingers. I've had a few of these to do along the way, else I'd have been here sooner."

Brock stepped back, thinking. "It's okay. I'm right here. We've got a ship waiting. Just as soon as you get it open, you can drop down and I'll catch you."

Anne struggled some more with the grating and soon it dropped down, hanging by its hinges. Her two feet appeared, dangling down as if on a swing in a park.

"Ready?" she asked.

Brock got underneath her. "Yeah, ready. Drop," he instructed her.

She wriggled forward and then dropped. Brock caught her, staggered back a few paces, then found his balance and put her down. "Wow, that went a lot better than I thought it would," he remarked.

Anne giggled to herself. "Thank you," she said shyly. She regarded the human carefully. She wasn't one to trust anyone, but this person was different. He had an easy air about him, and putting aside the fact that she didn't know who he worked for or why he was helping her, she felt there was a kindness in his eyes.

"My pleasure," he responded. "I'm Brock, I'll be your escape buddy today." He held out his hand not to shake, but for her to take. She put her hand in his and allowed him to lead her off through the double doors to the hangar deck.

"Okay, now stay close," he told her quietly. "There are some engineer types around. We just need to act casual and if anyone asks, you're an intern doing some work experience with me, right?" He squeezed her hand reassuringly before letting it go to walk ahead of her at a professional distance to sell his plan.

Anne absorbed the information as fast as she could. She nodded her understanding and then continued to follow him.

They got nearly all the way round to where they needed to be and Brock started leading her off the walkway and onto the deck.

"Hey. You there!" A voice called out across the deck.

Anne felt a pulse of adrenaline shoot through her chest.

They'd been found.

She spun round to see one of the engineers that Brock had warned her about.

"Don't suppose you saw a tool kit on the railings out here, have you?"

Brock looked around where he was pointing. "Uh, no. Not just now, but there was one there earlier," he relayed.

Anne stayed close, bracing herself, ready to run. She glanced furtively around trying to figure out which direction was going to give them the best shot.

The engineer nodded casually though. "Yeah. Just left it there while I took a break and some bugger has nicked it."

Brock frowned. "Some people just need a good beating," he said, matching the guys tone of annoyance. His accent twanged though. Anne could tell it was put on. She watched to see if it roused any suspicion in the engineer.

"Yeah," the engineer agreed, oblivious to the tell. "You're telling me!" He scratched his head and continued looking around.

Brock pushed Anne on in the direction they had been heading and they hurried onto the ship as soon as they were out of sight. Brock went straight to the cockpit and started running the final checks. The tailgate closed and Anne came up to the cockpit to join him.

"Grab a seat," he told her. "And strap in, this may be a bit bumpy."

Anne did as she was told.

Brock hit the bead in his arm. "Okay Oz, an exit would be great right about now."

Anne watched as he communicated with yet another person on this team. She wondered idly how many people they were. They weren't in any kind of uniform, so they weren't military or police enforcers. And this human, Brock, didn't seem at all stiff and disciplined. Anne watched him, puzzled, as he flicked switches and powered up the ship.

Within moments they were up and out and then away through the hangar opening.

Brock grinned. "Okay Oz, we're clear," he announced, glancing down at Anne. "Heading in the direction back towards Estaria to rendezvous with the *Empress*."

He turned to Anne. "Okay. Looks like we're out of harm's way. Everything's going to be okay."

Anne looked back up at him, tears welling in her eyes and emotion swelling in her chest.

For the first time since she could remember, she actually thought that she could believe him. She settled back into the console chair, feeling the tilting motion of the ship as it cradled her through the maneuvers away from the prison. She had no idea where she was, or who she was with now. But she *did* know that now she felt safe.

CHAPTER 16

Force field boundary of the Guard's dome, Aibek Moon, Orn System

Several kilometers away the freeze began to thaw. The six watched from the other side of their terraformed dome. Noses almost pressed up against the atmospheric shield, they observed the strange alien ship rise up out of the dust and rock, straight into the air above them. A second later it whipped out into the empty sky beyond and disappeared into nothing but a speck.

Gagai pulled himself up tall. "This is it," he announced. "We need to get down there and find out how far those intruders have gone."

Jendyg stood a few paces back. "My guess is they'll be stuck in the first chamber, frozen," he muttered, loud enough for Ammo and Mennynad to hear.

Gagai turned and headed back in the direction of the encampment. "We leave straight away. Get to your vehicles," he ordered.

The five Zhyn guardians lingered, each with their own

thoughts about what lay ahead for them with the arrival of the strangers. With the freeze locking them down there was little point in contemplating any interaction with them.

Koryss was the first to move. He turned quickly and jogged to catch up with Gagai. Naldrir followed next.

"Come on," Mennynad said, peeling his eyes from the spot where the ship had disappeared into the distance.

Ammo gruffed and started walking after the others.

"But what if they're the chosen?" Jendyg protested. "We all saw what they did on that bridge."

Ammo stopped in his tracks and turned to him. "The chosen? They weren't even Zhyn! They're intruders. Magicians from other worlds that have come to steal our power and our ancestry! This is exactly what we were warned about. What Gagai keeps telling us." Ammo's tone was determined, but sounded almost as if he were trying to convince himself.

Ammo and Mennynad gestured for Jendyg to start walking, ushering him onward. "But what if it's not true?" Jendyg insisted. "Why hasn't a Zhyn chosen one come forward? And where was it ever written that the chosen ones would be from our own race?" he protested earnestly.

Gagai and Koryss had already mounted their antigrav bikes and passed them, roaring through the dome towards the gateway.

"Come on, we need to hurry," Ammo insisted. "They won't want to open the gate twice."

He cajoled Jendyg on more quickly, willing him to stop talking and just get to his bike.

Naldrir passed them on his bike heading in the opposite

direction. He had his visor down, avoiding any kind of interaction with what he regarded to be the hoi polloi. Ammo felt the contempt as he rode past them. There was no doubt that facing the enemy had driven a wedge between them. Even if there had been a fracture from the beginning, the difference was that all of a sudden, all the points that were moot were now very relevant and real.

The three remaining warriors arrived at the bike shed and quickly strapped on their protective gear and weapons before mounting up. Seconds later they too rolled out of the wooden hut and rode towards the gate.

Gagai and the others were already there, waiting. As the remaining three pulled up, Gagai turned to confirm what he had heard and then hit the command on his wrist comm. The shield lowered, granting them passage out into the rocky desert beyond. No sooner had the last of them passed through when the shield door re-established itself, sealing off their home and keeping their atmosphere contained.

The six of them moved effortlessly and obediently into formation. Gagai led the charge, with Naldrir and Koryss on either side, slightly behind him. They would watch his movements carefully for signaled instructions, reading how he was shifting his weight for clues about direction.

The other three followed in a similar fashion but in a row behind. Jendyg fell in line on the right, slightly behind Ammo, who led the second row by a few bike lengths.

The rocky terrain sped away beneath them, their vehicles unencumbered by the pits and rocks. None of them could guess how long they had before the ship returned.

If it returned.

They all suspected that what Jendyg had said was true though. The two people they had seen were probably already dead, but, there was also the unspoken fear that they hadn't been neutralized, and the magic they displayed had indeed allowed them to venture further, beyond what even they could find in the cave.

Though their comm system would have allowed for some level of conversation, it was as if they each took the opportunity to be with their own thoughts. Thoughts of what lay ahead of them, and how their conscience would guide them to act.

The ground raced away as they headed towards what they knew to be the other exit of the chamber that must be guarded. It was indiscoverable but for those who had made it through the labyrinth alive - which no one ever had.

That exit was the point where they had been trained to wait. Wait for signs of life to appear. And the ship appearing back there to collect the two magicians would be a sure sign that they were still alive.

Jendyg prayed to their moon gods that they were indeed alive, and that they might stay that way long enough to get him off this rock.

Aboard the *Little Empress*

Anne had watched wide-eyed as he deftly flew the ship into the belly of a much larger ship and touched down with barely a bump on the cargo deck floor.

"Okay," Brock said letting go of the controls and glancing down at her in the next console chair. "We're here."

Anne looked out into the cargo deck, trying to make

sense of the dim lights and doors. She had so many questions she didn't know where to start.

"You okay?" Brock asked her. His tone was gentle and almost as if he understood what she was feeling.

She nodded.

He smiled. "Look. I know this can be a bit much, and I don't know what happened to you back there, but this is what I do know. You're safe now. Molly... our boss... she'll protect you. It's what we do. We're all here for you. We're friends."

He looked out at the cargo deck to see people approaching the door ahead of them. "You're going to meet the whole crew in just a few minutes, but you don't need to be worried. They're all good people and we're going to get you checked out in the med bay, okay?"

Anne nodded. She opened her mouth to speak but her voice didn't come out. Brock put his hand on her shoulder and gave her the space to say what she wanted to.

It took her a second but she found her voice, and her words. "Thank you," she told him. She smiled as much as she could, but right then she felt like she could sleep for a week.

Brock got up and helped her unbuckle out of her console chair. She put her feet on the floor and allowed herself to be led out and off the ship.

"Remember," Brock told her as the others approached with a clatter and a chorus of excited voices, "it's all okay now..."

Aibek Moon, Orn System, Temple

"Okay, great. Thanks Scamp. Giles out."

Giles turned to make eye contact with Arlene. "So, it looks like we can't be nearby when it happens and we have no idea how long this overload will take the force field off line for."

Arlene pursed her lips. "We'll just have to be ready then." She looked around, surveying the site. "I reckon we hang behind that pillar, and then when we see the ion trail stop, we can run in and grab it. Closest point of safety."

Giles nodded, then smiled with just one side of his face. "Who wants to do the running then?"

Arlene's eyes burned brightly. "I'm the fastest," she responded without hesitation.

Giles looked taken aback. He took off his glasses and started cleaning them. "I don't know why you'd say that," he told her.

Arlene smiled and patted him on his upper arm. "Come on, you know I am. Despite your unfair nanocyte advantage." She winked at him.

Giles narrowed one eye at her. "Speaking of unfair advantages, did you ever admit to the Federation instructors that you were using your special capabilities in the assessments?"

She smiled nonchalantly. "You want to bring that up *now*?" But she looked incredulous for a moment before answering the question. "I did. And they said it didn't matter, because it wasn't something that anyone would be able to take away from me."

Giles grunted, unimpressed. "Well then, I guess you should be the one to run in and grab it then. Since you're so kindly offering your services," he added, his eyes showing that he was playing with her.

She smiled and headed over to the column. "Good. That's settled then," she agreed. "Though, you might want to get your ass out of the way. Scamp is going to be firing in exactly that line of fire from *that* opening any minute now." She squinted to see the tiny bright spot in the ceiling that was heavily disguised in amongst the carvings. Had Beno'or not pinpointed it on a map with an overlay of the insides that Giles and she had painstakingly photographed, they wouldn't have a clue about the trajectory.

Giles ambled out of the way. "Two minutes," he confirmed, checking his holo.

They waited behind the column. Giles noticed his heart was racing. This was the thrill. The all-or-nothing situations he would seek out. The adventure, the mystery, the resolution. And he'd been waiting *soooooo* long to resolve this one. Although, even with this second talisman, he knew they still had many more to go. And some of the others might not be so easy to locate.

He remained lost in thought until Arlene nudged his arm. "Forty seconds," she told him, watching the count down on her holo.

They readied themselves, not daring to watch the opening in the ceiling now.

Scamp's voice came over their implants. "I'm on approach. Ready to deploy the beam. Are you out of harm's way?"

Giles nodded to Arlene. "Affirmative Scamp, you are clear to fire," he reported.

"Acknowledged. I'll pulse for two seconds, then you'll need to let me know if it needs longer. It will take me at least another five to reposition."

"Understood," Giles responded. "Good luck," he added.

Their audio implants went quiet.

Arlene positioned herself ready to move from behind the column as soon as the firing stopped. She kept her eyes on the target, waiting.

Giles could feel the tension as they waited. He leaned against the column on the other side of her out of the way. He could feel his heart beating in his chest. He tried to breathe to release the tension but nothing worked.

It'll all be over in a few seconds, he told himself.

Before he knew it he was jolted by the realization that there was indeed a beam coming through the cavern and piercing the box with the force field inside it. Then it disappeared, and Arlene sprinted out to the location, her arms pumping, propelling her forward.

She plunged her arm into the casket. Giles watched, emerging from behind the column, moving over to her.

She rested her hands on its edge, then stepped back, dropping her head as if recovering from the run.

"Did you get it?" he asked, hardly daring to speak in anything but a whisper.

She turned her head and peered at him. Then she straightened up and nodded, the tension flooding from her face, and leaving her with an expression of utter relief.

"Yes," she said simply, holding out her hand, revealing the talisman, which looked very much like the one they already had in their possession.

Giles exhaled. "Scamp," he called over his holo, "mission accomplished. Stand down."

"Acknowledged. Standing down," Scamp replied.

Beno'or's voice came over the audio channel. "Congratulations you two. Well done. Great job!"

Arlene smiled at Giles, still processing the relief. Spontaneously, Giles lunged forward and wrapped his arms around her. "We did it!" he whispered excitedly. "Or rather, *you* did it!"

Arlene nodded, barely able to move from within his embrace. "We damn-well did," she agreed. "Now let's see about getting the hell out of here!"

Giles released her, suddenly composing himself. "Yes. Of course." He took his glasses off and cleaned them, a little embarrassed by his outburst of affection. "Right," he grunted, looking around without his glasses on his face. "I think I saw something passage-like over that way earlier."

He started walking in that direction, replacing his glasses on his face, with Arlene trotting after him, smiling to herself.

CHAPTER 17

Aibek Moon, Orn System, Temple Caverns

Arlene had gone ahead through the passageway.

Giles followed, stepping into the darkness behind her. He paused briefly, waiting for his eyes to adjust. Hearing Arlene continue on ahead of him he added one more data point to his theory that she did in fact have eyesight that was far superior to even his own nanocytes-enhanced capabilities. Either that, or she was perhaps using her realm abilities to feel her way through.

He was about to turn on the light in his helmet he was carrying when he noticed a faint glow coming from up ahead.

"I think there's something out there," Arlene called back in a loud whisper.

Giles hurried to catch her up. "What is it?"

"I dunno," she muttered under her breath. "But there is light. It might be a long way off. Can't tell."

They kept walking.

And walking.

And walking. The small glow becoming incrementally brighter as they did so.

Eventually the light filled the tunnel and they could make out rock and sky up ahead.

Arlene's pace quickened. "We've made it!" she said, relief in her voice.

Giles hurried along beside her. "I think you're right." He clicked his intercom. "Scamp, do you read?"

"Scamp here."

"Great," Giles said, "Wanna run a scan for us? We're on the way out. We can see daylight up ahead."

Scamp's voice came back in their audio implants. "I have a lock on you. Moving round to intercept."

Giles and Arlene continued moving but realized that the air must be thinning as they found themselves struggling to get enough breath into their lungs. They instinctively moved to put their helmets and gloves on as they approached the end of the tunnel.

Despite the helmets they heard the ship before they saw it. Warmth, comfort, food, and restrooms were nearly within sight.

Scamp opened up the channel again. "Er. Giles?"

"Yes Scamp?"

Scamps voice was unusually serious in tone. "I'm sorry to tell you this, but you have company."

Giles frowned, trying to fathom what Scamp meant. At that same moment he and Arlene reached the mouth of the tunnel and stepped out into the thin atmosphere.

They squinted in the brightness and very quickly realized that indeed something wasn't right.

Arlene was the first to put it together. "Erm... Giles?"

she started. "I think what Scamp was trying to tell us was that the guards have managed to track us down, now that the freeze has passed."

Giles's eyes adjusted to the light to see a team of Zhyn warriors with blasters trained directly on them. Spontaneously he raised his arms in the air. Arlene reluctantly followed suit.

A voice boomed across the rock. "You're removing something that isn't yours," one of the Zhyn guards told them, their implanted translators making the adjustment for them. "Put your weapons down and surrender. Or lose your lives."

Giles shifted his weight awkwardly. He slowly turned his upper body to make eye contact with Arlene to decide their next move. She wasn't looking like she had a plan to take them on.

He turned back to face their accuser. "We're not here to cause any harm," he called out, relieved that at least the sounds coming from his mouth seemed odd enough to be some form of Zhyn dialect. The guard seemed to understand at least. "We have the support of the Zhyn Empire. We're trying to help," he explained.

The warrior in front of him looked angry. "Stealing the sacred treasure of our ancestors isn't helping anyone. We are sworn to protect it with our lives. You will hand it over."

Giles nodded his head, lowering his eyes. He slowly and carefully reached into his pocket. Arlene did a double take, knowing full well that Giles didn't have the talisman. She still held it.

He pulled out a metal puck. It was the same size and

shape as the talisman. At least from where she was standing.

"The man thinks of everything," she muttered to herself, careful not to be loud enough for it to be translated by her implant.

"We're not here for power," Giles continued, now holding the puck at head height between thumb and forefinger as if to show he had nothing to hide. "We're here to understand our collective heritage. This affects us all. We may all be in danger," he added.

Arlene knew that there was a reason the General had suddenly endorsed the trip, and at that moment she suspected there was something that they had considered or knew that she wasn't privy too. She didn't have the focus to consider it now, though. She kept her eyes carefully on the threat ahead of them, counting off the other warriors around them that might be able to get a shot of if they were to make a move.

There were five other Zhyn, clearly under the command of the bigger one that was doing all the talking. She tried to reach out with her awareness to see if there was anyone else. She couldn't sense anyone behind their line of sight.

That was something at least.

She wondered if Scamp might have a plan. In an emergency he was programmed to intervene as best he could, but they hadn't been expecting to have any more trouble from these guys. At least not without warning.

Giles was still talking. "This is part of a bigger picture. Your mission - you've done it well. But now there is a new task. I have others of these on my ship. We're putting them together to figure out where we all came from."

The Zhyn kept their weapons trained on he and Arlene. "You're putting them together so you can use their power!" the leader exclaimed, his eyes flaring with rage.

Giles hesitated, his muscles tensing throughout his whole body. The blaster could go off at any moment the way it was being jolted in the arms of this angry commander on front of him.

He changed his hand gestures and with open palms tilted them towards the ground to try and subconsciously calm the man in front of him. "We're working with the support of your empire," he insisted gently. "We have your Justicar on board our ship. He endorses this. We're trying to protect both our races," he explained.

The commander was having none of it. "Well then he is a traitor to our ancestors. And you will be terminated for your infraction on our sacred land!" he bellowed across the space between them.

Arlene noticed that one of the warriors had lowered his weapon, listening intently to what Giles was saying. She was almost certain Giles had noticed that too, as he could be seen a little behind the commander.

The warrior made eye contact with her and nodded. She clenched one fist in a symbol of fighting to see how he would react. He nodded again.

She hoped Giles had seen it.

The commander had raised his weapon higher and was about to fire at Giles.

"Now!" Arlene shouted, praying that her translator was working and that the defecting warrior would understand.

The warrior did indeed comprehend and in one swift movement turned his heavy blaster around and used the butt to knock his commander on the back of the head. The others, stunned, started shouting, their blasters trained now on the traitor.

Giles and Arlene took their opportunity and ran back towards the cave.

"Scamp," Arlene shouted into her holo. "Scamp are you there? Can you come get us?"

Scamp's voice connected over the audio. "I thought you'd never ask. Please stand by!"

A whoosh was suddenly heard over the shouting of the Zhyn warriors. It pulled their attention from the traitor and they began firing at the ship as it appeared from somewhere over the rocky cliff.

Scamp returned fire. Arlene could tell the ship's weapons were turned to stun, and the shots just seemed to miss each of them by a fraction enough to not hit them. Scamp wasn't trying to kill them, only effect an escape.

Arlene noticed a chain drop down from the ship. She nudged Giles. He nodded and they readied themselves for Scamp.

"Ready when you are, Scamp," Arlene called through her holo. "We can see the chain."

"Yes, apologies it's not something more substantial," Scamp told her. "Baba Yaga tended not to need fast getaways."

Giles rolled his eyes, and despite the chaos Arlene couldn't help but laugh at the dig that Scamp was making at having to rescue their asses from a violent situation.

Baba Yaga of course wouldn't have left anyone alive.

But then, Baba Yaga would only go after evil people who needed ending. Not trinkets and talismans guarded by dedicated but innocent monks.

The ship lurched forward, having knocked out a few of the warriors or rendered their blasters useless. Arlene noticed their friend running towards them, looking up at the ship.

"Wonder if I could catch a ride with you," he shouted over the racket of the ship's blasters and the roar of his comrades' bikes powering up.

"Of course," Arlene called back. She pointed at the chain that was now dangling above them as Scamp moved the ship into position to collect them. "Why don't you head up there first," she offered. The Zhyn thanked her and grabbed onto the chain when it came into reach. He tried to move himself up it but it didn't quite work at first. And then the chain morphed, giving itself footholds on either side.

Despite the noise and chaos and dust being blown up by the ship, Arlene felt sure she could see the relief on the Zhyn's face as he found he could climb.

Giles shouted over the sound of the ship. "You next," he told her.

Arlene was about to protest but he shook his head at her and gave her a stern look. She ran forward and grabbed the chain, hauling herself up as quickly as she could, vaguely aware of at least one or two blasters still firing at them to prevent their escape.

Giles waited a few moments, trying to shelter back in the mouth of the cave while Arlene made her way up the chain.

"Giles?" It was Scamp talking through his implant. "I suggest you get onto the chain too. We can start pulling you up."

Giles spied the one remaining Zhyn who had reclaimed his blaster and was doing everything he could to keep them from escaping. "I'm having a spot of trouble down here," he replied. "I'm pinned back in the cave."

Scamp was silent for a moment. Giles had a horrible feeling they had lost the connection. After several moments he got a response. "It's okay. If you can get onto the chain, you'll be mostly protected by the ship's force field. But you have to hurry. We need to put some height in our position soon else I'm going to drift into this cliff face."

Giles felt the pressure mount. He'd be *mostly* okay *if* he can make it to the chain. He didn't like the implied odds. But this was the life he had chosen. This was exactly the kind of trouble he went looking for, he reminded himself. And in no time at all he'd be back in the safety of the ship and back to finding his next adrenaline hit.

He took a deep breath. "On my way Scamp. Stand by," he called.

He sprinted out into the open, trying desperately to reach the chain before the Zhyn warrior could reset his aim.

He lunged at the chain, oblivious now to his surroundings, aware only of the awful fear that he might get hit by a blaster ray at any moment. He grasped the chain in his hands, pulling his weight onto it and fumbling with his right foot to find a foothold. He managed and then stepped up with his left to find a support there.

"I'm on the chain," he called over his holo. "Bring me up,

Scamp!" He turned to his left to see the Zhyn continuing to fire his blaster at him, but the rays exploded on the ship's shields. After a few more blasts the Zhyn gave up, slinging his blaster on his back, and turning his bike off in the direction the others had taken.

Giles turned to his right, relief flooding through his body. The cliff face was approaching slowly and he could see the ground disappearing beneath him. He glanced up to see Arlene disappear into the ship as she hauled herself up. The warrior had obviously managed to find his way up and was helping her in.

Giles turned. "Erm, Scamp... You remember the cliff face?" he asked.

"Yes, Giles," Scamp answered.

"It seems to be approaching pretty fast. Any way you're going to be able to course correct, or get enough height before this becomes a problem for me? I'm rather exposed down here."

There was a pause on the line before Scamp responded. "There is a 72% chance that we will clear the cliff with enough height to ensure your safety. I'm doing my best, but the laws of physics are the laws of physics."

Giles couldn't believe his ears. "So that's it? I might die being slammed into a cliff?"

"I do have another suggestion," Scamp offered, "if you'd like to increase those odds."

"Yes. Anything!" Giles exclaimed, now no longer bothering to keep the panic from his voice.

Scamp responded. "I suggest you start climbing the chain. I'll also start bringing it up, but if you can move up it too you'll increase the odds of survival significantly."

Giles didn't wait to be told twice. He was already climbing as he replied. "On it. Climbing now…" he reported.

The chain also started winding itself up. Giles could see the cliff face getting closer and closer. It was hard to judge distance in those circumstances and with no reference points, but he could see the rock surfaces were quite jagged. He guessed that meant that they were pretty close. Plus it was dark, meaning that the ship was blocking much of the light.

He didn't like his chances. He kept moving up the chain, his arms throbbing with fatigue. The others had made it looks so easy.

Suddenly there was a jolt on the chain.

"Scamp?" Giles called loudly about the noise of the engines and wind. "Come in Scamp. What just happened?"

Scamp's voice was calm. "Erm… it looks like the drop-chain has malfunctioned. As I've told you before, these parts are pretty old and-"

"Shit!" Giles shouted. "Scamp. Help? What else can you do?" Giles kept moving: hand, hand, foot, foot, up the chain, slowly closing the gap between him and the ship.

Looking up he could see Arlene shouting to him.

Scamp responded in his ear. "Nothing. There's nothing more I can do other than continue to try and reach the top of the cliff before we collide with it."

Giles could see the cliff coming at him. He kept climbing, his heart racing, though not enough to give him the strength to move any faster.

This was it.

This was how he was going to die: on the first part of a mission that held the mysteries of the universe.

And he was going to die by slamming into a rock.

...

...

...

Just then the chain jigged.

And then again. And then again.

He looked up to see Arlene still shouting at him, but two sets of blue, muscular arms pulling the chain up and into the ship.

It must be the Zhyn warrior and Beno'or, he thought to himself as the help renewed his determination to survive. He climbed higher and higher, the chain disappearing into the ship twice as fast as he was climbing it.

Within moments he was inside the ship, several pairs of hands hauling his exhausted body up and onto the deck. Panting and terrified, he glanced down at the space he had occupied just seconds before, and saw the edge of the cliff disappear beneath him.

"That was a close call," the warrior said, holding out his hand to help Giles up.

Giles waved at it, still panting, and then went limp onto the floor, showing he had no will to get up just at the moment.

Aboard the *Scamp Princess*

"You're bleeding," Arlene shouted over the sound of the wind as the door took a few moments to close itself.

Giles waved his hand. "I'll be alright..." he said, bravely.

"Not you, you idiot," she scoffed playfully, tapping his shoulder with her foot as he lay spread-eagle, his face planted on the meshed metal floor. "Our guest," she clarified.

Giles lifted his face just enough to see her heading over to the Zhyn warrior who had helped them escape. Finding it too much effort to be bothered to move, he lay his head down again and exhaled dramatically.

Arlene noticed out of the corner of her eye as she set about helping the warrior. "What's your name?" she asked, thankful for the translation device.

"Jendyg," he said, bowing respectfully to her.

Arlene put her hand on her chest, bowed to him and told him her name before cautiously advancing and examining the bleeding wound under his atmosjacket.

He allowed her, flinching only when it was obviously very painful.

"Come," she told him, taking him into their makeshift mess room.

Giles listened as the footsteps left. "Yeah. Go. I'll be through in a minute. I'll be okay…"

Unbeknownst to him, Beno'or was still in the cargo area tidying away the weapons and equipment that Arlene had stripped off the moment Giles was clear of the cliff face. "Come on, young man. Let me help you," he said, humoring Giles's drama.

In the mess room, Arlene had managed to help Jendyg out of his jacket and was already washing the wound and trying to determine how best to treat the extensive burn marks around the outer edges of it.

Beno'or guided Giles to a seat at the other side of the little table. "Wow," he said, noticing the interesting wound pattern. "That wasn't one of our weapons, was it?"

Giles glanced over, forgetting himself for a moment. "That's a blaster!" he said. He winced as he sat down, clearly playacting, in Arlene's professional opinion. She smiled as she continued working on the stranger.

Jendyg grunted. "Yes. I took some fire when I took out our leader. The others would defend him with their lives." He paused, bracing himself against the pain as Arlene dabbed some lotion around the wound. "I'm lucky this is all they did," he added. "Honestly, if they wanted me dead I think I would be."

Arlene turned away with the lotion and then pulled a small device from her med kit. She turned it on and it emitted a blue glow which she directed over the worst part of the wound. "This may tickle a little," she told him. "It's going to start healing the skin from the outside to close it up, but the inside will take a little longer. Or a nanite injection. That will speed things along. I'll need to find one though, and I want to avoid this getting infected first."

Jendyg nodded. "I'm grateful for your kindness" he said, looking up at her with puppy dog eyes.

Giles interrupted their moment. "Well, it's the least we could do!" he said, slapping the warrior's leg with way too much familiarity. "After all, you saved us from certain death down there."

Jendyg moved his leg away from Giles but made a polite kind of smile. With his Zhyn features though it unnerved

Giles more than made him feel socially appeased. Giles withdrew his hand and shuffled his chair back a touch so that it was around the corner from where he had been sitting.

Jendyg looked back up at Arlene. "I hope the talisman brings you the answers you seek. It was doing nothing on that rock. And I'm sure our ancestors intended for it to perform a function."

Arlene bobbed her head slowly as she carefully moved the device over his wound again and again. "I'm sure it will," she responded.

Beno'or was watching their interaction. "Well!" he said chirpily, "this calls for a celebration, and I have just the thing." He moved around Giles and headed for one of the top lockers above the sink area and produced a bottle of whiskey. "Who is with me?"

"Aye," the Zhyn warrior gruffed.

Arlene looked up at it. "I'll have one," she chimed.

Giles raised his hand casually, his eyes now fixed unfocussed on the table. "I'm in," he added.

Beno'or reached for some glasses and started pouring. He handed out generous shots to each and then raised a toast. "To adventures with friends," he said.

The others muttered their approval at the toast. "Adventures with friends," they repeated. They each went to drink, but Arlene stopped with the glass half way to her lips, one hand still administering the skin graft.

Jendyg's hand holding his glass suddenly started shaking. He moved to put it down but before the glass reached the table his eyes rolled back into his head and the glass tumbled to the table, spilled, and rolled with a clatter.

His whole body started to shudder. Arlene placed her own glass down on the table and was helping him to the ground as he shook. "He's having a fit," she told the others, panic rising in her voice. "Giles, we need a nanite injection. Fast."

Giles was on his feet in an instant opening lockers and scurrying for a med shot. "Scamp?" he called loudly. "Scamp I need a med case stat. Help me out?"

Scamp's voice came over the intercom. "There are two med cases on the ship. One in the cockpit under the pilot's seat, and one in the mess on the wall near the intercom.

Giles's eyes darted to the intercom on the far side of the room and bolted over to it. He pulled it off the wall and grappled to get it open. "Shit," he cursed, shaking his hand and then sucking a finger briefly.

He struggled with it some more before opening it. Rummaging inside he couldn't find what he wanted. "Arse!" he shouted in frustration. "It's not been replenished."

He ran to the cockpit and a minute later returned with another med case and an injection pod. He thrust it into Arlene's hand as she held the Zhyn down, holding pressure under his chin to keep him from swallowing his tongue. "Try this," he told her.

She took it and pressed the cartridge against Jendyg's neck. The shot administered, she pulled it away.

They waited.

A few moments later the fit subsided.

Jendyg looked like he was asleep. Arlene bent over him to make sure he was breathing.

"Agghhhhh!" the Zhyn suddenly screamed, sitting bolt

upright, knocking heads with Arlene. Arlene fell back out of his way, clutching her head.

The Zhyn gripped his chest where the wound was. "It's okay. I'm ready to die!" he sobbed.

Giles glanced over at a bewildered Beno'or. "I thought that was meant to heal him?"

Giles nodded, kneeling down next to the warrior. "It does. It's just the effect of the nanites pulling from his existing cells. It will normalize in a moment. It's just painful right now."

He turned to make eye contact with Jendyg. "It's okay. It's healing you. You're not going to die." He could see the panic and pain in the warrior's eyes. He realized the Zhyn may never have experienced medical tech like this before. How was he to know what was happening?

Jendyg's face creased up in trauma. "No. It's okay. It's my time to die. Just let me go peacefully..." he panted through the pain.

Giles held his gaze, his arm now on his shoulder as the Zhyn sat on the floor, rocking back and forth. "I know that feeling," Giles said, his tone slowly soothing the wounded soul. "I know what it's like to want to just give up. We get weary. But there is always more. Another chapter. We can help you. Show you a new world. One where you don't have to protect an old relic, where your efforts can mean something. Please, take this chance."

He knew he didn't have to convince him. Just distract him for another few minutes while the pain passed.

"But how?" Jendyg winced.

"How? It's happening now," Giles explained again. "That injection is a suspension of nanites which are tiny robots that are creating the cells that you need to heal. It just hurts because they are having to destroy non-essential materials in your body in order to give them the chemicals they need to reconstruct the damage around the wound. Trust me, my friend. You're going to be okay."

Giles glanced over to see Arlene watching him soothe her patient. They had bumped heads at the moment of Jendyg's revival and Arlene was rubbing her forehead at the point of contact. It seemed Jendyg had a harder head than she.

Jendyg had started to calm, the pain subsiding. "There now," Giles cooed, "Your mood may even improve too."

Jendyg nodded, releasing his grip on his wound and relaxing.

"Looks like he's ready for another drink" Beno'or said as he located the spilled glass and poured him another one. Arlene and Giles helped Jendyg to his seat again and put the glass in his hand. It didn't take long before Jendyg was looking almost fully recovered, but for the memory of the pain and experience he had just undergone.

Giles slumped into the next chair and Arlene took a pew too. They each took nice big swigs of their drinks and Jendyg watched their facial expressions relax into bliss.

Jendyg picked up his glass and examined the contents. He sniffed it suspiciously. Then he held it to his lips and took a tentative sip, trying to emulate the motion that Arlene and Giles had each just performed.

"Ewwwwww!" he growled in disgust, quickly replacing the tumbler onto the table.

The others laughed out loud.

Arlene touched his arm. "It's okay," she reassured him, "You'll get used to it!"

Beno'or stepped forward from the sink unit he'd been leaning against and sat down at the table. "All too quickly," he added, smiling and raising his glass at their new friend.

The others chuckled, knowing only too well how they had become accustomed to drink, mocha, and indeed the earth drink "coffee" that they had to wean themselves from every time they ventured far from the Meredith Reynold or the ArchAngels.

"So," Giles said, his own fatigue and injuries already dealt with by his own nanocytes from his upgraded state long ago, "How long have you been down there? On Aibek?"

The Zhyn searched his mind for the answer. Finally he shrugged. "I'm not sure. I've lost count. Probably several life times by now," he confirmed.

Giles frowned. "How? You say *lifetimes*. How come you're still alive?"

He glanced at Arlene, who was equally intrigued.

Jendyg looked sheepish. "Land energy of the planet I believe." He shrugged. "Though I'm not an expert."

Arlene's eyebrows arched high. "Hmm. Average life cycle of a Zhyn is what? Forty standard cycles?" She looked over at Beno'or for confirmation.

"Yeah," he agreed. "If you're lucky, or smart," he chuckled remembering something he'd read once about the human "Darwin Awards."

Arlene looked back to Giles. "Might be possible," she said. "Especially with the right conditions and training." She turned her attention back to Jendyg who was sipping at his drink while examining it in the glass. "Did you have any special training?" she asked. "You know, to draw life force from the rock?"

Jendyg shrugged. "Maybe. I don't remember. We were taught to meditate. And fight."

Arlene nodded her head, contemplating.

The conversation moved on, but later, when it was just Arlene and Giles in the cockpit, the subject arose again.

"So what do you think?" Giles ventured, tilting back in his console chair. "You reckon he's gone stir crazy down there?"

Arlene shook her head. "I dunno. I was wondering if maybe the elders he told us about did something to the place. Maybe something they wired into the force field." She swung her chair round to face him. "We both felt something down there. Maybe it wasn't just the land energy?"

Giles rubbed his chin. "Maybe. I'm thinking we should have Scamp run a full medical diagnostic on him though. Psych, physical, etheric. The works. Just in case."

Arlene tilted her head at him quizzically. "You're wondering if he just lost track of time without a normal star cycle and orbital period?"

Giles rolled his lips inward before he answered. "Either that, or it might give us some more clues. There's definitely a layer or two of technology we're missing with this whole talisman thing. We are almost certainly without pieces of the puzzle, figuratively as well as literally."

Arlene chuckled quietly. She leaned forward in her console chair and tipped herself out onto her feet. "I agree.

Okay, lemme know what Scamp finds." She started to leave. "I'm going to get some rack time while I still can."

She was halfway to the door when she heard the snoring coming from the two Zhyn in the sleeping quarters. "Actually," she said, doubling back and reaching into a compartment under her console. She produced a little box. "Ear plugs," she explained.

Giles chuckled. "Good thinking!" he agreed.

Arlene smiled and headed out. "Good job today, partner," she called as she disappeared out of the door.

"You too," he called back, turning to watch her leave, and wanting to talk some more.

CHAPTER 18

Approaching Kurilia, Zhyn Empire

"We're heading into orbit," Scamp announced.

Giles sat up in his console chair, suddenly more alert. "Okay. Take us in, Scamp. I'm assuming the skylift option will be most appealing to the Justicar."

Scamp remained on audio only. "Very good, I'll make the necessary arrangements."

Giles bounced to his feet and headed for the mess room. "I'll let them know," he told Scamp.

Arlene was sitting at the table talking with their new friends. "So you killed it?" she was asking Jendyg.

Jendyg nodded. "I had no choice!" he protested. "It was all a test to see if we were worthy of survival."

Beno'or snorted with laughter. "I'd love to know who these guys were," he said, noticing Giles hovering in the doorway. "All okay, Giles?"

The jovialities subsided. "Yes, yes…" Giles confirmed. "We're coming into orbit around Kurilia. I thought you'd like to know." He lowered his eyes, knowing that this was where they were going to have to part company.

The Justicar collected himself up. "Well," he exclaimed slowly and with forced levity, "I suppose I'd better get my gear down to the cargo hold," he said, pushing his chair back.

Jendyg did the same.

Giles took another step into the room. "May I just say," he said quickly and loudly, stopping them in their tracks. He looked down at his hands and fiddled with his fingers before bringing his eyes up to the Justicar. "It's been an honor, sir. I'm sorry to see you leave."

Arlene had been staring at her mug of mocha, but now turned to Beno'or as well. "Me too," she said quietly, a certain sadness in her eyes.

Beno'or shifted in his seat and took a breath. He placed a hand over Arlene's. "I'm sorry to go too. I'll miss you," he told her. He looked up at Giles. "Both of you," he qualified, with equal sincerity.

Giles nodded. "I'll meet you down there when you're ready," he said, retreating from the room to give Arlene a chance to say her goodbyes.

Jendyg understood what was happening. "I need to gather my things, as well," he declared, getting up and heading out of the other door. Though he had nothing more than his weapons and the clothes he was wearing when he jumped on board, Beno'or appreciated the gesture. "I'll meet you down there in a second," he said.

Jendyg nodded and bowed to Arlene. "You have been most kind to me. I thank you for rescuing me from the moon and for healing my wounds. If there is ever anything I can do for you, you know you have a friend on Zhyn."

Arlene got up and hugged the warrior who had been lost in time. "You're more than welcome," she told him. Releasing him, she smiled, looking into his eyes. "And you have a friend in us, too. I look forward to seeing you again in the future," she said, a tear forming in her eye. "Good luck, Jendyg."

Jendyg bowed respectfully once more and then left, taking his heavy mass through the door with a strange level of agility that was still odd for an Estarian to fathom.

Arlene turned back to Beno'or. She smiled a moment, just being present in the situation. "I don't really know what to say," she told him. "I mean… you're leaving. I just didn't think of this."

Beno'or nodded empathetically. "I know. When you're on an adventure that's all that exists. But, we both must return to our other lives."

Arlene nodded, sitting down again at the table.

"Although," he continued, "there is always a place for you on Kurilia, if you'd like to return there with me. Now, or any time in the future." He paused, immersed in his thoughts. "We have excellent anthropology departments across our academic institutions, and lots of space-going scientific projects if that's what you'd prefer."

He looked up to gauge her reaction.

Arlene took a moment to understand what he was suggesting. "Er… erm… Oh!" she exclaimed when the penny dropped. "I… I'm flattered."

From her reaction Beno'or had all the information he needed. He nodded his head slowly, his eyes lowered to the table. "I get it. Your place is here." He shifted his tone to make it brighter. "Besides, you have all these adventures to look forward to. You've only just begun to scratch the surface of this talisman quest."

Arlene took a deep breath and reached out to his hand over the table. "Yes. But this won't be forever, and honestly, I don't think I want to go back to my life the way it was before."

Beno'or's eyes brightened as he lifted them to look at her. "Well…" he said, clearly enthused, "that is good news. I think I can go back to my duties happy in the assumption that perhaps when this is over you will at least pay me a visit. Will you permit me to count on that?"

Arlene smiled at him, her eyes tearing up. "Yes. You can count on that," she confirmed, her own mood lifting.

Beno'or nodded, his manner much more jovial than it had been since Giles had told them they were arriving. "Very well then," he said, standing up. "I shall bid you *au revoir*, as the humans would say. Until we meet again."

He put his hand out to shake hers and she jumped up and hugged him. He was large, and even she had problems getting her arms around him. She felt like a little girl hugging a grownup.

But the connection between them was nothing of the kind.

He held her tightly as long as he could before propriety and a waiting ship forced him to release her. The two ambled down to the cargo hold ready for docking with the skylift.

"So, I take it you got his number?" Giles asked, once they were safely back in the cockpit, having delivered Jendyg and Beno'or to the skylift.

Arlene grinned. "Of course," she said simply.

Giles glanced at her sideways, the frames of his glasses obscuring the expression around his eyes. "And when do you think you're going to see him again?"

Arlene shrugged casually. "Dunno yet. If we're passing by any time soon I'll probably want to pop in. But he'll be around once I've finished chasing this talisman thing down with you."

She sensed Giles relaxing. He shifted in his console chair trying to mask his relief. "Ah. Right. Okay then," he responded.

Arlene smiled to herself. "You're not jealous, are you?" she asked. "Only... *we* got done a looooong time ago." She pointed to him, then herself, and then back and forth a couple of times.

Giles spluttered. "No... God no. No. Like you said. Besides, you know. Molly."

Arlene grinned to herself. "Yes. Of course. That girl you won't even talk to without a chaperone present..." She looked at him deliberately and he ignored her, pretending to perform some serious and urgent operational checks on his console.

It didn't go unnoticed that this was the first time he had openly verbalized that he had any interest in her.

Aboard the *Scamp Princess*, Sark System

Giles rubbed his face wearily.

Arlene looked over at him in the low light of the cockpit. "Last night's drinking sesh catching up to you?" she quizzed.

He grinned back at her. "You know my nanocytes handle that, don't you?"

Arlene shrugged. "Allegedly. But you always have a weary look about you after a late one." She flicked a couple of switches and closed a holo screen she had open before glancing over at him briefly. "I always assumed it was a psychological quirk of yours."

Giles shook his head and tipped himself out of his console chair. He stretched his legs and wandered around the cockpit a few paces. "I've been thinking about the Estarian talisman," he confessed.

"Uh huuuu," Arlene cooed, her eyes returned to her console work.

"Yeah," he said. "I think it's going to still be on Estaria."

She stopped what she was doing and spun round. He was holding onto one of the other chairs and stretching out his calf muscles like he was some kind of athlete.

"And what brings you to that deduction?" she asked, one eyebrow characteristically raised in skepticism at her partner.

Giles didn't look over as he replied. "Well… there was the Molly thing."

"You mean the Molly thing that you pooh-poohed earlier?" Arlene was impressed by his sudden confession that he was buying into Molly's visions and not just going along with her deductions.

Giles smiled over at her, daring her to tell him she told him so. "Yes," he answered simply, just as Arlene would.

The irony in his manner wasn't lost on her.

"Go on," she pressed, trying to keep her own expression straight. "What else?"

Giles shrugged. "I don't know for sure. I remember hearing rumors when we had the original escapades to get it out to Teshov back when we were hiding it from you. But they never shared the details with me as I was… compromised."

Arlene nodded. "I'd say."

Giles clocked the humor in her tone and grinned. "Well anyway," he continued, "I think they still had it. They wouldn't have sent it out to the Teshov elders to have them both in the same place. My bet is they kept it within the ranks of the order there on Estaria. Just cloaked, or something."

Arlene rocked gently in her console chair. "And you don't think I would have checked for it?"

Giles pulled his lips to one side. "I'm guessing if a bunch of them worked together they could conceivably have masked its existence from you… Especially if you didn't know the energy signature to begin with."

"Conceivably," she repeated in agreement.

"And besides," Giles continued. "why else would Molly see a place on Estaria in relation to it. And doesn't that room she described sound an awful lot like a certain religious order we know?"

Arlene took a deep breath. "Yes. It does. And I had the same thought myself. But…"

Giles stood up, waiting for her counterargument.

Arlene's frown deepened as she spoke. "How on Estaria are we going to find that particular building? And that particular girl she mentioned? We have no name. No description. No starting point."

Giles sighed. "We found the talisman on one moon out of eleven," he reminded her.

"True," she acknowledged. "But we need something else to go off."

Giles ambled back to his chair and leaned on the back of it. "Scamp, any chance you can connect us with ADAM? We could do with some information on Estaria."

Scamp's voice came over the intercom. "I've sent him a message. I'll let you know when he responds."

Giles thought for a moment. "Okay. Or better yet, could you outline our problem and see if he can get us everything available on The Order of the Sacred Ascenders on Estaria."

Arlene glanced at him. "That's going to be a lot of information," she warned.

He nodded. "Yeah. We'll just have to get into it and see what we can turn up," he said.

"Okay. Relaying the message now," Scamp reported. "I'll let you know when we receive a response."

Giles sat back down in his console chair. "Right then. In the meantime, let's set a course back to the Sark System. At the very least it may be worth paying our friends a visit…"

Arlene smiled, getting up. "I was wondering when you were going to make that suggestion," she said.

Giles ignored her jesting as he watched Scamp set their flight path for the Sark System. A moment later they opened a gate in a flash of blue light and disappeared to the other side of the galaxy.

CHAPTER 19

Aibek Moon, Orn System

Ammo helped Naldrir off his bike. He'd been wounded. So had Mennynad. Mennynad sat on his bike trying to inspect the damage himself.

"Come on, you're going to be all right," Ammo grunted, helping hold Naldrir up long enough to get him into the cabin.

Naldrir, reluctant to accept help, tried to hobble on his own, but then stumbled, forcing him to allow Ammo to help him.

Koryss leapt from his vehicle, unscathed and pumped from the action. "Where's Gagai?" he asked. By way of an answer their leader rolled up slowly, his face like thunder.

Koryss went straight to him and they talked, the sound of the bike masking their conversation.

Ammo in the meantime struggled into the hut with Naldrir, shouting for someone to help Mennynad. His requests were ignored, and as soon as he had deposited

Naldrir he went straight back out to help his friend dismount.

Mennynad tried to make light of the situation. "Could have been worse," he said to Ammo between grunts and winces as they approached the hut. "They could easily have taken us out with their ship."

Ammo shook his head in despair. "Something far worse happened. They took Jendyg, our brother." His eyes were sad and though he had no physical wounds bleeding out, his emotional heart was another matter.

Mennynad was about to comfort him when Gagai stormed in, followed by Koryss. "He's lucky he got away. For what he did, for losing the talisman, he will be condemned to a life of eternal torture by our ancestors."

Naldrir was slumped against the far wall and lifted his eyes in dry humor. "Sounds like those ancestors are one angry bunch!" he remarked.

Gagai glared at him. "I will not tolerate insubordination. That Jendyg was a bad influence. And he will pay the price for his lack of faith!" he growled.

Ammo helped Mennynad to the floor and then stiffly straightened himself up. "So what do we do now?" Ammo asked, turning to their leader.

Gagai seemed to have a valve open on his emotions and Ammo could see the anger and frustration escape from his over inflated ego as the post-battle exhaustion set in. "We regroup." He paused. "Although, with the talisman gone, we've failed. Our purpose is now obsolete."

Ammo glanced around at his brothers in arms. "But… we can get the talisman back. We can go and find it and bring it back. There's still a chance."

Gagai shook his head. "We have no space-going ships. And those strangers will be long gone. We've been here a long time, and who knows what else has been going on out there while we've been here."

Naldrir nodded, his skin paling from lack of blood. "He's right. We're removed from our own time out here. We've all known it for a long time now. We've lived far longer than any other Zhyn. It was something the elders did to us."

"So what?" Ammo insisted, "We just give up? We stay here and just exist? Until what?"

Gagai didn't answer. He just ambled out of the hut in a daze.

Ammo glanced over at Koryss. "Is he going to be okay?" he asked.

Koryss's expression was blank. "I expect, one way or another, yes."

Mennynad shifted himself upright, pressing on the wound in his chest to stop the bleeding. Ammo moved to help him. He started to tear up rags he had found in the hut. "You're going to be okay," he told his friend.

Just then there was a boom from a blaster.

Ammo looked up. "We're under attack!" he shouted, springing into action and grabbing the weapon that Mennynad had dragged into the hut with him. Like a shot he was at the front door looking out for signs of movement.

Naldrir shouted out to him. "How could they breech the force field around the dome?"

There was no response from Ammo. Instead, Naldrir

watched as Ammo lowered his blaster, realizing there were no enemies to fight.

The door ajar, he stood for a moment taking in what he could see. Naldrir shuffled, trying to get up. "What is it?" he asked.

Koryss didn't need to see to answer. "Gagai has moved on," he said. "It was the honorable thing to do," he told them definitively.

The others, stunned, tried to process what had just happened. Ammo looked over at Koryss. "Well, don't you get any ideas! This lunacy stops, right here. We're getting off this rock. We're going to find the elders and we're going to get our talisman back. No more waiting around forgotten. They chose us for a reason and we can deal."

He glared at Koryss, half-expecting him to challenge him physically. Koryss just looked back at him, and now without his leader or any other purpose, he accepted the new direction. "Okay…" he said slowly. "Okay," he repeated again, bobbing his head in surrender now.

He started walking across the room. Ammo got out of his way and let him out of the door.

Naldrir chuckled with a humorless expression on his face. "Looks like you just became our new leader," he told Ammo.

Ammo looked at him in shock for a moment, then remembered his friend needed his help. He returned to tending wounds, but now with a new-found confidence.

The dynamics had shifted. That was for sure. And what had just a moment before been an uncertain future for them was now taking shape with purpose.

. . .

Aboard the *Scamp Princess*, Sark System

"It's no good," Arlene huffed, her hands in her hair, elbows on the table in the mess room.

Giles pulled his eyes from the holoscreen he was reading and moved his feet that he had up on the table. "What if we had Scamp try and assimilate all the known locations?" he suggested.

Arlene shook her head. "They're either not mentioned or they have code names, which aren't obvious to an algorithm." She took a deep breath and pushed herself away from the table, despondent. "As we might have expected, they've gone to a lot of trouble to remain covert."

Giles threw a krib seed he had been chewing on into an accumulating pile of husks. He closed his holo and pulled his feet down off the table. "So what are our options?" he asked, genuinely at a loss.

Arlene thought for a moment. "I dunno. Keep going? Start canvassing any buildings that look like they may have belonged to the ord-"

She paused. Her eyes brightened and she looked up at Giles. "Hang on..." she said, pulling up her holo. "What about Oz?"

Giles had put another seed into his mouth and was chewing on it while holding the end of the husk with his fingers. "What about him?"

"Well, he was tapped into the Estarian systems for a while. Maybe he was able to spot patterns that ADAM didn't."

Giles rolled his eyes at her. "You do realize that ADAM is THE MOST advanced AI ever to exist, right?"

Arlene waved her hand as she plugged a search into her

holo. "Yeah, but sometimes local knowledge is better." She paused and looked up, knowing she wasn't convincing him. "It's worth a try," she added. "And if it doesn't work out, then maybe the crew can help us in some way."

Giles dropped another seed husk into the pile, gently shaking his head. "Well, it will be a break from this, at any rate," he agreed.

Arlene brightened and her purpose seemed to be returning to her. "I've had Scamp reach out to Oz."

Giles got up.

"Where are you going," she asked.

"To get showered and changed," he replied, as if it were obvious.

Arlene frowned. "How come?"

"Because," he replied, "you can bet that as soon as those AIs start talking they're going to be setting up a meeting for us to head out to Gaitune. And so I'll need to be presentable."

Arlene grinned. "Uh, ha," she uttered humorously, watching him disappear out of the door to the crew quarters.

Giles appeared an hour later, smelling much better and looking a whole lot less like an unshaven bum.

Arlene spun round in her console chair. "You were right," she said before she clamped eyes on him. Seeing him, she couldn't help but smile.

Giles grinned. "My favorite words in the universe," he said, savoring the moment.

"What was I right about?"

"The AIs," she told him. "Oz has started searching based on the intel we had selected out from ADAM's data dump, but in the meantime, he has suggested we liaise with Molly on the surface."

"Of Gaitune?" Giles qualified, confused.

Arlene shook her head. "Estaria. She's down there doing some big recruitment meeting. Apparently, she's setting up a university that's going to change the way things are done in this system."

Giles's eye brows lifted up. "Interesting," he said, after a moment.

Arlene leaned forward into her console chair so it tipped forward and allowed her to put her feet on the floor. "Oz seems to think that our search for the Order is a long-term thing, too."

Giles frowned. "*How* long-term?"

Arlene lowered her eyes and prepared herself for delivering the news. "Not a few days," she said.

Giles expression remained blank.

"Or weeks even," she added. Her face remained serious.

Giles narrowed his eyes. "You're meaning *much* longer then?"

Arlene nodded solemnly. She could see Giles's brain whirring behind his eyes.

"You're going to suggest we see if we can get positions at Molly's university while we wait, aren't you?"

Arlene's solemn expression slowly morphed into a smile, which subsequently brightened into a grin. "Oz already has positions picked out for us and has pre-approved us for Molly's selection, should we be willing."

Giles rubbed one hand over his face. "You're kidding?" he asked from beneath his hand.

Arlene shook her head slowly, eyes fixed on him, still grinning. "Plus," she continued, "he said it would be an excellent cover for any investigating we might need to do in order to track down this next talisman."

Giles dropped his hand. "Well, I guess it's all been decided then!" he remarked, his expression changing to one of amusement.

Arlene shrugged. "I guess. Anyway, it's a good job if you're ready. Her meeting starts in an hour and Oz has suggested we crash it and surprise her!"

Giles shook his head, chuckling to himself. "Well, let's do it then," he said. Then he looked Arlene up and down. "You might want to go and get ready yourself though, too!"

Arlene glared at him, got up from her chair, and stomped out. "Was just about to," she said, slapping him playfully on the arm as she left.

Giles carried on laughing to himself as he sat in the pilot's seat of the *Scamp Princess*.

On to the next adventure, he thought to himself. *There's always a next adventure...*

CHAPTER 20

Gaitune-67, Safe House

"I must say," Giles commented, taking a quick swig of beer and nodding in Molly's direction, "it was bloody lucky you offered us those positions, else we really would have felt foolish!"

Molly grinned. "Oz gave me a heads up," she confessed.

Giles's expression changed to one of more relief. "Ah, that explains it then," he added.

Molly shook her head. "Not *much* of a heads up. It was only when we were saying hello that he made the suggestion and admitted that he'd been talking to you. When I laid eyes on you at the back of the room I had no idea how you'd come to be there." She chuckled. "For a moment I thought I was having another realm walking experience," she admitted, her gaze falling to Arlene, sitting next to her.

Paige was grinning brightly. "I had no idea until you showed up either!" she shared. Then she looked at the others sitting around the common area, an array of empty pizza boxes and beer bottles strew around. "It was sooooo sweet!" she told them. "The whole audience clapped and cheered when they hugged, and I swear even Molly had a tear in her eye at one point."

Molly pretended to glare at her, and Paige, playing along, shrunk back in her seat looking sheepish.

"Anyway," Molly said, picking up the conversation, "it looks like we're in for a good academic year with you two on board."

Sean put his empty beer bottle on the mocha table. "Yeah, and I'll bet there won't be a dull moment now that you're back!"

The others laughed. Pieter reached out and patted Giles on the back, somewhat awkwardly, but Giles returned the gesture by patting his leg with a very flat hand, patronizingly, like he might a crazy person. Another round of laughter erupted from the group.

He grinned at them all, secretly thrilled to be back.

EPILOGUE

Giles remained in the now quiet common room, waiting for Molly to return from showing Arlene to her quarters. Paige was pottering between the common room and the kitchen, tidying up yet again after the gathering.

Most of the others had already shuffled off to bed, or whatever they did in their down time.

Giles's eyes were unfocussed as he drifted in the memories of the adventures he'd just been recounting.

Suddenly he had a feeling that he was being watched. He looked around and didn't see anyone right away. Then there was a movement he caught out of the corner of his eye, just behind the common room holoscreen, out in the main foyer area.

He waited, watching.

"Hello?" he said eventually. "Paige? Is that you?" he asked, despite hearing the clattering of pans and plates in the kitchen. He knew it wasn't Paige.

There was another movement, and a second later a

small Estarian girl stepped out from behind the screen. "No," she said quietly. "I'm Anne."

Giles, relieved it wasn't a realm-walker or an intruder, exhaled. "Ah, well... hello Anne," he said.

She took another step into the sofa area. "I heard your story," she ventured.

Giles looked a little smug and leaned forward to see if the bottle in from of him had another swig in it. It did. He picked it up and took a sip. "And did you like it?" he asked.

Anne shook her head. "No," she said flatly, breaking his pattern.

Giles did a double take. "Oh," he managed, trying not to choke on the beer.

Anne took another step and then hesitated. "But I may be able to help you," she said. "With the talisman that is. If you promise to keep me safe and not tell anyone."

Beer bottle half way to his lips, Giles paused, mouth agape, astounded.

FINIS

HOLO TRANSMISSION FROM OZ

Greetings of the day upon you.

Oz here.

Molly has asked me to be the liaison between her operation and your rather primitive earth communication methods.

I believe you call it *email?*

Still.

I am here to act as your interface. To help bridge the gap between the dopamine induced hits as you watch Molly through her trials and tribulations as she takes on all manner of shenanigans.

If you'd like to receive such status updates, please go ahead and leave your holo/ email address here:

http://ellleighclarke.com/

As you might have gathered, this transmission will not just be coming through space between our two galaxies, but is also traveling back through time.

I will attempt to send you updates in chronological order but do be advised that occasionally gravitational optics will interfere (no pun intended!) with the sequencing of these packets.

An understanding of all things timey-whimey will be useful in such instances.

Additionally, if you have any feedback for Molly - or her team - do feel free to pass that on through me. All you need to do is hit reply to any of my messages.

I process every communication personally.

Looking forward to hearing from you.

Oz

(on behalf of Molly, *aka the lady- boss*)

Sanguine Squadron 2.0

Gaitune-67,

Sark System,

Loop Galaxy

AUTHOR NOTES - ELL LEIGH CLARKE

NOVEMBER 6TH, 2017

As always I'd love to thank Yoda for the opportunity to write in the Kurtherian Universe.

The pages you have just read are a spin off from the original Molly series. It is the story of what Giles does to help Molly figure out the Ascension Myth, and something I wanted to write because I thought it would be cool as shit. Giles is a favourite character of mine, even though he's complex.

Maybe *because* he's so complex.

When I talked to MA about it he thought the concept was great and more than happy for me to go off on my own and figure it all out. Which was awesome. But about 40k words in I was so exhausted I just needed my friend to have a read so I knew someone was paying attention. MA graciously obliged and after his notes and a conversation I managed to finish the manuscript with very little effort.

To say that I don't like writing in isolation is an understatement. MA – thank you for caring enough to read it through and be involved even though that wasn't the plan with my little hair brained spin off. [I think you mean hair-brained... not "little hair" ;-) and more than happy to!]

I'd also like to thank Steve Campbell and the JIT readers. I met Steve for the first time a few days ago. He told me that I scrubbed up surprisingly well. The next day he told me that he didn't like me very much when we first started working together. [From Steve - I believe I may have said, "I wasn't sure about you," when we first started working together. The words *possibly high maintenance* may have been used as well.]

The consolation to this little tid bit of information was that he was telling me that he does like me now we've met in person!

Small mercies, eh?

Anyway, thank you Steve for turning the manuscripts around and working with the JITers. I appreciate your efforts, and professionalism, especially since you didn't even like me up to this point. [From Mike - Huh, he never told me he didn't like you.] I believe that you're currently trying to get this all set up to push the button on it between flights heading home after the long weekend at the Vegas conference. You must be exhausted. So I extra appreciate you.

Thanks also the JIT team.

Your enthusiasm and input is always such a blessing. It was also so great to meet a number of you at the conference: Jim, Sherry, Oggie, and Dan. Apologies if I've missed anyone who was there and I didn't clock you as a JITer! Thank you. You guys are awesome and I really hope as the Ellie-verse expands you'll want to come along for the ride.

I'd also like to say a massive thank you to Joe Brewer,

our editor, who took time to read a bunch of Molly books in order to learn the universe and work on this manuscript. Joe, you've done an awesome job and your efficiency at turning this around is awesome. You're the best. Thank you!

And last and by no means least, thank you to *you*, the reader, for taking a chance on Giles and reading through to these notes. I hope you've grown to enjoy Giles and his antics, as much as I have enjoyed writing them. And sure, I know that he will never replace Molly in your heart, but I think he has an important story to tell in The Ascension Myth, and offers a complimentary vibe – and er, shall we say *tactical approach* - to the Molly badassery.

I hope you'll continue the adventure with us! We've got one hell of an arc planned.

MA and Jousting

So for those who have found Confessions of a Rogue without having read Molly, let me fill you in on what these Author Notes are at the end of a book.

They're basically where MA (Michael Anderle – my co-author) and I go into a rampant joust and extreme banter.

There's been a progression, so if you like these notes you may want to go back and check the ones in the Molly series: The Ascension Myth starting from Book 1. (We also have a story in the main part of the book if you're into sci fi, too!)

Some people find our silly-isms amusing. I hope you find the same.

Since meeting other authors in the 'verse though, I've

come to realise that this is kinda unique. MA is *nice* to his other collaborators.

He doesn't take the piss out of the way they talk. [Mike - This is English 1.0 way to say I don't give them a hard time. I would like for the record to show I *do* talk shit back to some of the collaborators and NONE of them were editing my OWN author notes. You did this to yourself.]

Or their quirks.

Nor does he tease them relentlessly.

[Mike – I tease Martha relentlessly too (that Willen)… and SM Boyce for her cover charges and Justin about covers. However, they aren't in Author Notes because they are usually in private messages or in a group chat area Ell doesn't read, so she is unaware.]

But on the other hand, they don't get to see his notes (for adding in their mischievous comments!) either.

So I guess that evens things out 😏

But anyway – if you want to read more of these, feel free to check out the back of the other Molly books (The Ascension Myth is the series. Book 1 is called Awakened).

And there's podcast he and I do. It's called Author Shenanigans: www.lawnfairies.com, which is basically us doing it live and talking all kinds of rubbish. It's like the version of our private conversations. Except MA shaves.

And I get out of bed and wear make up. It's a novelty [Mike – *This is true*]. True story. Check it out.

Giles worried me

So here comes another big confession.

I was worried about writing a Giles spin off.

My heart longed to write it. I mean – **Indiana Jones in frikkin' space**.

What's not to love?

But I've long been aware that you love Molly. "We want more Molly!" you've told me on the reviews and on the fb page. "When's the next Molly? Thanks for writing Michael with MA... but really. Come on now."

And what do I do?

I brutally land you with a spin off where Molly has a mere cameo role.

So to say I was nervous about sharing this one with you was an understatement. Layer in the other anxieties around Vegas surprises, and the parent-teacher meeting I'm going to share with you below... and honestly I've hardly slept for the last two weeks.

No joke.

Luckily I'm still relatively young and have an eye cream that does wonders at sucking up the bags under my eyes... but it's been intense.

And still, writing this note I don't know how it's going to be received. Are you going to love it? Are new people going to find it? There are so many series in the Kurtherian Universe now, maybe it just gets lost? Maybe the cover doesn't really speak to scifi people?

Maybe I've screwed up.

I'm going to try and stay calm and collected, but I guess I'll hear what you think over the next few days and beyond.

Waiting with bated breath...

Vegas, Baby

So I haven't really talked about this with MA yet

because he's been swamped by 400 adoring fans and deep in conversations since I got here. But right now I'm sitting in bed in the MGM Grand in Vegas getting these notes written because Steve Campbell, my task master, (er... I mean, the wonderful gentleman who makes sure the books get released on time, proofed and pristine) hit me up on slack before I even managed to peel my eyes open, giving me his schedule for needing my notes.

...which I'd carefully forgotten about under a deliberately administered haze of tequila last night.

My point? I'm in Vegas, and I wasn't going to be here.

I had mixed feelings about coming. But in the spirit of adventure, and after some careful prompting from Jen, a dear friend and editor in the Kurtherian world, I decided to make it happen.

That was a while ago because we needed to register and get our hotels booked.

As the conference drew closer and closer, I figured at some point MA was going to ask me if I was going.

You know, like friends do.

2 months out... He still hadn't mentioned it. I mean – not a word.

1 month out...nothing.

3 weeks out.... Still not even a whisper of anything that's happening at the conference.

2 weeks, he mentions he has it coming up.

Four days out... he tells me he's going to be busy because of this thing but he'll try and touch base.

I said nothing.

When I rocked up and he realised I was there, it was going to be a surprise.

I hoped it was at least going to be a nice surprise.

He looked shocked.

I see in his notes he's sent me he said it was good shock and not bad. So yay. You'll see his notes next.

Anyway, despite my aversion to noise (casinos!) and people generally, I was glad I came.

I met some wonderful authors who I've heard MA talk about over the last several months since I started working with him, and even some readers and JIT people who have helped on The Ascension Myth... which was pretty damn awesome.

Plus, I got to hang out with some existing friends who I never get to see otherwise. It's been a great few days.

Oh yeah, and MA gave me the opportunity to flip him off (English style, two fingers,) in front of 400 people.

He translated for them. That was a thing. :)

[Mike - For the record, we also had Andrew Dobell over from England in an Age of Expansion meeting with Ellie – he was able to translate English 2.0 (American) to English 1.0 for us!]

Story Gurus, and the budding Bromance that terrifies me...

Have you ever had a situation when you've got two very important people in your life... either personally or professionally, and for the longest time they've known about each others' existence, but they've never actually met?

At best it's just a gap that has never been bridged. At worst, it can create the feeling of two different worlds colliding.

It's kinda like taking your first boyfriend home to meet your parents.

Or your first parent-teacher's evenings when you're at school and you've developed two different personalities for the two environments.

Well... several weeks ago it became relevant to introduce MA to a friend of mine, John. John Truby, henceforth called JT because I'm lazy about typing.

JT is a story guru extraordinaire. We've done a bunch of projects together and he's been a *huge* influence on me for the last several years since we met at one of his classes in London. (Which is a funny story... but I'll save it for another, more relevant, time.)

So when I say JT is a story guru, I'm not quite doing him justice. He's the grand-daddy of story structure, and over the years his students have generated over 15 billion at the box office. That's without even mentioning the number of novelists and tv shows he's influenced.

Anyway since I got into the indie game with MA he's been watching with interest to the point where I suggested he got himself along to one of these conferences... Like the one where I met MA.

To my surprise, he eventually agreed to come to Vegas.

After I picked myself off the floor, I suggested he talk to MA, to see if he could introduce him to the guys who also help writers, and would interview him on their podcasts etc. MA was more than happy to help out. In fact, he's gone above and beyond to facilitate this... which just goes to show what a genuinely nice guy he is, despite having a million other things to do in the midst of a conference like this.

Anyway – back to the parent-teacher meeting.

In order to set this up, JT had to "meet" MA on a zoom call. So I sent an intro email and they arranged a time to speak. To say I was concerned about these two big pieces of my life colliding was an understatement. I mean, JT knows me from my business consultancy world, and even calls me by a different name.

Logically - I mean, what's going to happen? Even if they don't like each other, or they talk about my failings, so what, right? But I still felt like a little girl waiting to hear the verdict after a school meeting of parents and teachers. (And no – I still haven't figured out who would be the parent or the teacher! It was just an overall irrational feeling.)

Anyway – they both promptly reported back in and said they had a GREAT conversation and they were going to talk some more.

Super!

I was relieved, and soooo glad they liked each other.

And neither reported back anything like: "Oh yeah, MA doesn't like the way you do xyz, Ell." Or "yeah, JT told me you can be a pain in the ass when it comes to blah blah blah…". Or whatever.

Anyway - a few weeks later I heard they had spoken again.

This time for "two hours!" they both exclaimed excitedly to me on different occasions. When I had the report back, both were gushing about each other, saying how much they liked each other. How much respect they had for their insights into their particular areas.

MA even mentioned the word "bromance".

It was *adorable*.

And heart-warming.

And absolutely terrifying at the same time.

Who knows what they might get up to... What plotting and planning they might hatch. What ideas MA might give JT about his webinars to undo that which we've already painstakingly mapped out. What story stuff JT might fill MA's brain with and cause me any number of rewrites?

My life could be in disarray at any moment.

[Mike – I wouldn't touch your webinar stuff with JT, I value your business expertise too much to think I'd be able to offer something better.]

But worse still - they could gang up on me on the mickey taking, and put me at a *distinct* disadvantage.

My dad often ended up doing this with my boyfriends. In fact, there were moments when they were both teasing me and I had flash backs to those moments during the conference.

(I think MA had the same feeling when he introduced me to Sarah Boyce at dinner the other night. When he realized how well we clicked, he was like: Oh *hell* no! Nothing that comes from this can be good. Maniacal laughter and massive author shenanigan levels of piss-taking ensued.)

[Mike – This is true. Sarah already has an evil ... err, mischievous bent and when she was eyeing Ellie as a serious *'let's go get into trouble together'* partner, I believe in my heart of hearts I'm screwed.]

Anyway, needless to say *I* survived the conference, which is the most important thing in my book.

MA went above and beyond in introducing JT to all the people he could think of. He gave him a shout out or two from the stage, which resulted in JT signing a few copies of his book. (Yep – apparently writers travel to conferences with his book in their bag!)

MA even confessed to their bromance to room of 400 people. I'm sure I saw JT blush, but look very happy at the compliment.

It seems like my two worlds have indeed collided.

And though I haven't managed to raise the blinds yet (still sitting in bed typing), it appears the earth is still turning and the sun came up this morning.

JT and a New Frontier

Normally my author notes are very focused on the interactions of MA and myself... because well, that's where the funniest and most relevant stuff happens. But what with the conference and MA travelling we've not had as much go on since out last lot of notes.

So I'll mention a JT moment that might be interesting to you, which foreshadows some of what is to come.

Since the day I first published Awakened with MA he's been encouraging me to go down the publishing route – finding my own collaborators to take them along for the ride on the indie adventure. I was resistant at first, because, well, that would involve talking to people – which I generally find hard. But over the months I've become more and more open to it.

Especially if it means just spending more time with my favourite people. (Have you noticed that all my work so far has been with one certain collaborator? ;P)

So fast forward to Vegas, and JT and I are sitting in the food court area in the hotel/ casino. He had convinced me try some burritos from a fast food place. JT is not normally an enthusiastic kinda guy. His brand of humour is extreme sarcasm and sometimes he can come off as... well, cynical. So for him to get enthusiastic about a particular type of burrito told me there was something to this.

He was right. It was great.

But that's not the point of the story.

After I'd finished battling with trying to get my mouth around this thing, (and having resorted to a fork and a plate) I was flicking through some messages in slack. I had received the image of a cover for a concept I'd been working on for a new universe I was starting on my own. It's sci fi. Female protagonist and totally bad ass.

I showed JT.

He had "opinions".

But then a few minutes into the discussion his manner changed and he suddenly became excited. (JT doesn't tend to do 'excited', despite what I just told you about the burrito. So for the second time in an hour I was intrigued.)

He uttered a two-word concept that blew my mind.

"Yeah. That's cool..." I said slowly, letting the concept sink in.

It took a few moments, but hell yeah he was onto something.

And he smiled. Which was a shock too.

What followed was an exciting and fascinating brain storming session about how we could take the beats of a specific (secret for now!) origin myth, twist the beats and come up with something totally profound.

Something that would also allow us to track the building of a new society. A new way of leading people.

And forge a path from the semi-dystopia we have in the world right now, to something far more evolved.

And tell one hell of a story along the way.

We spent a lot of the following days mapping stuff out and recorded several hours of audio (which JT has gone home to transcribe.)

We have a plan.

If you guys end up loving it it could be a whole universe of scifi/ fantasy with deep, deep layers of high concept thinking that will push the boundaries of any scifi that had gone before. (I know a lot of folks who read Molly are also thinkers, and love the serotonin hits that you can get when clever shit happens in your stories.)

We're talking arcs upon arcs and themes and ideas within plots and world that continually unfold, changing the very neurology of those embarked on the adventure with us.

I don't want to over sell it (she says!), but we're both excited about it.

This could truly be epic – in every sense of the word.

And I wanted to loop you in on it because you're such passionate supporters of Molly, I think this story will be interesting to you.

I'll keep you posted as things progress, but would love to hear your thoughts. And if you'd like to be a beta reader for this, and check out the sample story we're going to write to test the idea, then hit me up on fb: www.facebook. com/ellleighclarke, and I'll get you hooked up.

AUTHOR NOTES - MICHAEL ANDERLE

NOVEMBER 5, 2017

First, THANK YOU for not only reading this story, but making it through Ell's author notes, to read these as well.

Further, thank you for getting past any subtle shenanigans she setup to author-note block me. If you think she didn't try to do that, just consider that it was *subtle*.

[I expect her to argue this here…]

We (and by 'we', I mean Ellie and many others) just got finished attending the first 20Booksto50k Las Vegas author conference and I'm tired as %*#%#@.

(Sorry, too tired to make up a string of expletives.)

However, for some reason, I'm not too tired to try and regale you with an Author Shenanigan story or two.

So… *picture this:*

I'm sitting with MD (Michael) Cooper, his wife Jill, their daughter, Tee Ayer and a couple of others I can't remember in my foggy brain when Jen McDonnell and Ell (who hadn't told me she was coming but was an absolute delight at the event) show up.

We are at Sam's Town on the East side of Las Vegas

(truly Henderson.) This casino has an old west motif, and the middle area has a large forest / mountain area. There are paths through the area, trees, lots of water places (including a 3 story waterfall) and animatronic animals.

That is the important part of the story, the animatronic animals – specifically the bear.

So, the group is talking about survival and stuff, when Michael Cooper says something that causes Ell to conflate concepts.

Because that is what Ell does.

MD: *Is speaking about a survivalist.*

Ellie: (raising her hand) I need a bear drill!

MD: (looking up at Ell) … We were talking about Bear Grylls, you know, the TV adventure guy?

Ellie: Oh, I thought a bear drill, you know, like an earthquake?

--

During this same discussion, Michael (MD Cooper, who is a good friend of Ell's) remarks to Ell that he has watched our Author Shenanigans videos (http://lawnfairies.com) and says a few really nice comments…

Then, he smiles to her and says, "You are so *delightfully* clueless."

I think Ell wanted to flip him off with her two version of the correct one finger version hand gesture.

[Ell edit >> Actually it took a couple of times of someone translating for me to understand what he was saying. And, to my credit I think I just gave him what y'all call "stink eye". (That's the right expression isn't it?]

If you have not watched our conversation video's, you *really* need to do it.

We have received many encouraging comments on how fans have watched and laughed as the two of us try to figure out how we can be *two authors separated by a common language.*

She speaks English 1.0

I speak English 2.0

She speaks the *King's* English…

Just saying.

--

During our conversations, the Mystic Falls Park Laserlight show goes off (See: https://www.samstownlv.com/experience/mystic-falls)

Ell's eyes get big, does that "ooo ooooh?" stuff with her voice as she looks around with a dazed and slightly shocked expression.

Ell: Oh my god, is that a bear?

MD: It isn't real, Ell.

Jen: It's animatronic

Me: Oh shush! We could have had at least a half-hour of entertainment. She *is* that gullible.

Ell stares daggers at me.

If you want to hear about Ell's story, her author and previous stuff I imagine (I wasn't there for the live recording) set a reminder to watch for her interview with the amazing Stephen Campbell and his Author Biz podcast. The interview will eventually come out here: http://theauthorbiz.com

[Ell Edit >> yeah I don't think we talked about authoring and stuff. We mostly goofed around – but it was fun.]

As I close these author comments, I want to tell a

slightly less humorous, but no less proud moment in our time(s) together.

Last week, Ell and I are chatting on a video call, and we are discussing what she plans to do in her near future (you should ask her, it's cool stuff) and discussing where she is challenged, burnt out, and frankly fighting physical fatigue among other things.

She had just had a whole weekend of partying (which for her meant two parties on Friday Night and another on Monday Night... Probably a year of going out with people all crammed into four days.

You see, while she is charming and fun, Ell isn't the biggest on actually *leaving* her apartment in California. It was a substantial amount of energy for her to start making the effort to work alongside human beings at the WeWork (co-working space) which is about a ten minute Uber trip away.

So, the two of us were supposed to do another set of video's for Author Shenanigans (see: http://lawnfairies.com Yes, I'm pimping the videos because they are so fun) but I'm under the crunch to finish my next Bethany Anne book **Ahead Full**.

So, I ask to push the video recording from Friday to Saturday.

Saturday morning, I call Ell and explain I'm really sorry, but would it be ok if I push back further, as I need to do about 15,000 more words. She is fine with that, but mentions some stuff about her night.

She had gone to a local Halloween party at her apartment complex, and followed that up with a party out with those from WeWork (I think I have this right.) She wakes up, old and decrepit, tired beyond belief on Saturday, bones creaking and bruises on her feet and legs.

With no remembrance of how she got stomped on or what table she might have bumped up against during the dancing to acquire said bruises. She ends up sleeping all day because she partied till ... like...

Maybe 1:00 in the morning? She is getting old, no 4:00 o'clock in the morning for her.

[Ell Edit >> What? I was hauled away from the party by get this... NEW FRIENDS... at 1.20am, and we went to eat Korean food in Korea Town! I was awake and alert and the life and soul, I'll have you know Anderle! What's more it *was* at least 4am before I got home!! Honestly.]

[Ell Edit 2 >> And my bones weren't fucking *creaking*!]

(I can't WAIT to see the stuff she plugs in response to that story ;-))

Anyway, I go through the weekend typing my little fingers off and she recuperates. I have stuff during the day Monday and she has another party Monday night, so we speak on Tuesday.

During the conversation, we discuss that our publishing business (as we do it, with rapid releases, social interaction on Facebook and that each of us are actually small publishers) is very tiring. She explains her concerns and we chat about options she has to make her own publishing company while she is challenged with flagging physical energy.

This would not even remotely be a problem if she wasn't tired a bunch of the time.

So, we end our call about her publishing company

future and I go about my week with the conference and the early, early meetings. The conference hits and It is a constant barrage of people, speaking, listening, taking notes, talking to more people and trying to work with friends and collaborators.

On Sunday morning, Martha Carr is smiling, a glint in her eye.

Why you ask?

Louie Carr (the offspring Martha calls him) had been helping Craig Martelle *livestream* the event and therefore taking in all of the main stage information as he worked to respond to notes and other items.

Now, sometime early Sunday morning Martha whispers to me that Louie has been talking *story* ideas.

About five hours later, after the event closes, I find Martha and Louie with their luggage in the Mystic Falls area of Sam's Town about to head for the airport and I say goodbye.

Martha looks at me again, a larger smile on her face and leans in. "Louie has been talking about his stories with Ell Leigh Clarke who might *publish* him!"

My collaborator is not a fellow author at that moment, she is just Louie's *mom*.

Ell Leigh Clarke has officially spoken from the role of a publisher, looking for talent and changing lives.

I'm so damned proud of my friend, I can't express it well enough.

[Ell Edit >> Well damn. It's not like you're a wordsmith or anything... Mr. 20-billion-books-published! 😉]

Go Ell, go...

You got this.

[Ell Edit >> Thank you Yoda. If it wasn't for your encouragement and constant support, I don't think I would have even entertained the idea. I mean – adding more stuff when all I was to do is Nap-flix?? Am I insane?... But you took the time to have a series of long conversations about this and the connecting considerations, and helped me see how it might be possible. So thank you.

And thank you for not sending me home when I showed up in Vegas. I know that must have been a shock for you, but I was shooting for it being a nice surprise. (I had to swear three people to secrecy to make it happen. And no, I'm not telling you which three!)]

Ad Aeternitatem,
Michael Anderle

with Michael Anderle

Darkest Before The Dawn (3)

Dawn Arrives (4)

Interplanetary Spy For Hire

with Michael Anderle

Expelled

Exposed

Deuces Wild

with Michael Anderle

Beyond The Frontiers (1)

Rampage (2)

Labyrinth (3)

Birthright (4)

Resolution (5)

The Sword-Mage Chronicles

Awakening

Taken

Heist

Resistance

Legba

Storm

www.ingramcontent.com/pod-product-compliance
Lightning Source LLC
Chambersburg PA
CBHW020354110726
47899CB00006B/1718